Chapter

The offices were just within the border of the District of Colombia. The three ancient men behind the top-secret location's doors officially did not exist. No one knew of them or their classification. The secret they held was so tightly held, to their knowledge, no one knew the absolute truth about their mission and purpose.

However, for the first time in more than six decades, long since these curious aged men first met, the atmosphere in 3G indicated that something ominous was afoot.

For more than half a century, before the start of the new millennium, they knew. Ever since the middle of World War II, when this small group of anointed government officials first came together because of world events they, and they alone were made privy to a finding which became so secret, so devastating in content, that each pair of eyes when laid upon it, read the super-secret section of text in awe.

The wording began as one simple paragraph in an intelligence report generated by an obscure intelligence analyst serving in the OSS, the nation's intelligence service at the time and the forerunner to the CIA. His analysis was simply based on a short message intercepted through two very high-profile parties in Berlin. And so, on that day the analyst decided to add the passage as a short paragraph to his daily intelligence briefing synopsis.

The merit of the findings made its way up through busy intelligence channels and ultimately landed in an obscure section of the OSS. A small committee was formed, and they studied the matter. The control of the operation became the responsibility of a young OSS official who was new to the agency. He received his dubious charter along with the names of two lower ranked young coworkers assigned to the committee. The three studied the matter and issued a paper on the topic's plausibility.

Seconds, minutes, hours, days, days, weeks, months, years, decades, a century, and a millennium changed as the group of three, who met monthly when their inquiry began in the near dawn of the 20th Century, met daily after the birth of the 21st Century. The wind was changing…

But, among the trio, each with white and silver hair, had stoic expressions and facial wrinkles earned having lived a long life, faced facts that caused more than a rise in their blood pressure. For apparent in their eyes was what had been taken to heart, change was coming…

Two sets of eyes concentrated on Dr. Tom Miller as he rose from his chair and stared at the American flag which stood majestically in the corner of the impressive conference room. He scratched at his full scalp of thick white hair resting atop his intelligent expression as he turned around and faced two men he had known and trusted since they had come together in the early part of the 1940s.

For decades these three men brought soul to a group that unknown to them held the possible future of the civilized world.

Miller softly cleared his graveled voice. "To this date, around the world, we think we've identified seven-hundred and twelve of them. As we've become aware of them, we've documented their lives, some since childhood, some since their teens, some since adulthood. If you recall, at one point, over sixty years ago, we statistically calculated that there were literally ten million possibilities. Many millions of them passed on, and as they did, we figured out that they may have met some of the criteria, but not all of it. Also, there were hundreds of thousands of them that committed suicide over many decades, and they were able to be ruled out. Even when Hitler in his sick twisted and perverted mind exterminated millions under the shroud of ethnic cleansing…"

Miller's face flushed as he traumatically recalled those years in his mind's eye. He paused for a few silent seconds, lowered his head and looked down at his shiny black shoes atop a thick regal gold carpet. His head slowly rose to make eye contact with his team members as he swallowed and told them: "We've found him."

Miller sat down at the large circular conference table, folded his hands and fixed his eyes on his colleagues, who looked at one another with stoic expressions. He reached out and poured some crystal-clear water from a crystal pitcher into a crystal glass and drank it.

"Over these sixty-five years, an infinitesimal amount of time in the scheme of things, we've known it to be true, and now, although we have not yet been able to exactly pinpoint when, or how it will come about, we can say we know a lot more. Over all these years we've been able to rule out millions, some naturally, some sadly, and some horrifically. And now, as you know, we're down to seven-hundred and twelve. Today, I'm convinced, we are down to one."

There was always a serious tone in briefing room 3G. On that day, however, each person's concentration now seemed even more intense. The room appeared brighter for some reason.

Dr. Kushner, one of the two other men who sat in the room that day reached out for the pitcher, poured some water into a glass, and then took a small pill out of a little box he kept in his pocket. He popped it into his mouth and swallowed it. An ageless intelligence official, Kushner, in fine shape for a man of eighty-seven years appeared to understand. Hornet, the unofficial top-secret computer network used only by federal government officials with the highest top-secret clearance delivered an encrypted communiqué which was deciphered by top intelligent officials and turned over to Miller.

Miller took a pair of reading glasses from his shirt pocket, put them on and read: "Quote: Confirmation received through Hornet. At four o'clock yesterday afternoon on February 16, 2010, it was confirmed that a man admitted into the West Los Angeles Veterans Hospital Psychiatric Unit two-south, at two thirty-seven pacific standard time, a week prior to this communiqué has now been conclusively identified as genuine. He has met every one of the criteria. End of quote."

Dr. Kevin Allison, the most insightful of the group, subtlety looked as if he refused to believe it. He slowly shook his head from side to side. His deep forehead wrinkles twisted as his bushy silver eyebrows communicated his feeling of ambiguity. He leaned forward in the high-back red leather chair he and the others occupied exclusively for sixty-six years, and his aged face then provided only a hint of what he thought which was skepticism. He folded his leathery fingers together, which revealed his dedication to keeping his nails well-trimmed. His deep base voice delivered a dark melody to the room as he articulated his opinion: "I believe this message and its messengers require a complete investigation before we can launch our own inquiry into this matter. Gentleman, do you realize what we have here?"

Miller and Kushner seemed to sigh simultaneously.

"We can't just make our move as if it is an unadulterated fact. Think of what it means," Allison expressed passionately. He then dismissed even the possibility of it in his voice tone.

"We know our enemies are preparing an all-out disruption of our infrastructure. This may be the start of such an operation."

Miller's ripened eyes returned a hint of disbelief.

"How on earth could they know, Kevin?" Miller stated emphatically. "How could they ever pull off such a hoax?" He added.

Allison turned his six-foot frame towards Miller, his most trusted friend and stated: "Hey, remember these are the same people who called the holocaust a hoax."

The three men without words expressed the complexity of how they felt at that moment. A long pause delivered an unnerving message to Miller, a proportionately healthy man at age eighty-four, who was at the helm since the group's inception. "I understand," he relinquished.

Dr. Roland Kushner, who practiced psychiatry before earning his doctorate in political science almost sixty-years ago, pulled at his bottom lip as he contemplated the consequences. His olden almond shaped eyes peered out from what his mother always called: "A nice face" and they spoke volumes to anyone interested in reading them. "We should just observe... Learn more about him," he said, haltingly.

"I think we should sleep on it and look at it with a fresh set of eyes in the morning. Let's wait until tomorrow, for the morning report," Allison chimed in.

"But you know our protocol is before we can even consider our next option," Kushner said, categorically. "We need to know more, much more," he added in haste.

"What's his status now, at this moment? What's to happen?" Allison asked coolly.

Miller took a very deep breath, exhaled. "We do what you said, Kevin. We wait for the morning report. I've dispatched staff in Los Angeles to surreptitiously interview this guy. We've got a live digital feed, both audio and video going and it's staffed twenty-four, seven. And, of course, we use the same cover story." Miller stood up from his chair, looking earnestly at his colleagues. "At all costs, we mustn't give even the slightest hint of what is possibly the arrival of what the Jews have called the Messiah for five-thousand years, and the beginning of the Second Coming, the birth of Armageddon."

Chapter 2

Daniel Sherman drove in to Bakersfield with concrete plans, but he lacked the mortar in which to build with. He had plenty of bricks when he made his way into the town his gut suggested as its destination. He reasoned that California, and its medical marijuana program was the place to be. Oregon and Nevada's programs completely sucked, and only the golden state's plan to deliver on the state's promise to those in need of the 'medicine' appeared like the service worked.

His body took a lot of punishment over the decades since childhood compared only to that of a defeated boxer who by some force still stood. He had lost the fight long ago. The bell for round-twelve silently sounded but the broken and beaten athlete in the ring was too exhausted to hear the sound or the sound's echo. His body was puffed and swelled from blow after blow. His knees were weakened by successions of bad times. Each terrible second, each dreadful minute, each awful hour, each horrific day, each unpleasant week, each appalling month, each wicked year, and each immoral decade, only resulted in a new purpose for Daniel in life: He was to serve no purpose, whatsoever. No purpose at all. That was his purpose.

For once he had a purpose in life. He served the mentally ill, but eventually even his presence there unfortunately served no purpose. In some way he lost his purpose and any value he once held, they could not be found, or somehow, they were stolen. But no police report could be filed to locate something so priceless.

Perhaps his value to himself and society was damaged by life's circumstances or consequences and the poor thing waited just like a lost dog in the pound that passed time as the poor pooch slept its hours and days away, lying on a cold slab of concrete inside a caged enclosure. And just as the dog tried to block out its dismal surroundings, the brave canine dreamt. The dog dreamed its master would soon arrive, identify and rescue him, and the owner restored their faithful friend to its warm, dry and beloved home and family.

And he, Daniel Sherman, which was the name assigned to his soul when his spirit, which was presented to this world, was responsible for it. He took possession of it when he became of age. Its keys were handed to him. He was given the proper tools in which to maintain it. He was its caretaker. He owned it. It was the most important gift he would ever receive, because it was a bequest so priceless the masterpiece of the Mona Lisa paled in comparison, intrinsically. All these years, ever since his brain fully developed, it was he who held the key to its salvation. He was to serve it. Only He could really help it and no one else. It was his obligation. He did not do his best. He was to ensure that it was properly cared for. That it was kept as healthy as humanly possible. That it was kept clean and kept safe. He didn't. Instead, he misused it. He mindlessly punished it, repeatedly. He performed no maintenance on it. He let it go. Maybe he never had a full grasp of it to begin with. Whatever the rationale, he was a glutton with cold and calculated amounts of unhealthy gusto inside him. He forced enough food down it a day some entire families do not see in this world for a month. He neglected it. He abused it. He held the controls, and he was its pilot. He placed unhealthy drugs into it or used it as a sexual object. He forced it into an unhealthy lifestyle and damaged it beyond recognition. He robbed it of beauty and innocence, and of charm, character and personality. Daniel Howard Sherman aimed only toward the destruction of it. His vehicle for life: Self.

Every soul presented to this world starts out as good, but not every one of them ends up leaving that way. He had arrived where his gut told him to be, and he now faced the battle to end all battles, the final enduring blows, the last round that would settle this long, costly and ugly war once and for all, sink or swim, finally, the time arrived, and the scheduled showdown was to take place in Bakersfield, California.

His mind paused and then he thought about his mother. How much she loved her life, her grandchildren, and her friends. He summarized that she was a good person who did not deserve the ghastly end to her life that she experienced. She gasped for every precious breath during those last days, and he believed that she deserved better.

He stuck to his usual routine. He got a room at a motel, bought the local newspaper and identified living arrangements that he could afford. He stayed at a motel that had a computer in their lobby that guests were allowed to use. He searched for information about medical marijuana, and he found a useful site that gave all the details: One needed to obtain a "Physician Recommendation for Therapeutic Cannabis," under the State of California Health and Safety Code 1136.2.5, Compassionate Use Act of 1996. The law required the patient to be certified by a medical doctor who examined them in their office. The law required the certification to state that he/she had a serious medical condition which, in their professional opinion, may benefit from the use of medical cannabis. The medical doctor must discuss the potential risks and benefits of medical cannabis with the patient. The physician must state their approval of the patient's use of cannabis as a medicine.

He scratched the top of his bald spot and looked around the Vega Inn. He needed a pen to write some of the information down. He walked across the clean tiled floor and stood at the front desk. There was a small careworn woman who reeked of cigarette smoke behind the counter. She waited for a customer who needed a room. The sixty-room motel sat just off the 99 South freeways. The motel was a typical choice for Daniel, for every single place he stayed each night on his nightmarish journey back and forth across the nation was always just off and off at an interstate or in California, a freeway.

He waited for the appropriate time to interrupt, which was a skill he taught to his mental health clients during psychosocial rehabilitation. The clerk handed the waiting customer his plastic key cards and said in a froglike voice: "Thank you, sir." She smiled at the customer and adjusted her lime green polo shirt which bore the logo of the Vega Inn. "What can I do for you, sir?" she asked.

"I just want to borrow a pen."

"Sure…"

She pleasantly replied, which pleased him, because for some reason he always had a problem with any kind of customer service clerk who treated him unkindly. He took their unprofessional tone and attitude as rejection.

"Here you are, sir," the kind clerk said.

"Thank you," he replied.

The information he sought stated that there was a clinic for "William E.

Marks, M.D. and Associates, and that the clinic was located at 3828 F Street, Suite D in Bakersfield." Daniel jotted the name, address and phone number down on a piece of scratch paper.

When he returned to his room Pearl greeted him. Her little tail wagged, and she offered her unconditional love as she always did. He realized she may need to go out. He placed her collar and leash on and walked her through the parking lot to a grassy area under a palm tree. Pearl peed and he praised her.

When he returned to his room he called and made an appointment for the marijuana program. The appointment was a week away at 10 a.m. and he needed to obtain a California ID, which meant he would need a permanent address.

His presence in Bakersfield was as fresh as a newborn colt. He retrieved a pen from his car and walked back to the motel's lobby. He Googled directions from the Vega Inn to the doctor's office, and it wasn't far, but he had a habit of getting lost so he decided he would leave a little earlier that morning.

When he got back to the room he started his apartment search. There were numerous listings. He called a few places and got the details. One place caught his attention. There was a studio available at an apartment complex and the dwelling was in its price range. He called and spoke to the property manager, Gilberto Ruiz. At one point during the brief conversation Mr. Ruiz asked him to hold on one second, because he needed to tell his maintenance man something. The bi-lingual man spoke in rapid Spanish which Daniel did not understand a word of, because he flunked Spanish in high school.

Mr. Ruiz gave Daniel directions to his complex and Daniel told him he would be there in the morning. He circled the classified ad and folded up the newspaper. He pulled out his one-hitter and self-medicated.

The Vega Inn looked better to him when he walked outside and around the corner to a nearby fast-food joint. He put in his order and took it back to the room. He bought enough food for a family of four. He was busting out of the jeans he had worn every day for a week, which included his underwear and socks. He managed to change shirts daily and he applied a heavy amount of deodorant, but he was a disgusting mess, and he knew it.

He pulled the curtain in the room back and turned on a light. The television was tuned to the weather channel, which was another ritualistic habit for the soon to be ex-vagabond. He caught a glimpse of himself in the mirror with the TV and he was repelled. He hated looking in a mirror because it only reinforced the notion that he really was a disgusting mess.

He took a shower, put on fresh underwear and socks and put on his lounging clothes, which were an extra-extra-large pair of grey sweatpants and the same sized white T-shirt.

He relaxed and spent the hours watching the weather channel, petting Pearl and smoking his one-hit pipe over and over. With his special stash greatly diminished he calculated if he had enough to hold him over until his medical marijuana appointment next week, at least he thought he did.

The following morning, after walking Pearl, he gathered his keys and cell phone. He was medicated only on a Xanax, choosing not to be high when he met with his potential new apartment manager.

People do not always think about the fact that when they smoke something they reek of it. Cigarette smokers are bad, but marijuana users are worse, because they carry the pungent smell around as if they had a block of Limburger cheese in their pocket. Daniel was sensitive to cigarette smokers since he quit smoking at the turn of the century, and he knew from some of his mental health training on substance abuse about the tell-tale sign: The smell. So, he was wary of it and used a lot of Febreze to mask any odor.

He smelled good when he arrived at La Casa El Norte on the corner of Green Street. As he approached the rust-colored buildings, he saw nicely manicured lawns and several well-maintained mature palm trees and other shrubbery native to California. He walked past a bank of mailboxes and followed the sign to the manager's office.' He noticed a surveillance camera and beyond it a small nicely maintained gated pool.

He knocked on the manager's door which had an "open" sign posted and he was waived in. Daniel introduced himself to the manager he spoke with yesterday. Gilberto Ruiz was a tall Mexican American with a bit of a gut on him. The proper gentleman appeared to have a command type demeanor. His dark brown hair, mustache and eyes complimented him greatly.

"So, Mr. Sherman… shall I call you Dan or Daniel?"

"Daniel…"

Gilberto walked Daniel around the corner of one building to a rust-colored structure which stood behind his office. He showed Daniel a well-maintained studio apartment. It was roomy enough, had a small convenient kitchen with a breakfast bar, a small half-wall which separated the bedroom from the living room and just off the bedroom, around a small corner was a large mirrored two-door closet and off it a small full bathroom. The rental price was good, and they accepted pets, with a deposit.

The whole thing came to just over one thousand, which included the first and last month's rent and the pet deposit. Gilberto had one stipulation. Daniel reported that he was not employed but that he would get a job soon. Gilberto wanted to verify that Daniel had the proper resources to pay the rent each month until he got a job. Also, he did not take cash. Daniel would have to get a cashier's check and present the check and a bank statement to rent. "You are just the type of person we like to have here at La Casa El Norte," Gilberto said with his Mexican accent.

Daniel moved three days later. He unloaded his car and waited for the new bed and recliner which would be delivered that afternoon. "If there is one thing to say about Daniel Sherman, he knows how to relocate," he said to himself. "After buying three beds and two recliners in the past few months, you ought to know," came the reply inside him.

California was known for its stars and Kern County was one of them. Bakersfield held ownership of the county seat since 1874 and geographically the area was almost the size of New Jersey. Located in the southern central valley of the state, the county is California's top producer of oil and

Kern County can lay claim to a significant amount of the oil produced in the United States.

Bakersfield boasted low humidity, and, in fact, Daniel believed the weather was a lot like Nevada's. The town was spread out and covered a lot of land in the county. His first days in the new town were spent trying to find simple things: Grocery stores, gas stations, a Wal-Mart, the Post Office, and he managed to find them.

When he searched for directions for the Marijuana Doctor on F Street, he believed he would find the office all right. Even so, he took off an hour before his appointment in case he became lost. He found the location and waited in his car for half an hour before his appointment time. He noticed that Bakersfield was not a small town which he believed was the case before he arrived. The city's architecture was not spectacular but when he learned how large a population lived in Bakersfield, the number surprised him.

He did not want to move to one of the major cities in California, because San Francisco, Los Angeles or San Diego, "they'd be too large and difficult to live in," he reasoned. When Bakersfield came to mind, he remembered it being the town mentions in Joseph Wambaugh's book "The Onion Field," though he could not confirm this.

The weather was a cold dreary wet day in mid-December and the air outside had a chill. He felt apprehensive before his appointment for legal marijuana. He brought his two prescriptions with him to show what he used to combat cluster headaches.

When the appointment time came, he entered the doctor's office and saw the receptionist. Well skilled at handling new patients, the young Hispanic receptionist with dark eyes and hair had him fill out an information sheet. He produced his new California ID which he obtained a couple of days ago from the DMV, and he signed the required "warning" forms which indicated he read the statements which stated: "Use of this medication alone, with alcohol or other mind-altering medications, may produce physical or mental impairment affecting the performance of potentially dangerous tasks." The statement he signed went on to say: "Use the least amount of medical cannabis needed to relieve symptoms. We recommend that you not use tobacco. Please use discretion and respect the rights of others. We recommend that this approval be renewed within one-year from the below date." Daniel also signed a form which stated that cannabis is potentially "cancer causing," which slightly made him think twice since a couple of weeks ago he had come from his mother's hospital bed side and saw what she went through with Stage-Four Deep Rooted Lung Cancer.

He signed the form, paid the $125 fee for the office visit, which, once approved, included the certificate he would need to go to one of the many dispensaries. He wrote down a couple of dispensary names and their addresses, but he had no idea how to get to any of them and the medical staff was prohibited from giving out that information. That was State law.

Daniel sat in the waiting room to be called back. A Hispanic man seated next to him began to talk about his problems and which dispensary he would use once approved. Daniel asked him if he could follow him after their appointments because he did not know where any of them were. The heavy-set man agreed just as his name was called. When he stood up and walked toward the door which led back into the doctor's offices he turned and told Daniel with his Mexican accent: "I will wait for you when I get done."

Daniel thanked the man, and it suddenly dawned on him: "Legal marijuana… the best marijuana… whatever I want… whenever I want it… I'll be like a carnivore at a fancy steak house."

He went through the routine office visit with no problems. In fact, at one point the doctor asked him to stop talking: "You've convinced me, already." Daniel showed him the other medications he used, and the doctor dismissed them with a wave of his hand and said: "Just smoke."

Daniel received his certificate which indicated his name and date of birth. The piece of paper also bore the signature of the medical doctor as well as a patient declaration: "I, Daniel M. Sherman, the undersigned, declare that all the information provided to the above physician is true and correct under penalty of perjury. I am a California resident. Daniel signed and dated it: December 18, 2009."

Angel, the Hispanic man who he sat next to in the waiting room, waited for him. He was hunched over a black sports car talking to another younger Hispanic male.

As Daniel approached the flashy car the young male gestured with his eyes and head to Angel who turned around and spoke: "Hey, man… I can't go with you, because I must go somewhere... this is Marco," he gestured at the young man inside the car, "he can lead you over there… I've got to go."

Daniel looked through the open window at the young man behind the steering wheel of the black shiny car. Marco was an extremely handsome young Hispanic male in his late 20's. His wide eyes were black, and his short full head of thick black hair was nestled just behind his thin ears. The striking young man wore a white V-neck t-shirt under a black leather jacket along with black jeans and black sneakers. Marco kept his left arm around the top of the custom steering wheel as his athletic body leaned forward to see Daniel. He motioned to the obese white man to come closer.

"Hi, I'm Marco… I can lead you over to the shop."

Daniel was awe struck by the young man's attractive features. Daniel eyes were drawn downward to a half-smoked marijuana joint in the car's ashtray.

"Yes, um… I'm new to town… I don't know my way around."

"It's okay… I'm going there anyway… I'll wait for you."

Daniel pointed across the parking lot and told him: "I'm parked over there."

The weather had not improved, but the cold dreary wet day did not seem to faze him. Handsome Marco somehow put a little fuel into Daniel's engine.

He followed Marco through the rain. The drizzle turned to drops and subsequently, the clouds poured. Marco's black sports car twisted and turned through so many streets he could not keep track of where he was. Finally,

Marco's car turned into an alley way beside a small, unmarked store front. He turned and saw Marco make a left into a parking lot behind the unmarked building. He followed.

He could smell pot before he entered through the first heavy solid black security gate. The pungent smell of smoked marijuana was never a pleasant one to Daniel's sense of smell, but he never seemed to mind the odor when the smell came from the stuff he smoked.

The rain kept coming. Marco's car window opened enough for Daniel to see his almond eyes, "tell them Marco sent you… they'll take good care of you," he said.

He watched Marco's car take off. The old blue baseball cap he put on when he got out of his car was drenched. Drops of precipitation dangled from its brim onto his sneakers. The rain quickly sent the oversized man who wore an oversized sweatshirt and sweatpants through the first opened security gate. He walked along the covered path which led to a second heavy security gate. That entrance was locked and closed. There were two posted signs above a doorbell button. One read: "Please Ring for Service." The other stated emphatically: "No Entrance Without Proper Identification & Proper Documentation." He rang the bell, pulled out his wallet and prepared himself for entry into a world he only dreamt of all these many years.

Hal had introduced him to pot in the early 1970s when Daniel was thirteen. The day his older brother left to go to college in Philadelphia he placed a small envelope with a small amount of it inside. He placed the envelope in Daniel's top dresser drawer without him knowing. He wrote on the front of the envelope: "Have fun," and signed the note: "Love, Hal."

When Daniel discovered the contraband, he felt conflicted. He knew his mother was against the craze sweeping the country from the hippy days of the 1960s. He watched her snatch a small bag of it out of Hal's hand one day, and she ran and flushed it down the toilet as Hal through a fit.

Daniel used one of his grandfather's pipes and he and a friend smoked the weed, but nothing happened. The two teenage boys shrugged their shoulders and concluded that there was nothing to this stuff called: "Pot."

As he waited below a metal canopy which amplified the sound of the pouring rain, Daniel thought back to the first time he really did get high. The euphoric experience was some months later at a high school fraternity convention at a Holiday Inn in another town. As he played poker with his peers and smoked, joy suddenly hit him and hit him hard. His first experience elevated him into an enchanting realm that greatly enhanced his sense of well-being.

A heavy solid door opened behind the security door, and a white man stood there wearing a black t-shirt with "SECURITY" silk screened on the shirt. The tough looking middle-aged guy wore a black baseball cap with "SECURITY" printed on hat, as well. He asked Daniel for his California ID and Medical Cannabis Certificate. Daniel held them up and even though at that time it was daylight, the security man shined a flashlight on the ID, the document and Daniel.

Daniel watched everything with keen interest. The security guy turned his head and nodded to someone. A buzzer buzzed and the medical cannabis employee turned the knob and pushed on the strong black gate Daniel stood in front of.

He was led through a maze of corridors. The inside of the place looked like it was under renovation, because wood frames and plastic sheeting were everywhere. The security man took a closer look at Daniel, his ID and his certificate. He prompted Daniel toward a desk where a young heavy set Hispanic man who wore a baseball cap sat.

"You're new here."

Daniel looked at the young man, nodded and disclosed more information than he was asked for.

"Yes, I just moved to town about ten-days ago, and I got my California ID, and I went to the doctor this morning and he gave me permission to use medical marijuana because I get these really bad headaches called cluster headaches…"

The young worker just looked at him.

"Marco led me over here from the doctor's office… He told me to say that he sent me."

The dude at the desk was named Benny. He opened a side desk drawer and pulled out three forms. He got up and opened a nearby filing cabinet and pulled out a digital camera.

"I need you to fill these out and then I've got to take your picture."

The youngster gave Daniel a pen.

"Take your time… We're real relaxed around here."

Daniel grinned and he looked at the forms which solicited basic information.

Daniel put the pen down and looked around the large open area the maze of corridors led him to. Benny was busy bouncing a blue rubber ball off the floor as cannabis consumers came and went around another corner. The odor of marijuana was everywhere. "I've never been in a place like this," Daniel said. Benny snatched the ball out of the air and squeezed it a few times before he opened another side desk drawer, plopped it inside and quickly closed it.

Benny looked at the completed documentation and asked: "What are cluster headaches?" The employee quickly discerned, asking an open-ended question like that to Daniel Sherman was like feeding a piece of steak to a dog that has not eaten in a week.

Daniel offered up his usual monologue on the subject only with something new added: "I'm used to smoking the cheap stuff because that's all that was available where I'm from. The pot was green but not potent. When I was your age, all we had was low-quality weed. The weed was brown, and we had to smoke a couple of bowels to get a buzz."

Benny picked up the camera and said: "We've got all the good buds here… Let me take your picture for your file and then I'll assign you your ID number you'll use when you sign in the next time you come." Surprisingly, Daniel said nothing, nodded and sheepishly grinned.

His amenable host led him around the corner where a group of people snaked in a line directed toward a young woman who stood behind a counter. To her left and to her right were two long panes of glass where three shelves filled with large air-sealed glass jars sat. Each of the containers contained a great deal of cannabis. Benny readjusted his baseball cap, patted Daniel on the back and told him: "They'll take care of you now. I'll see you later Daniel." Daniel thanked him and observed the young woman behind the counter, the array of people who stood in line, and the jars.

The thin young woman with short multi-colored hair that resembled a rainbow had a pierced nose and helped a stocky older man who knew what he wanted. She removed a jar from the shelf, opened it and stuck her hand inside. She grabbed a small handful of buds and delivered them to a small electronic scale. The transaction neared completion when she placed the man's order into a small plastic bag and wrote on the label. She collected some cash from the guy, turned and rang the purchase up on a cash register, handed the guy a few bills, bagged the plastic bag into a small brown paper bag, stapled it and handed it to the customer. "Thank you," she said.

Daniel was next. As the customer in front of him was being helped by the young lady, a second employee came to her aid. She was a young woman with a kind face. She smiled at Daniel and motioned for him to step forward. The carnivore at the steakhouse did not know much about the wide selection of goodies displayed on the shelves. Each big jar had a white sticker on it which indicated a name for the content inside it and a price: An eighth of an ounce for cherry bomb was $60. There were so many to choose from he told her his sob story about his cluster headaches and asked her to select what she thought would be best for him. She chose Jamaica Jam: $45/ an eighth. He smelled the bud when she unsealed the jar. "That's very potent," he said.

"If you don't like it once you get it home, just bring it back tomorrow and we'll exchange it for another kind, but I think this one will work for you."

Daniel looked at other jars as if he needed to stock up on the stuff. He realized his foolishness and just asked: "Do you have any hash?" The agreeable young lady steered her body orientation towards an area where she collected another air-sealed jar and opened it. She took out a hunk of black hash, broke it open, smelled the hashish and allowed him to smell the merchandise.

The entire affair lasted a few minutes. Daniel spent $100 and thought he had enough to last him for a while. He slowly headed back in the direction from where he came and observed Benny sitting at his desk lighting up a joint.

"Hey, Daniel we'll be seeing you."

Daniel felt shaky, because he needed a Xanax. The left side of his brain felt tender. He waved to Benny.

"Thanks for all your help, Benny."

Daniel's first legal marijuana transaction was complete. He was escorted out by the security dude who was holding the leash of a guard dog, a Doberman Pincher. "Thank you," Daniel said as he looked at the pooch. The second security door buzzed, and he laughed to himself that he was leaving to get buzzed.

Daniel's first night of legal marijuana use did not go well and the next morning he was at the dispensary door when it opened for operation. Benny was still wearing his baseball cap and acknowledged Daniel with a look and a wave. Daniel waved back in despair.

The bleary-eyed heap of fat signed in and went to the counter. Behind the counter was the rainbow-haired lady with a pierced nose. He felt nervous as he approached.

"I've got to return this. This stuff was no good for me. It didn't mellow me out and my brain didn't shut down into the stages of sleep. I was up all night."

"No problem, we're here to make sure you get just the right bud which will treat your illness… let's see…"

Daniel looked worried and desperate. He did not have a cluster headache in the last twenty-four hours; however, he would have gladly accepted one in replacement to the way he felt. The depressive feelings were severe.

He waved to Benny and was excited. The security person opened the gate, and the Doberman was busy drinking water and was not leashed.

When he got home, he was determined to smoke until he slept. The new bud made him sleepy and that is all he did for days. Pearl looked worried. Daniel neglected her and his body. He put down food and filled her water bowel and he used extra deodorant too, however, he smelled funky, and when a depressed person is to the point that his body's odor offends even him, it spells trouble.

Over the next few weeks, he went to the dispensary almost every other day. He spent hundreds of dollars and kept himself highly sedated. The retched reeking body he carried around like a heavy load of concrete offended him and the people who were unlucky enough to encounter him. He bought large amounts of food and consumed it quickly. He did not shower. He did not change his underwear or socks, or his clothes. His sheets and pillowcases went unwashed. He would just sit in his recliner staring out the window in a daze when he wasn't asleep. A DVD is always played on the TV. Again, they were old black and white movies he had seen a hundred times because he had no cable and no reception:

"Today's television programming is all garbage, anyway," he said out loud.

Pearl looked at him as if he ought to know…

He was slipping fast, and his speed was faster than a roller coaster descending after its last big incline. The faster he went the more he felt like he needed to end his ride as a human. After he finished about ten one-hitters, Pearl coughed. He realized that she had not been out all day. His responsibility for taking her out still weighed on his mind, up until today. He decided to just let her out. It was a cold, damp ugly day and the ugly man opened his door and slurred out:

"You hurry up now Pearl… do your business and come right back…"

Pearl was gone for almost an hour until he realized her absence.

"I'm going to give her the biggest slap on the butt she's ever had," he said through his clenched teeth.

Light rain fell through the grey skies and Daniel's teeth were still clenched when he found Pearl around the corner at another rust-colored apartment building.

"Pearl!" he said, loudly and forcefully.

Startled, Pearl turned her little body around and cowered. His gritted teeth were evident to her wise little mind. Daniel held her at the back of her neck and with his other hand he smacked her so hard on the behind that she turned around and bit him.

Blood ran down his hand, as blood always should when the juice of life emits from a deserving wound. The owner of one of the finest little toy poodles ever to take a breath on this planet gave Daniel a good dose of the medicine he so badly needed: Humility.

He yelled at her and tears came into his eyes. He wrapped his finger in a used tissue he had in his sweatpants pocket, apologized, picked her up and went back to his apartment.

The next day came, and he had a bandage wrapped around his right index finger as he looked out the window. A man, a very tall and large man moved into the vacant studio apartment next to him. Daniel cringed as he could hear every word the man uttered: "Yeah, man… just wait till I get my woofers all set up… It'll be awesome, dude… I'm goanna be jam men to AC/DC."

Daniel started to cry. As he turned his head away from the TV screen which was playing his DVD of Bela Lugosi in the original "Dracula," he stared up at the perpetual grey sky of Bakersfield, California. He began to reason that he had made another big mistake:

"I can't sit here and listen to AC/DC blasting through the wall all the time. It'll drive me nuts," he thought.

The man's name was Dave. He moved in and never blasted AC/DC through the wall while Daniel soaked and sulked in morose.

A couple of days later, there was a crisp blue sky with gigantic cumulous clouds and Dave was just outside Daniel's window as he sat in his recliner doing one-hitters.

He heard Dave talking with another neighbor and the upbeat giant-sized man with long left-over hair from the 1960s said: "Yeah, man I'm a veteran…"

Even before he heard those words Daniel's gloom had finally reached its peak. He finally put down the brass one-hitter pipe and walked outside to meet Dave.

Chapter 3

The Veteran Outreach worker arrived at Daniel's apartment complex the next day and interviewed the veteran. At 5am the following day, the worker showed up again, as the veteran waited, Daniel had decided to voluntarily admit himself into a psychiatric unit at a Veterans Hospital in Los Angeles.

Daniel opened the back door of the sedan and placed his gym bag inside. Daniel nodded a greeting as he positioned himself in the passenger seat and fastened his safety belt. Barry Hammett was a younger man, well built in his features with a chiseled jawbone, a full head of thick light brown hair, shaved short, and a man he soon found out had some marital discord.

Barry performed outreach work and helped veterans' access benefits from the VA. He lived and worked in the Bakersfield area. But he also traveled Monday through Friday to West Los Angeles and covered territory there as well. Barry's wife often complained that he cares more about his stupid job than he did about their marriage.

Barry was pissed at his wife. He complained that she did not contribute financially as much as she could to the marriage, she also worked for the Veterans Administration in Bakersfield, in an administrative job, and he said: "She gambles all the time."

For years other men complained to Daniel about their spouses. He listened but he did not offer any advice to Barry, but he thought:

"We need to get along with each other, enjoy each other's company, find things in common and focus in on that." At least show respect for each other, look for things you admire about the person, not things that make us angry and resentful."

Of course, at that moment, Daniel realized he's not a psychiatric caseworker anymore. If he took off his mental health hat now, he would be better off, especially before he checked in as a patient.

Los Angeles was about 200 miles south of Bakersfield. Freeways all the way, with two people in the car, Barry zipped into the diamond lane and zoomed on.

"Did you sleep okay?" Barry asked.

"I guess so," he replied. They listened to music most of the trip.

After Daniel was processed in on the hospital's ground level, he arrived at the unit. He was issued hospital garb and over the next eight hours he was interviewed an unknown number of times by a host of different staff members, a nurse, a doctor in residency, a social worker, a dietician, and a recreation therapist, who all took notes.

Daniel gave an accurate history of himself every time, which he kept secret from the other patients. But only a few staff members who interviewed him believed him.

Later, one staff person admitted: "I've had people come in here saying they were the CEO of Pepsi Cola."

Daniel told staff that he interviewed him that because of his background he felt totally at ease on the locked unit. Some staff thought, which was not true, that he had been hospitalized for psychiatric purposes before, he never was. He later told his brother Hal:

"I think the past twenty-years or so prepared me for what I experienced there."

When asked about mental illness in his family, Daniel recalled when his father left the family. His mother checked herself into a locked psychiatric ward in Pennsylvania. After three days, against medical advice, she discharged and claimed:

"I've to get home to my kids."

Daniel recalled when his mother was really upset one day, she saw a local car dealership's commercial on television. They used a man in a strait jacket to attract business, "I go crazy for Fulton Ford," the man uttered deliriously "My mother called the car dealer and complained," he said.

The nurses on the unit were very good at what they did. Daniel was interviewed individually by several of them on his first day. Each took copious notes.

Daniel was asked about his religious convictions, and he reported to the psychiatric nurse who interviewed him that his mother and father were both Jewish, as was his family. He had a Bar Mitzvah and went to Hebrew School for six-years, but: "I misbehaved in class, and I was silly and goofy." He also told the nurse that his father and his side of the family were not religious, opposed to his other side of the family who were very religious and Orthodox: "They kept kosher and attended synagogue regularly."

He could guess what the note-takers might write:

Parents divorced when he was ten-years old… Lived primarily with his mother and two siblings, one older, one younger… Grandparents influenced him as he grew up… As a child worked for them selling shoes at flea markets… Patient says he held a host of jobs in his youth.

"Maybe that's why I had so many jobs as a grown-up," he reasoned out loud.

When asked about his first job Daniel recalled:

"I was a paperboy."

The psychiatric nurse, who wore a shiny diamond wedding and a bright gold engagement band that light reflected off of as she wrote suddenly stopped her pen, looked up at Daniel. and said:

"Tell me about that," she said.

He had been staring at the nurse's shiny diamond wedding band with its matching ring and now he looked at her as her eye contact delved back into her note.

Daniel delved back into one of his favorite memories which he must have repeated a thousand times because he believed people would laugh and then like him.

"I didn't manage the money very well, I had to go around each month and collect from each person, once, I remember there was one house that never answered their door when I came to collect, they owed for three months, so I left a note on their door, that night a cop came to my house with the note in his hand, he thought I was a blackmailer, when he found out I was a ten year old collecting for the newspaper, he laughed," he mused.

He talked about his other jobs, about how he mopped floors in a donut shop, washed dishes in a restaurant, mopped floors, washed dishes and scrubbed pots and pans in another restaurant.

"They were all after school jobs," he summarized with a hint of pride in his voice.

He fought with his mother a lot, but he never raised a hand to her, and he was never in a physical fight with anyone ever. So, when some kids picked on him, which some did, he would "run away and avoid them," he told the nurse.

One thing not mentioned as he was interviewed that day was a job he held one summer when he visited his father in California. Daniel's mother breathed a sigh of relief every time she was able to cart the difficult boy off to the absent sperm donor.

His father had a new wife, Eve. She was the reason his dad left his mother and three children after thirteen years of marriage. She had become Daniel's stepmother, something that she probably regretted sometimes in future years. A smart slender pretty woman with golden hair, Eve was kind to Daniel. She knew how to handle children, she was a teacher once. But she was not Jewish, and Daniel always felt conflicted about this as he remembered his mother's mantra:

"You must marry a Jewish girl," he recalled out loud to the nurse mocking his mother's voice.

The job Daniel failed to mention was another donut shop that employed him. At age fifteen, he had no male role model. With his father 3,000 miles away, most of the boy's days were dominated by females. His grandfather was in his senior years, so he did not experience much quality time with him. At that critical time of development, the main male influence in his young life was Don Vito Corleone from "The Godfather." From his earliest years Daniel loved movies. He attended the inexpensive weekly entertainment at least once a week, and in the early 1970's when the motion picture was released Daniel became heavily swayed by it, he attended at least a couple of dozen screenings. He didn't like sports, even though at his mother's orders he tried. He was never any good at it, basketball, baseball, floor hockey, he never excelled at anything, really.

So, when the important work of art came into his life, he emulated it. He bought the motion picture's music soundtrack and listened to it a lot. One summer when he visited his aunt in Arizona, he and his favorite cousin Stevie made their sixteen-millimeter version of the film, and a couple of years after the original motion picture was released, Daniel was first in line on the first day's release of "The Godfather, Part II." Robert DeNiro portrayed the young Vito Corleone, and Daniel was mesmerized.

So, in the fifteenth year of his life when Daniel worked at his second donut shop job, sometimes he worked with a couple other grown-ups in the morning and he made donuts, and sometimes he worked in the late afternoons and early evenings, alone. Despite being a small shop, the impulsive fifteen-year-old decided to commit a robbery; he would rob himself.

One early evening when business was slow there was $100 in the cash register. Daniel was instructed to take any money over $20 out of the register, and for him to store it in a cash box in the back office. Daniel took the $80 out, but he stuffed it into the headlight of his bicycle which sat in the back of the shop. He called the police and the owner, and reported that he was robbed, and when both parties arrived, Daniel put on a performance that even Robert DeNiro may have envied, he believed. He tearfully described the suspect as a young white man with a knife dressed in an orange muscle shirt.

Daniel got away with it. He quickly quit the donut shop, "My dad won't let me work here anymore," he told the owner in convincing fashion. The young thief learned his lessons well from the "Don," he shamelessly believed.

But that was not his only foray into the world of crime.

When Daniel was sixteen, he worked at a drug store after school. He was the delivery boy; many prescriptions went from the store directly to the person's home. He drove the store's car around the town, which he knew well. During his rounds the music blared when an AM radio station played Elton John's music.

The lad delivered twenty or thirty bagged and stapled packages a day to people's homes. The bags had a prominent receipt attached which indicated all the pertinent details.

Daniel loved going to the Jewish Community Center. The JCC was a half hour's walk from his modest row home, and the youngster frequently made the trek back and forth, almost every day before he was sixteen and was able to drive. His imagination ran wild as he fantasized along these long walks to and from the community center, his refuge.

One day, soon after he started work at the drug store, he found himself at the JCC. He drove his car there, a 1958 Ford he bought for $300 from one of his uncles. He sat on the bleachers in the gym and watched a basketball game in progress.

A fellow, four years older than Daniel, entered. He knew Jack Auerbach, a tall handsome young man with long dirty blonde hair, who was Daniel's sister's age. Jack went past him up to the back of the bleachers. He called Daniel's name out and signaled for him to come up, Daniel obliged him.

The plan was Daniel's idea, his idea alone. But Jack became a good friend, strictly in business. The older fellow told Daniel that he used to work at the same drug store as a delivery boy. He went on to tell the young protégé of Don Corleone's about a drug, "Quaaludes," a drug that was:

"Really good and simply stored on a shelf in the store back where the pharmacist worked," Jack explained.

Jack proposed a business relationship that Daniel accepted. Already into marijuana, introduced to him by his brother, Hal. Daniel loved to get high.

On a Sunday, Daniel had to show up early at the drug store. He and an older guy had to stuff the Sunday papers with the comics and supplements before the store opened. Daniel's deal with Jack was for him to take some Quaaludes, put them in a paper bag, and deliver them to Jack's house. Religiously, Daniel carried out his duty every Sunday and was paid one dollar for each pill he stole and delivered to Jack, normally that amounted to about $40 to $60.

After a few months, Daniel got an idea. The Quaaludes which sat simply on a shelf back where the pharmacist worked were stored in a big bottle.

Five-Hundred powerful pills were packed into each bottle, and there were two bottles, the one being used and a full unopened one behind it.

Daniel had the idea of stealing the whole bottle. There was always just one pharmacist on duty at the drug store. Daniel made one fruitless attempt to obtain the bottle when the store was opened and manned by a pharmacist, he was unsuccessful, the moment never presented itself.

So, he developed a plan, a plan "even the Don would approve of," he bellowed to himself.

One day, assisted by two peers, a male and female, the group sat in Daniel's car parked a block away from the drug store. The store was almost closed. Daniel reviewed the layout, Mike who lifted weights and it showed, entered first and was instructed:

"Look on the back shelf adjacent to the drug store's lunch counter at the foot powder. Mike, you're to ask the pharmacist for assistance. The old man will stop what he's doing and assist you," he told his comrade.

Daniel's associate in crime was to be paid $100. Sally, a blonde girl who was one of the girls who worked behind the lunch counter looked at Daniel as he instructed:

"You're to enter and distract the other girl who's working behind the lunch counter."

She was to be paid a carton of cigarettes and $40.

Mike entered first and carried out his assignment. Three minutes after Mike entered Sally entered and carried out her assignment. Two minutes after that Daniel was to enter, go through the store and down into the basement of the building, where he was to sit in darkness until the store closed and there was no one there.

When no footsteps could be heard above him, Daniel emerged from the basement. He grabbed a big brown paper bag, unfolded it and carried out his plan. He took a couple of cartons of Marlboro, the kind of cigarettes he smoked, a carton of Salem, the kind of cigarettes Sally smoked, as well as a full bottle of Quaaludes.

Daniel did not have a key to the store. He planned to go back into the basement. He emerged through a door that was simply bolted from the inside. Mike was there at the appointed time and stood by the door. Daniel knocked twice on the door, and when Mike saw that the close was clear he knocked twice, Daniel unbolted the door and came out. They took off in Daniel's car, the mastermind was proud of himself.

The bolt would remain unlocked when he left. But the next day when he was scheduled to work, he would go back down into the basement and bolt it again.

"The burglary came off without a hitch," he thought.

He sold the bottle to another drug dealer Mike knew for $800 and his accomplices were paid what they were promised.

"Score now two for the Don, and zero for authority," he mused.

In later years Daniel's opinion changed, he was not proud of his actions then. He was not addicted to Quaaludes, because he loved pot more. But he started to learn more about pharmaceuticals and when he delivered some narcotic prescriptions, he kept a stapler and a staple remover with him. Sometimes, he opened the bag, took a pill of whatever it was, and later that night consumed it, Demerol was his favorite.

He told Mike years later when he ran into him one day:

"I am not proud of my actions back then. I may have gotten away with it, but I was sentenced to ten-years of low self-esteem."

He did get caught once. In his last year of college, just two months before he graduated and earned his bachelor's degree in journalism from Penn State. He was in a grocery store. He stood in line and impulsively the immature criminal tried to steal a pack of Marlboro. Casually, he pulled the pack from the display and slipped into his coat pocket. Little did he know that a store detective stood behind him and saw the whole thing, as he was about to exit, the detective flashed his ID and grabbed Daniel by the arm. "You're under arrest for shoplifting," the detective said seriously.

Daniel tried to wiggle his way out of it. "I didn't steal anything," he cried out.

"You took a pack of Marlboro," the detective replied.

"I did not," he claimed.

Daniel reached into the other pocket of his coat and pulled out another unopened pack of Marlboro he had bought in a vending machine at school during a break just hours before. He showed it to the detective and said:

"I bought these at school."

The detective looked at the bottom of the package and did not see the code he was looking for. Taken aback for a second, the detective looked at Daniel who had the most innocent expression on his face, he reached into the shoplifter's other coat pocket and pulled out the other pack of Marlboro, Daniel was in trouble.

With evidence and the culprit in hand he marched his thief to the rear of the store. His days as a thief were over. With his head down Daniel was marched through the store handcuffed by a uniformed police office. He escorted the shoplifter to the town's small police station. The police officer removed the handcuffs, fingerprinted, photographed, and interviewed Daniel who was in total shame. The young criminal was issued a Summary Offense citation, which is all they did in those days to shoplifters.

He was never behind bars, and he had to pay a $75 fine, which he did the next day. But he took the whole incident hard. A couple of hours after the stupid stunt happened, he was released and driven by the same police officer back to the store where his car was.

Daniel returned to his dorm room and sobbed into his pillow. Angered, he stood up and went to his desk. He grabbed a stapled stack of papers and tore them up. He felt like his life was over. As he threw the application in the trash, he understood he would now be rejected for the special program he planned and wanted to enter after he graduated in two-months, a fellowship to work at a kibbutz in Israel.

"I don't know what made me do it. I just wasn't thinking. Why this? Why me? Why now?" he cried into his pillow.

When he thought how close he was to graduating from college the consequences of his actions started to sink in.

"I'm a loser… I'm a loner… I hate myself…"

However, employers were usually not interested in an offense where the criminal act resulted in a citation and a small fine, as if the prospective employee broke the speed limit or did not curb his dog. A summary offense was of no significance to most, as Daniel learned later.

So, when the social worker who interviewed him later asked him about his past criminal convictions and incarceration dates, Daniel recounted on his fingers as he looked at her:

"I have no criminal history, no misdemeanors, no felonies and I've never been in jail."

He told her the absolute truth, but in his heart, he knew the truth.

He never stole again after that incident, because it was powerful enough to dissuade him and place him on a path towards goodness.

The nurses interviewed Daniel for hours. They turned to the topic of military service.

He was sexually assaulted three times while he served his country. In spite, he excelled during his military service. He was a company clerk. And he did well. He was promoted from private E-1 to Specialist E-5 in just over two years of his three-year enlistment.

But at least five times that day when he recounted his life history, which included the sexual assaults, each time he revisited those memories he lost composure.

When a future psychiatrist interviewed him, she was mostly interested in his medical history. Daniel looked at the lady that was young enough to be his daughter. She was well dressed in brows dress slacks, a tan shirt and a chocolate brown cashmere sweater. She smiled at him and interviewed him in the nearly emptied day room. She sat right next to Daniel in one of the heavy plastic and steel seats bolted to the floor in the long row along the wall. With a clipboard rested on her folded legs she took notes. Daniel admired her stylish brown shoes. She had a warm soft way about her which also appealed to the patient.

"Tell me about any hospitalizations you've had in your life," Dr. Beth McDaniel said.

Daniel shrugged his shoulders. "I was in the hospital once for less than 24 hours," he said.

"Where were you in the hospital?"

"In Arizona,"

"When was this?"

"In 2006…"

"What were you in the hospital for, Daniel?"

"I had kidney stone blockage, and they had to go in and zap it."

"That's pretty painful."

"Yeah, it was."

Silence came between them for a few seconds as she wrote it down.

"And that's it? That's the only time you ever been hospitalized?"

"That's it, accept when I worked in a hospital."

"Yes, I heard about that." "You were a psychiatric technician one at the Nevada State Psychiatric Hospital on the admissions unit in Las Vegas."

"Yes, I was."

"So, you're used to a place like this?"

"I am."

Dr. McDaniel continued, she asked about childhood diseases, all normal. And then she talked about the depression and cluster headaches Daniel experienced.

"How long have you've been depressed."

Daniel sighed, thought and said: "Probably many decades to be honest about it."

"Have you ever had psychiatric services before?"

"Back in the 80s when I first started working in the field and learned about depression, I sought help from an outpatient clinic."

"What was the name of the clinic?"

"Pottsville Psychiatric Services,"

"And tell me about that."

"Well, they determined that I was depressed and placed me on an antidepressant."

"And which antidepressant were you on?"

"Nortriptyline…"

"Tell me about the medication."

"It was effective. But I stopped using it."

"Why did you do a thing like that?"

"Because I was ignorant, when I got to Nevada, I threw them away thinking I'm fine now, I don't need these anymore."

"So, the depression returned. When did it return?"

"In 1994, that's around the time I started feeling the pressure in my brain and the cluster headaches started coming."

"Tell me about the cluster headaches?"

Dr. McDaniel watched her patient's eyes sink to the left as the crease in his forehead rose.

"They are without doubt the most pain I've ever endured."

"Have you ever had brain imaging done?"

He was taken aback by the question.

"No, I never even thought about it."

"Well, MRIs weren't common back in those years, I'm going to order an MRI."

His forehead unfolded and his eyes glazed with gratitude.

"Oh, thank you. I would've done it years ago, if I'd only thought about it. It never crossed my mind to ask."

"Well, it happens. I'm going to start you back on a low dose of Nortriptyline, gradually we'll increase it every few days, just to see how your body is adapting to it. Also, I saw what you were taking before you were inpatient, I'm going to stop the Lortabs and I'm going to start weaning you off the Xanax."

A worried look came over him.

"But they're for my cluster headaches. I don't have anxiety."

"I know but you're on a very high dose and I'm going gradually reduce one-half a milligram every other day, that ought to make it easier for you."

He shrugged his shoulders.

"Okay," he relented.

"Okay then, I'll see you tomorrow. That's when have community day when everybody's here, all the patients, regular staff, and the resident supervisors, the psychiatrists. They go around an interview all the new patients."

"I haven't told any other patients about my mental health background."

"I understand. When he asks you about the kind of work you do just tell him you'll talk about that later with him."

"Okay," he said.

Dr. McDaniel left the room. Soon after, long enough for everything, she just told him to sink in a social worker entered and asked Daniel to join her in her office.

Mrs. Bernstein was old. Her white thinning hair and her shriveled skin was a curious thing to Daniel. Of course, he had been around old people before, but in all his years in the field he never met any professionals who looked as old as she did.

"I'm Mrs. Bernstein, I'll be your social worker while you're here."

Daniel grinned a little and thought:

"Here's a nice old Jewish lady who'll be providing social services to me."

He looked around her small office which bore a framed diploma, a calendar, and a framed painting of a red barn surrounded by lush golden pasture. She logged on to her laptop computer.

"What is your level of education?"

"I have a bachelor's degree."

Mrs. Bernstein typed his response into her computer.

"From where, in what?"

"I went to Penn State, and I have a degree in Journalism."

Mrs. Bernstein looked at him for a second and then turned her attention back to the computer screen.

"But I've never worked in that field. Except for a job in the business world for a couple years after I graduated, I've always worked in mental health."

He was honest about all the information she and the other staff solicited, but he knew sometimes he bent the truth.

Mrs. Bernstein offered her new patient the use of her office phone to call his father. Daniel had not spoken to anyone in his family about what happened and where he was at. Grateful, because he didn't have any money on him to use the payphone, Daniel accepted. Mrs. Bernstein had to dial the number for him. It was VA policy. When she handed the phone to him, he became nervous.

"Hello, Dad…"

"Daniel, where are you?"

Daniel looked down at the floor, breaking any eye contact he had with Mrs. Bernstein.

"I'm in Los Angeles in the hospital."

"In LA in the hospital, what the hell are you doing there?"

"I'm in the West Los Angeles Veterans hospital's psychiatric unit."

"What is this…? Why are you there…?"

"Because I'm depressed, Dad..."

He looked at Mrs. Bernstein for a split second and he could see she was concerned.

"Are you living in LA, I thought you were in Pennsylvania?"

"No, I'm living in Bakersfield…"

"Bakersfield! Why the fuck are you in Bakersfield? Who the fuck told you to go to Bakersfield?"

"No one, my gut told me to go there."

Daniel began twisting the telephone cord.

The phone conversation between Herbert Sherman, as he was known, went on for another few minutes. Herbert softened his tone for the boy he called "a mistake," and told him he'd call other family members and let them know where he was.

"What's the number I can call you at?"

"Um…"

Daniel looked at Mrs. Bernstein with a curious gaze.

"What's the number you can call me at?"

Mrs. Bernstein consulted her address book and gave him the number to the day room pay-phone. Daniel repeated the numbers to his estranged father.

His father tried to end the conversation in a compassionate way and Daniel welled up in tears.

"You just get well, Daniel…"

"I'm sorry Dad… okay, I will…"

He handed the phone back to Mrs. Bernstein and she hung it up. The social worker said she would meet with him again tomorrow.

Daniel slid back into the seat at the checkerboard table where he established his seat from the first hour he was on the unit.

It all started after he dressed appropriately in hospital clothes with some of his own personal clothes beneath. As he sat in the seat he sought, he quickly surveyed the room full of patients, some of whom watched television, worked on art projects, played chess, or just sat doing nothing except staring around.

Earlier he spotted a man sitting aside one of the tables and there was an empty seat on the other side of it. Daniel walked over and sat down. The man ignored Daniel at first and rubbed the top of his shaved head. After a few seconds Daniel turned his body and eye contact towards the man on his right and in a friendly fashion said: "Hi, I'm Daniel."

Robert Jones didn't make friends quickly. He had learned in the "joint," that was a mistake. In fact, he spent 9 months in solitary confinement so he could stay out of the general population. It fucking drives you crazy, man," he later told Daniel. Jonesy, which was the name he went by, swung his body to his left, reached out and shook Daniels outreached hand. "All right," he coolly announced. Jonesy surveyed Daniel and looked him over. Daniel wasn't proud of his appearance, he always had low self-esteem when he was overweight. Even so, Jonesy asked: "What are you doing in here man?"

Daniel raised his eyebrows.

"I've been depressed for more than a year."

"So, you're here voluntarily?"

"Yeah…"

"Man, that's fucked up.,"

"What kind of work you do?"

"Well, I don't work now, I quit my job."

"What was you doing?"

"Oh, I was working helping people and shit…"

Daniel rolled his head a little and looking up at the back of it softly hit the wall.

"What kind of help?"

Daniel sighed, crinkled his forehead and looked at Jonesy.

"Oh, it had to do with weatherization of their house or apartment."

"Oh, that's fucked up, man."

The pay phone rang, and Jonesy popped up out of his seat to answer it. "Hello?" he asked, "who?" he inquired, "Rodriguez here?" Jonesy yelled out. A short Hispanic man wearing large, framed glasses was dressed nicely in a white business shirt, unbuttoned at the collar and dress slacks, Daniel remembered: one outfit was permitted, but no belt, Daniel declined taking only the undergarments which were allowed.

Mr. Rodriguez rose from his seat at one of the heavy long tables in the center of the room and pushed his glasses closer to his face. He said nothing until he took the phone from Jones. Rodriguez listened for a second and began talking in Spanish to someone. Jones sat back down and looked over at Daniel.

"So, man, you married?" he asked.

Daniel hated that question; his face could not show it.

"No, I'm not."

Jones and Daniel seemed to hit it off. They talked, shared stories and appeared to enjoy each other's company. As the days went on, they would each get to know each other even more.

A tall thin man who unlocked the therapeutic recreation closet entered and approached Daniel.

"Hi, I'm Bob, the recreation therapist," he announced.

Daniel stood up; he was still a bit nervous. He always liked to make a good impression even when he was depressed. But often he felt awkward and uncomfortable with himself when he said things.

"Hi," he replied, sheepishly.

He looked at Bob's ID, it read: "Robert Cohen" Daniel quickly surmised that Bob was obviously a Jewish man. He looked Jewish, Daniel could picture him with a yarmulke on his head standing in synagogue, praying.

Bob invited him to come to his office.

They exited the day room and walked past a locked blue cage door which allowed the staff access to the nurse's station and allowed patients the opportunity to stand there and make requests or complain. A patient stood by the cage door with his head up against it as he peered in. He moaned to someone who walked by inside:

"I need my medication," the patient wallowed.

Bob and Daniel walked down a long hallway past a series of three huge thick glass bay windows. Behind the glass were nurses typing information into computer terminals. One peered up at him for a second as he walked past Bob.

Daniel thought about his journey through two-south, from his room located at the far end of one bright hallway near an exit door, around a corner that went past the day room entrance and the nurse's station to where he stood now was unchartered territory. They walked down another long bright hallway, past the far end of the nurse's sanctuary and three large thick bay windows on one side of the hall.

Bob's slinky tall frame twisted round the next corner in the bright tiled hallway, past a series of blue doors and finally to the last hallway, at the end of it was a big blue door with one of those 8X11 eye level safety pane, above it a bright red florescent sign read exit. Smack in the center of the door was big placard warning: "Patients at risk for flight, please close door behind you: Thank you." The door was not locked, it had one of those silver bars at waist height that needed only to be pushed, and it would open.

"It sounds an alarm," Bob mentioned.

At each end of each hallway mounted near the ceilings were cameras recording all activities, the hallways were also equipped with unknown and unseen audio devices picking up any sound activities, as well.

Bob bent over at his blue door and grabbed a key housed behind his ID on a string. Still bent at the waist, he stuck the key in the door and reached out to the door handle. He pushed down on it and removed the key simultaneously.

"Please," he said.

As he erected himself, Bob gestured for Daniel to enter first. The office light was already on, and Daniel sat in a chair with arms next to the desk cluttered with paper on top one of those large desk calendars, there were doodles drawn on it and lots of notations in each day's square. Bob sat at his desk, logged on to his computer and began to type. Daniel watched him as his long slender fingers manipulated the computer keys like Liberace on a piano.

A minute later Bob spoke: "So, Daniel, what brings you here?"

Daniel's expression sobered. He broke eye contact and looked down.

"I've been depressed for more than a year."

Daniel went on to give his testimonial, sexual trauma, tears and all. After which, Bob gave Daniel his take...

Bob's assessment of Daniel: "You're known as a late bloomer."

Daniel's eyes shot upward in his head as he introspected and thought: "Late bloomer."

Bob's therapeutic recreation assessment was that Daniel needed to focus on three things:

"Coping skills, leisure interests, and support systems." Also, Bob implored:

"you need to attend groups."

Daniel and Bob stood up and they shook hands.

Daniel slowly walked back through the hallways feeling drained by the day's activities. Suddenly, a nurse wearing new white sneakers that lit up appeared in the hallway from around the corner and called out:

"Mr. Sherman…"

Daniel halted; his name had never been called so many times in one day.

As his pace paused his voice managed to peer out:

"Yes…"

"I've got an order to escort you down to radiology, they're going to do an MRI on your brain."

Chapter 4

Daniel worked with kids before at a residential treatment program. So, when he accepted the position of substitute teacher, he knew what he was up against. He believed it would be a little easier because:

"After all, these weren't emotionally disturbed kids," he thought.

His first year on the job he was challenged. He worked every school day, even in the summer because Nevada had twelve-month schools. He faced hundreds of kids at many different locations around the valley. Each day he would call into a computer system which announced the assignments, the school's name, and the grade he would teach. The assignments were numerous, and he could pick and choose what school and grade he wanted to teach.

He would show up a half hour before school started, check in with the office and receive the classroom keys. Then, he'd make his way to the classroom he would work in that day. There was always a long note which outlined the class lesson plan and the kid's special needs:

"Johnny Smith needs to go to the nurse at eleven a.m. for his medication," he read. "Watch out for Billy Michaels he limits tests a lot." Daniel would look at the desk and the day's lesson plan materials were usually organized for him.

It was a good job. It paid ninety dollars per day, but there were no benefits. He could work every day, except weekends, holidays, and in-school service days which is when the teachers were there, but the kids were not.

The first year Daniel struggled. He gained weight and had more cluster headaches. His attitude towards his new job became negative and sometimes, he did not want to go to school and sometimes he stayed home and smoked all day. The headaches were just one reason why he struggled.

Daniel's moods were unstable. He mourned the loss of a favorite pet for weeks and things were not going much easier at school. One day he took an assignment in a fourth-grade classroom. The kids misbehaved all day, and the normally mild-mannered man showed them an angry facial expression with angry eyes and an angry voice tone. It was enough to push the kids to write a letter. They placed it on the desk and some point in the day. It said:

"We hate you…"

The substitute teacher had some lessons to learn. He retreated to his comfort zone and self-medicated. Later he was motivated and by what is still an unknown. He thought the motivator was some sort of drive which started in motion, and it only needed a spark which kindled the movement, because something inside him was triggered either by events at school or the death of pet, or perhaps both. Welled-up energy released its way through his mind, body and soul and he started going to the gym and for the first time in his life, he really tried to get in shape.

By that summer he was in better shape, and he continued to substitute for teachers. On one assignment he selected a two-day class assignment for first graders. He liked teaching elementary, especially second and third grade.

When he showed up at the door of the first-grade classroom a woman was there.

Her name was Mrs. Roberts, and it was her last two days before she was to retire after 35 years on the job. Mrs. Roberts smiled broadly when she met him. Mrs. Thomas was impeccably dressed. She wore a blue dress which complimented her dark brown skin. While waiting for the children to arrive, Mrs. Thomas explained that this would be a team-teaching day. Daniel occupied the desk and seat of the absent teacher.

Mrs. Roberts told him:

"Just sit there and watch."

And that was just what he did for two days. Her facial features were warm and lovable, and her delivery was so smooth and effortless, she possessed just the right attitude the substitute needed to learn to emulate. He observed her calm and collected manner and her commanding and compelling voice tone along with her perfect inflection and precision timing, even down to her body posture and hand gestures as she showed how to keep the children in the palm of her hand. For two days, he saw a pro in action. Mrs. Roberts may not have been aware of it, but she showed Daniel that you can manage a classroom with goodness.

After he left Mrs. Roberts classroom he thought about her a lot. His mind developed a different attitude, and he had begun to reason with himself more. He thought about those two days with Mrs. Roberts all the time. He even used one of her lines:

"Who is talking?" she'd ask. "Pencils don't talk," she reminded them with a song in her voice.

Mrs. Roberts was an inspiration and Daniel's attitude shifted and showed that he wanted to make the most of it.

He started setting the right tone and expectations at the beginning of each day when the students were first brought into the classroom. He wrote of the chalk board: "Mr. Sherman," and below that he wrote three-rules: "(1) SHOW RESPECT. (2) BE NICE. (3) LISTEN AND FOLLOW INSTRUCTIONS."

Once a challenge, now teaching developed into a labor of love. Daniel delivered about a seven-minute speech along with it. He developed the words, and he worked on it seriously and the poetic verse evolved from there. He started to get so good at setting the right tone and expectations that he presented it like it was a song. It had a rhythm. It had a heart. It had a soul.

One day, he accepted as an assignment to be a substitute music teacher for the day. He showed up in the classroom and there was nothing there. No note, no lesson plan, and no instruments. In this large empty space sat one folded metal chair. There were no other seats in the music rooms and the students would have to sit on the floor. Daniel unfolded the chair and sat down. His first class of the day consisted of students from three classrooms.

There were to be forty-five children in attendance that period, along with two student aids, which was because one of the classes was a special education class. Daniel got up and wrote his three rules on the chalk board. As the students arrived, he stood by the metal chair. These were students from second and third grade regular classes, and six or seven students from a third-grade special education class, along with their two adult special aides.

"Good morning class and welcome. My name is Mr. Sherman, and I will be your teacher today. I have three rules that you must follow: Number one: SHOW RESPECT. Number two: BE NICE. And number three: LISTEN AND FOLLOW INSTRUCTIONS."

Daniel surveyed the class, and they all had their eyes focused on him.

"EVERYBODY has a good side to them and a bad side. And when you come to school, you need to SHOW your good side. You need to SHOW it to your teachers. You need to SHOW it to your fellow classmates. And you need to SHOW it to yourself. Because you need to be aware that it's there, because your good side is a very important part of you, and you need to bring it out and USE IT."

Daniel held the attention of everyone in the room as he looked around at all their faces.

"Now sometimes when we are at home a brother or sister, or somebody will show us their bad side, and we automatically turn around and show them our bad side that's because it's a natural reflex and just like when the doctor hits your knee, your knee's going to pop up every time and it's the same with the bad side because when somebody shows us their bad side we turn around and automatically show them our bad side. So, when someone is mean or mad at us, we turn right around, and we are mean and mad back at them. But you're not at home now, and so you've got to act differently. You don't act the same way you do when you're at home. Because when you're at home you show everybody everything that's inside you, sometimes you're laughing and being silly and goofy, and sometimes you're crying and fighting. And, so, it's important to know where you're at. Right now, you're in school, and school is a very important place, just like when you go to the mall or the library, or to grandma and grandpa's house. So, there's no place for your bad side here or any other important place. There's no place for being mean and mad and there's no place for being silly or goofy, you can save that for the playground. Now, what do you think would happen if your mom or dad went to work and showed their bad side?"

Some students responded in unison "they'd be fired."

"They'd be fired, or they'd get in to trouble, that's right. Because when your mom or dad goes to work, they're going to their job and so they've got to show the very best that's inside them, and when you come to school you've got to show the very best that's inside you. You may not have realized it, but when you come to school you're coming to work. This is your job and you are a student and that's a very important job to have because you'll have this job for many years, and when you're finished with this job you will be ready to go to a job just like your moms and dads do, and so it's very important to learn how to show your very best when you are at work. Now sometimes when we come to school things are hard. But just remember when you tried to ride a bike for the first time, you fell off. But you didn't give up. You got right back up on it, and kept trying and trying, and now you're an expert at it. That's the same thing you've got to do when something in school is hard. You've got to keep trying and trying, and soon you'll understand it and become an expert at it because you'll have mastered it, and then it becomes something easy for you. Another thing to remember is boys and girls people talk all the time, and we say thousands of words a day and sometimes some people say things that's just not worth listening to, and so if you hear someone say something you know is wrong, and they know it's wrong to. We simply ignore them and don't ever give them the satisfaction of a response. We don't give them any attention. Only give your attention to people who are nice and kind and friendly and who show respect, because sometimes some people like to push our buttons. What is respect? It's when we are nice and kind and friendly to each other. I respect you and you respect me."

He turns, picks up an eraser and starts using it like it's a remote control for the television.

"Because some people walk around just like they've got some kind of remote control in their hands and if I push this button she'll cry and get mad and if I push that button he'll yell and scream. But by ignoring them you're saying: Your remote control doesn't work on me, it might work on somebody else, but it doesn't work on me, because what works on me is when you're nice and kind and friendly and we show each other respect, so we ignore people that try to push out buttons with their remote control and we try to only give our attention to someone who's being nice and kind and friendly. Just remember when we show the very best that's inside of you, you're showing respect toward yourself and toward others… And when we show our good side, good things happen… And when we show our bad side, bad things happen..."

The classroom was so silent it was hard to believe that it was a music room filled with children. Every pair of eyes in the room demonstrated that they understood what was said.

Daniel put the eraser back on the chalk board ledge. "Now," he said. Today, we're going to play a little game…

And for the next forty-minutes Daniel ran the classroom as if he were the host of the game show Jeopardy. "I'm going to give you some clues and you have to guess what I am. If you guess what I am you get to come up here and sit in the chair and give out the next set of clues. Now, it's important that you raise your hand if you know the answer, because if you call out an answer you will be disqualified. Okay, here we go,"

Daniel paused, thought and said: "I'm big and green, and I welcome people, what am I?"

Several students had their hands up and Daniel chose one of the kids from the second grade.

"The jolly green giant," a little girl said.

"No, that's not it."

Next, he picked one of the kids from the special education class.

"You are the Statue of Liberty," the boy answered with pride.

"That's right," Daniel said enthusiastically. "Come on up here," he told the boy.

The child unfolded his legs, jumped up and came forward. Daniel looked at him when he sat in the chair and told him: "Man, you are good at this game."

The game went on until the end of the period, and when time ran out, Daniel had them all stand up, stretch and form a line to exit. The two adult special aids stood in line next to their students. One of the ladies was a Hispanic woman and she looked at Daniel, and he saw that her eyes were a glow and vibrant. Daniel had seen that look before in the kid's eyes and to the substitute teacher it communicated the utmost respect.

Suddenly, Daniel loved his work with the young people, and he always treated them with dignity and respect.

"The same dignity and respect ever person should have towards them self and towards others," he said to himself one day.

He worked as a substitute for three years, until one day, his phone rang. He had applied to the State of Nevada, which announced he was deemed qualified for a certain position: Psychiatric Caseworker II.

Chapter 5

Daniel noticed the woman through the window as he reached for the door handle. His very first impression of her was that she was like no other nurse he had ever seen. As she searched through a page on a clipboard with a pen in her hand, he entered and introduced himself, whereby, she introduced herself as:

"Ethel Braveman."

Instantaneously, he gripped on to the notion that she had the stuff to make a great leader. She had a strong physical presence, and she looked like she had an intelligence level that could rival a Nobel laureate, and he believed that she possessed a very calm disposition which matched her appealing facial expression.

When Daniel sat down in to the small music room on two-south he believed that he was to meet a nurse to be assessed again. The new patient knew it was common practice for a couple of assessments to be conducted to illicit a patient's history. First there was the clinician's assessment followed by a psychiatric assessment conducted by a psychiatrist then there was the psychiatric nurse's assessment and finally the case management and therapeutic recreation assessment and Daniel knew they all had to be in a chart because when the chart was reviewed by auditors and higher echelons and they wanted to see a pattern of consistency between interviews, not to mention the treatment plan and treatment goals. But this was Daniel's fourth that day and although that was odd in and of itself, because these types of assessments usually take place over a period of weeks, but he did not care. He may have looked worn-out, but he was never exhausted when it came to talking about himself.

"You look pretty tired, Mr. Sherman."

Daniel quickly noticed her ID, but he thought that Nurse Braveman looked more like President Braveman because of her body posture and mannerisms. He thought she looked like a cross between Hillary Clinton and Margaret Thatcher.

"I'm doing all right, I guess."

Her posture never sagged, and her elegant hair style never shifted as she looked down at the clipboard atop her lap. "Well, I'll try and get through this as painlessly as possible."

It was eight o'clock at night and Braveman looked and smelled as fresh as a bag of popcorn that had just finished popping.

"Are you on the night shift?"

"No, actually I'm not."

She pulled her crossed ankles closer to her. "Now, I have a series of questions, and we'll see how good of a historian you are."

"I have a good memory," he replied unable to keep his mouth shut.

"Well, let us work chronologically backwards, if we may."

Daniel shifted his lower extremities from the edge of the seat back. He kept his hands on his upper thighs as his back rested against the seat and his large waistline protruded only a few inches shy of his hands and knees.

For a few seconds Daniel studied Braveman as she consulted her clipboard. He thought the middle-aged woman with brown hair and eyes seemed out of place. She looked more like a psychiatrist than a psychiatric nurse. From what he saw that day she looked nothing like the other nurses he had contact with since he arrived. She was dressed much more properly, and her grooming was impeccable. Nurses usually looked as if they'd been cleaning house, a bit disheveled. And most wore a scrub with little hearts or teddy bears on them. This lady was dressed as if she were at an important conference, and she was about to give the keynote address.

"Let us start with your job history."

As her fountain pen glided over the page like a professional figure skater on ice, Daniel began.

"I worked for a state-run mental health agency in the rural areas of Nevada for nearly five-years. After two years in northern Nevada, I transferred from one out-patient clinic to another, and then to another, following a conflict with a co-worker at the previous rural location."

"What kind of conflict?"

"It was so petty, and I did overreact, but I didn't do anything wrong, and the division's investigation concluded that. I received no reprimands, and I wasn't disciplined."

"What happened with your coworker?"

"She told me she hated the classical music that was played in the waiting room. I told her that she hated everything. Basically, that was all."

Braveman observed Daniel's facial expression and jotted down: "Flat affect." She smiled at him, and he did not smile back.

"You say you were transferred to another clinic," she asked.

"That's right. Ultimately, I ended up living and working in a dusty rural area about sixty miles from metropolitan Las Vegas.

"Tell me about your life there."

"I never went out. I had no life outside my work, and I stayed primarily to myself. I bought a puppy and named her Pearl. I self-medicated with marijuana. But, by then other prescribed drugs were added to the mix, which ultimately altered my brain chemistry, and my behaviors towards self-destruction. I messed myself up physically and mentally, and the whole mixture contributed to my downfall.

"Your downfall, what happened?"

Daniel fidgeted in his seat for a second.

"After three-years I made a mistake one weekend night by visiting a client at her home during non-working hours. One of my other clients saw my car and reported me. I didn't have to resign, but, after I was called in to the Director's office and the incident was brought to my attention, I voluntarily resigned from my position as a psychiatric caseworker for medical reasons. That one mistake and my impulsive decision to resign from my career in the mental health field that dates to the 1980s."

He noticed Braveman's writing hand and her wedding and engagement ring, which was a simple diamond set which seemed to compliment her soft hands and impeccably manicured nails lightly coated with a soft clear polish.

"I read that you've been getting cluster headaches for quite some time... talk about that for a moment."

"I've suffered from cluster headaches since the early 90s. They started when I was working in another mental health position for the State of Nevada as a house parent relief. And, one month shy of five-years serving severely emotionally disturbed youth, I resigned. That was my first resignation for medical purposes. I was sick because in those years, the cluster headaches had the upper hand."

"How so, describe it for me."

His stomach expanded as he drew in a deep breath. When his abdomen deflated, he looked down at his hands which were partly obscured by his sizeable waistline.

"For years I endured the punishing pressure on the left side of my brain and down into my left eye. I wrote about the pain once and I remember what I said…

"It's like my head is between the jaws of a vise and an unknown force is holding it firmly in place as it slowly winds and tightens the screw. The pressure builds every second, and for an hour or more the force focuses on my brain during its sadistic mission. The pain inflicts sharp twisting jabs into one specific section, and the throbbing pain continues to pummel and ravage the same area repeatedly. A never-ending feeling of dread encompasses my being. And the quality of my living experience is waning.

It's like this force has O.C.D. (obsessive compulsive disorder) and could really use some meds coupled with some therapy because the grinding pain and pressure never stops. The sadistic enchanter just keeps going on and on..."

Braveman stopped writing and observed him.

"The cluster headache is not merciful. The cluster headache has no consciousness. The cluster headache does its job and it's damn good at it. There's no knock-out blow leading me into my unconscious world. I'm totally aware of every excruciating moment. At first, I tried beating my head and that never helped. Now I just cradle my head in my hands and caress about it. But a soothing touch doesn't help much either. My head remains locked between this ever-closing grip. And, after a short period the pain begins to spread out. As the torture continues punishing the brain it spirals downward and squarely lands in and around my left eye. The pressure becomes so great many times I cry out in sheer agony because it feels as if my head will explode." Daniel paused and looked around the room. Can I get some water?"

"Yes, there's a water fountain in the hallway."

"Thank you."

Daniel stood and left the room. Braveman wrote more notes and observed her interviewee through the thick glass as he bent over at the fountain. When he returned, he resumed with a verbal prompt.

"You felt like your head would explode."

"Yeah, the cluster headache is a symphony of pain, and it heightens into a crescendo as it continues to relentlessly pummel its favorite territory of my brain and my eye. It's as if I were a door being pounded on by an abusive husband desperately trying to gain admittance into his petrified wife's house to beat her up once again. With true persistence he pounds as he tortures his spouse with his most hateful words. My brain torture is compounded by a similar flood of negativity because everything that's going on in my head thought wise is things I hate. Sometimes it's a song repeating itself like a broken record, and it just won't stop. Also, people I hate come to mind along with other hateful moments in my life. They bubble up and reach my surface of consciousness as they float around in the cesspool of misery. There's no stopping the audio of cluster headache attacks, just like there's no stopping the deluge of pain. And between the pain and my brain trash, I'm stuck like I'm in some med evil torture chamber. At least, until it decides it wants to stop."

Daniel eyes welled up and he could stop his emotions from surfacing, as well.

"A cluster headache is like a home invasion of the most personal nature, but the robber steals nothing material only spiritual. It used to be every day and night, sometimes five times per day, just like clockwork, while one part of my head and face is beaten to a pulp and the other side of the head is left untouched. Before the Xanax my favorite line was:

"I do not want to be here. I do not want to participate anymore, he noted.

"And since the Xanax the frequency of having one was cut to a third."

"That's really something, Mr. Sherman. So, you thought about suicide?"

Daniel sighed and looked at the poster on the wall. The picture was a beautiful scene of a lush green forest, and the sunlight shined through its breaches casting spotlights of sunshine on the earth's floor.

"During the cluster headache I think about killing myself, but I never try to. After I'm released from the jaws of agony I have frequent suicidal ideations. In the 90s, I sought help through the same agency I worked for when I first moved to Las Vegas. I used to be a psychiatric technician in the locked admissions unit of the State's small psychiatric hospital. When all of this started happening, I received out-patient services, as well as counseling and medication. The services I received were the State's best effort, but nothing worked, and the cluster headaches and depression grew steadily worse, and that's when I was approved for Social Security Disability."

Braveman thanked Daniel for his complete cooperation and cogent answers. She pulled her materials forward and referred to a section in her binder briefly.

"So, you left your job. What did you do next?" she asked.

"I drove and moved all over the nation. I kept thinking if I moved here, I'll feel better or if I moved there, I'll feel better, I'd tell myself. I set up a residence in almost each location I went to -- Las Vegas to Northern California, Northern California to Pennsylvania, Pennsylvania to Florida, Florida back to Las Vegas, Las Vegas to Alton, Illinois, Alton, Illinois back to Pennsylvania, Pennsylvania back to Las Vegas. I moved a lot, but I never felt any better," he told her.

"Where did you get all the money to do all of this?" she wondered out loud.

"Some of it was from savings. Some of it was cash advances from credit cards. And some of it was from my brother. I went into deep debt. And later, I had to declare bankruptcy, which my brother also paid for. I still owe him and his wife a lot."

Braveman looked back through her notes. "This is a complicated case. Let's move forward. I believe I read that you rebounded. Talk about that."

"Well, I finally settled back in the desert southwest I was accustomed too. One day the phone rang. It was a nurse from the Mental Health out-patient clinic. She told me that lab results indicated I had a high thyroid level, and she said I must see my primary care doctor to see if that could be the root of my depression and the cluster headaches. I went to a few doctors over the years. 'You're just depressed,' they all told me. No tests, nothing.

But I followed the nurse's advice, and I went to the VA out-patient clinic and sought the services of a new primary care physician. The young doctor who saw me told me that he could tell what the matter was when I held out his hands and looked at my bulged eyes: You have Graves' Disease, hyper-thyroid.' Sure enough, after blood work and a thyroid scan it was all confirmed. I had radiation treatment to ultimately kill the gland.

It took more than a year because the radiation treatment acted slowly as it was supposed to. That year I stopped smoking cigarettes and drinking diet coke, which my brother, the ex-nurse, said was the cause of my headaches and other medical problems. They weren't the cause, but I quit anyway."

"Well, that's good."

"I didn't miss the cigarettes at all, because at that time I took a small part-time job, which was permitted by Social Security, if I didn't work too many hours. That's when I started smoking marijuana for the cluster headache pain. I made a good drug connection. I was convinced that only marijuana combated the cluster headaches. But I never had a steady supply of the weed, and I could never tell from week to week if I could find it. But once I moved into the studio apartment and started my part-time job at a video store as a clerk, I met this guy, Alden. He became a reliable source of the drug for me."

"Alden was a lucky development. Alden who…"

"Yeah, Alden was tall and strong with dark hair, and I don't remember his last name. He was a soft-spoken man, he had become the perfect connection because at any time on any day, I needed only to knock on his door.

When the cluster headaches came, I retreated to the darkest spot in the studio which was the bathroom, which was also the quietest, because during a cluster headache noise and light were akin to being punched by a heavy-weight boxer. I used marijuana in the morning, noon and night. For the first time it felt like I gained the upper hand on the cruel cluster headaches. I still got them but, now I fought back. Marijuana did influence the pain. Sometimes it would instantaneously take the pain completely away and I'd be back to normal, but sometimes the pain would subside only for a few seconds as I held the smoke in, I could feel marijuana combating with the pain in my brain. I smoked hit after hit, until it went away."

Braveman unfolded her ankles and stretched her long handsome legs out. Another odd thought came to Daniel's mind: She was wearing black stylish high heels with short pumps. All the other nurses wore sneakers.

Nevertheless, the interview acted like a tonic on Daniel. He felt more relaxed.

"Daniel, have you ever left the country?"

Daniel was taken aback by the question from left field. "Well, yes, I, I did."

"Can you tell me about that?"

"Can I ask what's that got to do with anything?"

"Well, I'm just trying to show in my report that you're a reliable historian and that what you say is accurate."

Daniel shrugged his shoulders, and said:

"My thyroid ordeal left me in extra trim condition which helped boost my morale. I feel really depressed when I'm fat, but back then, when I trimmed down, I felt better even with the cluster headaches... Sometime that fall I received an invitation in the mail to attend my brother's youngest daughter's Bat Mitzvah in Israel. I was living off a small amount of money each month and my brother wrote that he would cover the cost of the trip and my other expenses. It was 1999, and at first, I was excited about going. I looked good and I felt better, as I said, thanks to the marijuana. I wrote back to my brother I told him that I would love to come. But really, I was still depressed. I was isolated. I didn't socialize. But smoking pot made those days pass more pleasantly. However, the more I thought about the trip to Israel the more my troubled mind stirred and brewed. I'd have to see my mother and a lot of other relatives I wasn't comfortable with.

"I remember just days before I left on the trip, my ex-stepmother, Eve, found me in tears. I do not want to go... I do not want to participate... I told her. She told me to go because after all, the plane had one stop where he had to change planes: Amsterdam, which excited me because I always wanted to live in Amsterdam because of the coffee houses which sold marijuana. The thought of seven-hour lay-over in Holland's city of canals meant I would travel from the airport to where the coffee houses were, get high and still make my flight to Israel. I also decided that since there was a layover in Amsterdam on the return trip, I'd plan to stay a couple of days there and then return to Las Vegas. When the itinerary was set it reduced my apprehension about the trip."

"So, Amsterdam was a great escape."

Daniel nodded and told Braveman:

"Yes, I made it to Amsterdam. I went from the airport into the heart of the city. I found a coffee house and was self-medicated. I was intoxicated even before I was intoxicated. I approached the first coffee house I could find, made a small purchase and indulged. I made it to the airport in time and I was still high. There was tight security at the Israeli airline, El Al, and when I arrived in Israel the security checks were even more stringent. It didn't matter; I wasn't carrying anything. I was just feeling good."

"Tell me about Israel. Did you like it there? Where did you go? What did you do?"

"I spent a week there, shared a hotel room with my younger sister, Kelly, who left her family in the care of her husband, and for the first time in decades I joined my family to celebrate my youngest niece's special day. My mother and stepfather were there, but I didn't spend any time with them. I can remember clearly that I rarely looked at them or spoke to them.

Israel was no fun. I was without marijuana for a week and my depression and cluster headaches didn't take a vacation. But I do remember that my sister-in-law Becky impressed me a great deal. She was an American from our hometown in Pennsylvania, and I enjoyed when we interacted, she was nice to me. Becky was very successful in life. She's always in great shape. My brother, Hal, is equally impressive. He's handsome and in fine shape. He's also quite successful. Becky and Hal had three children at the time: Allison, the oldest who was sixteen, and there is Elliot whose fifteen and Maggie, soon to be thirteen. Each of their offspring was bright healthy youngsters, and fortunately were raised in a functional family, unlike me and my siblings who were brought up in a dysfunctional household. In retrospect my mother provided for us but with an absentee father who ended up leaving the family when I was ten, and was lackadaisical about his child support responsibilities, not to mention his responsibilities as a father, life for our family when I was a boy was never harmonious. We were almost constantly at each other's throat. Hal was unkind and short tempered with me when we were children. He'd hit me, pull my hair, and throw a fit any time I came around him and his friends."

Braveman tried to direct Daniel as he swayed off course.

"What about Israel. We can talk about your youth later."

"Well, I was just going to say that I picked on my little sister too because I knew how to push just the right buttons to get her upset, and Kelly cried a lot. And I just wanted to add as for me and my mother, we fought constantly, and as a result, we never correctly bonded. I lost the love of my mother.

Braveman stopped writing and slowly looked up at Daniel.

Oh yeah Israel. It was on my first day in Israel that my family members piled on a chartered bus which made its way through the streets of Jerusalem. It was a peaceful period in Israel's history because the Palestinians and Israeli's were not openly hostile towards each other.

The bus stopped at the Western Wall, where everyone got off, except me, I stated that I felt a cluster headache coming on. With no tools to combat it I stayed behind. I watched as they made their trek down towards the wall.

An hour passed and I did indeed endure a severe cluster headache. The pain was unbearable, but the negative thoughts that surfaced were ugly. I paced the length of the bus back and forth rubbing the left side of my head and face, my body heated up as usual, but I did not strip off my clothes. I could see my family heading back and as they reached the bus and boarded, my brother could see that I was in pain. My left eye was puffed red and tears dripped from it, while snot trickled slowly from my left nostril. 'See,' I remember crying out. I remember my brother did show compassion and told me: 'You've got to do something about this.' All I could think of was to shout, 'What!' I shouted."

"So, the trip was hard on you."

"Yeah, but leaving Israel and my family was not painful. Once I got to Amsterdam, I was much happier. I checked into a small cheap hotel, and I immediately went to the first coffee house I could find, bought marijuana, hashish, and a small pipe, and retreated to my room. I smoked, it relaxed me, and I fell asleep. A couple of hours later, I was awakened by a very strong cluster headache. I stripped my clothes off, again, because my body heated up tremendously when I was in the grip of the pain, and I retreated to the bathroom, which I kept dark. I caressed the left side of my head, down to my puffy eye. I tried to blow the congestion out of my left nostril, which was another part of the cluster headache because the right nostril always remains unclogged and completely clear. The clogged left nostril prohibits oxygen from getting to the back left side of my brain. But the congestion wouldn't budge. My hands shook as I loaded the pipe with quality marijuana, and I felt increased pain when my left eye was exposed to the flicker of the flame. I inhaled deeply and I could feel the drug moving through me up into the left side of my brain. Instantaneously the pain stopped, and the left nostril cleared, and I could breathe through it again. I felt victorious. The victory was as if I scored the winning goal for my team."

Braveman studied her notes for several seconds and Daniel watched her as she contemplated her next question.

"So, you were in Israel for a week."

"That's right, just about seven days."

"Did the experience change you in anyway?"

"Change me? No, I'd say that it reinforced the notion that I needed to keep smoking pot, and that was around the time that states like California and Oregon legalized marijuana for medical purposes and I was determined to go there and do that, someday."

"But you didn't, did you?"

"No, when I returned to Las Vegas from my trip and Eve moved in with me. She was renting a room on the other side of town and wanted out of it. I offered her my room in the one-bedroom I rented and moved my bed out into the living room. After a few months, I decided to quit the video store and move back to Pennsylvania. My brother and my stepfather loaned me more money and that allowed me to move into a one-bedroom apartment. I bought furniture and moved in. I applied for a job and was hired. But a cluster headache began as I was being trained, and I quit. I stayed in the apartment for seven months, before I retreated once again to Las Vegas."

"Why did you return to Las Vegas? I thought you said you wanted to move to California or Oregon."

"I guess it's because I was so familiar with Las Vegas and because my father was willing to help me. By the year 2000 life started to get a little easier because that's when I got the job at the video store and met Alden. I smoked, worked at the store and lived in a studio apartment nearby. For two years I did that. I stopped going to Mental Health and stopped the psychotropic medication. But I continued to see the Endocrinologist at the VA who treated my thyroid condition."

Braveman was looking for something concrete and posed a direct question: "When the turn of the century came was that a time of change? Did the fact that it was a new millennium enter in to your mind?"

"Millennium, no I can't say that had anything to do with it. I did change a lot though. That was the year I stopped smoking cigarettes and drinking soda. And by the year 2001, I was well enough physically and mentally to stop receiving disability and I obtained full time employment as a substitute teacher."

Braveman's panache never changed during the interview. She did not seem to be impressed with Daniel Sherman, not on his first day in the hospital. "I do have one more question. What made you want to become a substitute teacher?"

I don't know. It was a step up from the video store I guess, and it was an easy job to get. I was hired because I had a bachelor's degree, a clean criminal history, and three references."

Braveman looked at her watch and Daniel could see it too, upside down. As she stood and shook Daniel's hand it struck him: Her watch was set three hours before, for Eastern Standard Time. Why, he wondered?

Chapter 6

Miller, followed by Kushner and Allison entered room 3G. Each man wore a perplexed facial expression. Miller turned around and watched as his two colleagues as they took their seat. Miller believed that his pronouncement would hit the room like a thunderbolt.

"All the signs are there."

Kushner's facial expression was strikingly apprehensive toward the announcement.

"Can you read that report again?"

"I've read it, and it matches."

"Please, indulge me."

Miller pulled an envelope from inside his suit pocket with the words TOP

SECRET printed on the front in huge red letters. He opened it and pulled out the document covered by a page which read: TOP SECRET.

"Wednesday, February 17, 2010 – 9 a.m. Subject: Sherman, Daniel M. Location: West Los Angeles Veterans Hospital - Los Angeles, California. Factors and Determinations – Subject interviewed: Five initial trials and two surreptitiously."

Miller looked at Kushner, who looked impatient and Allison who appeared focused.

"Undercover – Findings: (1) Sherman, Daniel M. – marital status: single – never married – Confirmed. (2) Religion: Non-affiliated – Jewish – Confirmed. (3) In-patient psychiatric status: One admission – Confirmed. (3) Israeli connections: Brother – sister-in- law reside in Israel – Confirmed - Nephew married to Israeli - residing in Boston – Confirmed. 1999 Sherman, Daniel M. enters Israel - stay: 5 days – Confirmed. 1983 Sherman, Daniel M. attempt made to earn fellowship in Israel - withdrawn – Confirmed. (4) Birthmark – back of neck – Confirmed. (5) No tattoos – no piercings – Confirmed. (6) Cluster headaches – left brain – Confirmed. (7) Brain tumor: Cavernous Hemangioma – no protrusion cerebrum – MRI Pending. (8) College Education – Graduated Penn State University, Bachelor of Arts in Journalism – Confirmed. (9) Sexually assaulted – three times – Confirmed. (10) Sexual orientation – Non-affiliated - sexual orientation (Conflicted) – Confirmed. (11) Criminal and incarceration history: Felony convictions: None - Confirmed. Misdemeanor convictions: None – Confirmed. Incarceration history: None - Confirmed. Other convictions: Summary Offense: April 1983 Petty Theft – Confirmation unavailable - original records destroyed in fire at local Justice of the Peace - November 1983– Confirmed. Summary findings: "Mr. Sherman is genuine."

The room was silent even before the findings were read, but the non-verbal communication between the group's members stood starkly contrasted from one another. Miller folded up the papers, returned them to the envelope and cleared his throat. Kushner with notes in front of him looked ready for rebuttal. Allison leaned back in his chair, and he had his two index fingers together over his mouth as he looked down at his notes on the conference table.

"Well, gentlemen?" Miller inquired.

Kushner looked at Allison. Both men communicated with their eye contact, their facial expression and body language: "You go first."

Kushner took the lead.

"Everything this guy has done over the past 50 years or so is dubious and I think it points in the direction of doubt."

Miller sat forward in his chair, picked up a pen in front of him and wrote a note. Allison repositioned his body to an erect posture as he sat forward in his chair and offered his point of view staring intently into his colleague's eyes.

"Gentlemen, Mr. Sherman has been on our list since the 50s…"

Miller slowly nodded in the affirmative as his head turned to Kushner.

Reluctantly, Kushner nodded and added:

"There were also over 10,000 names on our list back in those years. We never had the hard data we needed. His inpatient psychiatric hospitalization was negative…"

"Until, yesterday," Miller countered.

"Marital status, single," Kushner chimed in again.

"Never married, this guy doesn't even date," Miller supplemented.

Kushner's voice tone increased a decibel as his eyes widened and his brow lifted to its highest point.

"Cluster headaches were always negative."

Kushner rolled his eyes and cracked his knuckles.

"We had reports in the early 90s. And today it's been confirmed," Allison added in his soft gravel voice.

Kushner readjusted himself in his high-back leather chair and emphatically insisted:

"Wait a minute…. Let's hold on here for a second. In addition to that he must be born with at least one Cavernous Hemangioma brain tumor which must be like the type of Joseph Merrick, 'The Elephant Man' was plagued with."

"And remember," Miller added, "However, this tumor must develop internally and not protrude as it normally does."

"Yes, I've read that part a hundred times," Allison responded.

Kushner looked like he held the trump card as he gestures with his index finger waiting for his mouth to utter the words his had already formed in his mind.

"Most importantly, there must be a solid Israeli connection – which in his formative years never developed."

"He tried, didn't he? They've just developed slowly," Allison reasoned.

"Roland, he's been there, for Christ's sake," Miller added.

Allison eased back in his seat and diligently listened to his colleague's interpretations.

"This is the same man identified in the 80's who sought psychiatric services if you remember, but he never went in-patient, which is the most crucial indicator," Kushner professed.

Miller's eyebrows rose as he admitted:

"That was here back east. We were almost certain he'd go inpatient, but he just didn't."

"And when he had that automobile accident back in...

Kushner paused, glanced at his notes and then looked at Miller and Kushner.

…1985, November 22nd to be exact."

"Our analysis indicated that he would be a psychiatric inpatient in a matter of weeks, and we selected him then as probable," Dr. Allison stated as a matter of fact.

He smiled and looked at Kushner and told him:

"Remember the subject has never been in any hospital of any kind. There were no cluster headaches, no brain tumor, and all we had back then, Roland, were the facts that he was brought up in a Jewish home and was non-affiliated with Judaism or any other religion, and that he had a birth mark on the back of his neck, and he graduated from college with a bachelor's in journalism. Now we know his sexual orientation is conflicted."

A smidgeon of sarcasm broke into the forefront of Kushner's mind:

"He had that kidney stone blockage back in '06 and that was done in a hospital."

But, with his next progression of thought he argued convincingly belittling his own hypothesis.

"And let's not forget that he went to work in the mental health field and that pointed him in our direction. He wasn't impatient, but because he worked in mental health with absolutely no connection to it whatsoever, especially without a degree in the field. That tells us something."

Allison took Kushner's reasoning one step forward: "It could be quite the opposite. When he moved from the business world into the mental health field in 1986, we never dreamed to consider that the historical criteria we've followed since this began could be wrong and maybe he wasn't supposed to be inpatient. Maybe his mental health status as a provider of services was what it meant. After all, he worked in an inpatient setting. Roland, it may have not met the criteria, but it was always pointing us in the right direction," Allison told him.

Kushner leaned back in his seat, broke eye contact and replied mainly to himself: "I don't know."

"Consider one more thing, this man's life was always pointing us towards the right direction and even so, we dismissed him. Roland, he just had us stumped for six decades. It's him I tell you, it's him," Allison argued.

"Roland, back to your inquiry about the brain criteria, none of our information ever pointed towards a connection between the two. In fact, the cluster headaches and a brain tumor issue are not connected, even if the MRI does show that he has the tumor."

"Well, in my book one plus one equal has got to equal two," Kushner added.

Just then a red landline phone on the conference table rang twice. Miller was closest to it and picked it up.

"Actually, the report from the neurology team states that they don't know what causes cluster headaches and that there's no connection between a tumor and the headaches," Kushner said.

"Did they say anything, Tom?"

Miller looked both men in the eye. He searched for the facial expression of his old friend Roland Kushner for even the slightest hint of concurrence before he broke the news. "Roland, the MRI is in, and it is now confirmed: Daniel Sherman has at least one Cavernous Hemangioma brain tumor and he was born with it.

"And remember," Miller added, "this tumor developed internally and does not protrude as it normally does."

Mr. Sherman's brain tumor is in the exact location it's supposed to be, and it's benign Roland, benign," Miller reported.

"So, what are they going to do about it?" Allison asked.

Do? They do nothing. They're not going to touch it. It's in such a delicate area that any attempt to remove it could cause paralysis or death," Miller stated.

"We certainly can't afford that," Allison stated emphatically.

"If need be Daniel Sherman must be protected at any cost," Miller said.

"Or, if need be, Tom, stopped," Allison said.

Kushner had that wait and see attitude in his eyes as he looked at his colleagues in the thinking man's pose.

They all knew the reason why, of course because even though Kushner still harbored some doubt, they all agreed that Mr. Sherman must be stopped if he is to lead this country and the world to its demise. On the other hand, as Miller saw it, if their principal man was, however, this country and this world's only hope toward salvation, then he must be preserved and protected to insure victory over the forces of madness and mayhem.

Miller and Allison agreed, and Allison put it best:

"Since he's the one we've been searching for over many decades and a turn of the century and a rollover to a new millennium, then we've got to document his every move and his every word. We must be aware of his every shortcoming and his every success. We must be as aware of Daniel Sherman as Daniel Sherman is aware of Daniel Sherman. We have no idea where his mind is. And we've got to know at least that before we can proceed."

The three wise men were, in hard to believe territory: Agreement. And they reasoned that their man had to be on 24-hour surveillance.

"I want to know everything he does," Miller told his contact in Los Angeles. "It's set up. Even in his car?"

The men in 3G knew that the world almost self-destructed during World War II and there was a possible principle in place at that time who could have led it.

"He did not and most likely it was not time," Allison once said in a meeting.

On the other hand, engulfed by events, the special soul could not, even if he wanted to, initiate the process, nor could he have brought harmony among beings, because, as Miller, Allison and Kushner saw it:

"He was stopped by a mysteriously magical energy before any outcome was determined," according to an assessment made by Miller in the late 40s.

Allison later wrote in the journal he's been keeping for over 60 years: "The majority of the world hoped for man's common humanity to have, by now, unified humans and Daniel Sherman is the world's one chance for the planet to be unified."

The three seasoned intelligence officials also understood that there were forces in this world who desired most mankind to be destroyed or to self-destruct, so in their sick and twisted reasoning, they and they alone would end up in paradise.

Later that night, Allison looked out the great window of his study. He had not drawn the curtain. It was dark and life seemed calm inside and outside. He sat back and read what he wrote as his final entry for that day.

"For whatever reason, this man, Daniel Sherman, has endured. He's made it this far and very few chosen souls ever have or as history shows us, ever do."

Allison closed his journal and in the deep silence of mind turned his attention toward one distinct sound in the room: The ticking of an antique clock on the wall. His eyes smiled with humility as the seconds passed. He stood, reached over and turned off a nearby lamp and his eyes were still humble, but, for the fact that they were now lit only by the glow of the full moon.

Chapter 7

Depression existed in every nook and cranny of space on two-south because the mind crippling disease was everywhere. It came through the door cracks and the thick sealed unbreakable windows. It helped itself with anything it desired and mingled around inside people's brains like undesirables at a party. It constantly came and went, always at its own free will. Sure, the tougher diseases of the mind existed there too, like schizophrenia or personality disorders and even psychosis, but depression was unique, because it was the most treatable of mind's illnesses, and if one of many medications worked then, eureka!

On the third day of Daniel's presence on the unit he started to feel much better. Some color returned to his face. He slept the night before and gradually, as it was supposed to, the Nortriptyline worked. Daniel began to bloom. Coming out of a deep and long depression was like moving from a run-down shack out in the sticks to a tall white mansion on a hill. If depression was one of the most rigid and destructive things to self, then it seemed only logical to Daniel that when depression lifted it readjusted a person to their most flexible level and pointed them in the right direction. It was a second chance, an opportunity of a lifetime, and if he followed the right path, he started to believe that maybe he would finally get it right.

A soaring flight of fantastic energy embedded in his soul began to emerge. That flighty feeling twinkled throughout his entire body, from the top of his head down to the tips of his fingers and toes. The energy was euphoric. It was the cherry on the top of a hot fudge sundae. The finishing touches to a great painting. A landside so momentous any politician would kill for it.

Daniel knew what had happened. He could not help but shoot through his big brown eyes. He wanted to control it and maintain his composure, but it was strong, so strong that he just went along wherever it took him. He was the prized dog being led around at the end of the leash, and the leash was tender and loving in its treatment of him, as if he was the Best in Show at Westminster.

He shook his head and held up his cup. He walked out of the day room and exchanged smiles and head nods with a couple of people. He passed the nurse's cage door, and he stood at the water fountain and filled up his cup. He looked to his side as he watched his resident psychiatrist, Dr. McDaniel, coming toward him.

"Can I talk to you, Mr. Sherman?" she asked.

He followed her into the music room and they each sat on one of the comfortable padded seats. Each turned to face each other, and Dr. McDaniel reported to Daniel that the results of his MRI brain scan were in.

"Now, I first want to tell you that we're going to do a second MRI tomorrow, because I ordered it with contrast, and they didn't do that. So, we want to confirm the results because Daniel we found a tumor in your brain."

Daniel's forehead crinkled as he continued to listen.

"First of all, it is not cancerous it is benign, which is a good thing, and secondly you were born with it. It's on the left side of your brain. The type of tumor you have is the same kind the elephant man had, only his grew out which is what normally happens with this type of tumor. Yours grew inside…"

Daniel's eyes widened as he uncharacteristically stayed mute.

"This tumor is called a cavernous hemangioma. It sits deep inside your cerebrum and it's rather large. The dimensions are 1.2 cm X 1 cm. As I said, we are going to do a second MRI with contrast to confirm it and I don't know what the Interventional Radiologist Neurology Team is going to do. They told me after the second MRI the team will come up and meet with you."

He was dumfounded by the news.

"A tumor… and I was born with it…" he thought. "Just like the elephant man," he silently announced to himself."

He was familiar with the elephant man he had seen the movie several times in the 1980s and was touched by it.

He thanked Doctor McDaniel for all she was doing for him. She wrote down the information on a piece of scrap paper and handed it to him. After they departed and went their separate ways, He looked dazed as he walked back into the day room and sat down. This all had to sink in.

"The tumor is on the left side of my brain," he thought. "This just might be what causes my cluster headaches," he reasoned.

He sat down in his usual seat in the open dayroom, across from a black man who used to rob banks. He told Daniel he robbed four of the before he was caught, a man with schizophrenia and other health problems. They sat in silence. When the payphone rang someone popped up out of their seat and answered it.

"Yeah, hold on… I'll get him," he told the caller.

"Daniel, it's for you," his peer said.

"Hello…"

It was a birthday call from Hal in Israel. Daniel thanked him for calling. They talked briefly about their mother and Daniel implored:

"I had no idea that she was going to die. I never went back there thinking about that. I didn't want her to die."

"I know, but it was good that you were there and I'm glad you were there back in April and that you and she buried the hatched."

"Yes, I feel so, too.

Daniel swallowed and told him about the news he received a few minutes ago. The phone went silent for a few seconds.

"Hal are you still there?"

"Yes, I'm here. Um, I'm sorry Daniel… I'm sorry about the news… Becky and I will support you anyway we can. I'll stay in touch with you now. We'll email each other, okay?"

"Sure, Hal…"

Chapter 8

When the staff on two-south received notice that Mr. Sherman was one-hundred percent genuine, college degree and all, two-south came to attention. Floors simply mopped were now buffed and polished, and professionally speaking staff appeared to be on their toes.

Mrs. Bernstein sought Daniel out and talked to him about programs to help with his PTSD over sexual assaults and one that was in Kansas. The special PTSD facility primarily helped veterans returning from combat in Iraq and Afghanistan who suffered from the illness. The other option was for Daniel to be treated by an expert in the field located in Culver City, California.

Daniel believed all this special treatment was because he had a degree in journalism: "They must think I'm on some undercover assignment for The L.A. Times, or something," he thought. But he told the truth because he had never worked in the field he studied for. Besides his job in the business world after he graduated and except for his two years as a Substitute Teacher, he always worked in mental health. Whatever the reason, to Daniel the staff looked and acted differently.

That morning, he awakened to the sound of Marlene Goodwin, the lead mental health technician. She knocked on patient's doors and announced: "Vital signs." Daniel emerged from his room and soon felt something was different because in Daniel's observation the staff changed their tune. He thought that most professional people amplified their professionalism.

He went through his morning routine like a seasoned NFL player goes through a practice drill. Done a half-hour before the day room opened and breakfast was served, Daniel decided to walk.

He popped a mint through his lips to combat cotton mouth and took off on the same route he usually takes.

Ken wanted to walk with Daniel and so together they went from one exit door on one side of the ward through all the halls to the other side of the ward. Sam saw them and asked if he could join them too and he did.

Daniel's depression was history. He felt wonderful. Anti-depressants don't take away depression, as he knew. They only elevated the mood, and his whole attitude towards life, himself and others had changed. No longer depressed, he felt the beauty of the world in and around him.

After breakfast Daniel, Ken and Sam walked through the halls again. Daniel made a commitment to himself:

"I'm going to walk for twenty-minutes, three-times per day, morning, noon and night."

While Daniel walked, he began to think. He had been wrong for so many years about so many things. The resentment he held toward his family, all the anger, all the bitterness, was now addressed in his mind. He understood that he had another chance now to change and this time he knew he couldn't just say that he's changed, he knew he had to show that he had changed. He started with his respect for self...

Sam dropped out after a few laps. Daniel and Ken walked in their powder blue no slip slippers up and down the shiny tiled hallways.

At the end of the hallway Ken stopped and asked Daniel if he could tell him something. The young man looked down and softly kicked at the floor. With his facial expression flushed, he looked at Daniel and shyly spoke to him like a young man who just asked his girlfriend if she would go steady.

"Daniel, I… I think I'm the son of God."

Daniel looked at him and smiled. He turned and started to walk again. Ken quickly caught up and looked at Daniel for his response.

Speechless for a moment, Daniel's face flushed at the coincidence, he too had thoughts which he shared with no one:

"You are the Messiah," said the little voice inside his head.

Daniel dismissed the idea as total gibberish, but the thoughts continued:

"You are…" it said again.

"I am not because that's gibberish," he responded in his mind.

"You are… you are the Messiah."

"I am not," he responded silently. Emphatically, he added: "That's totally utter nonsense."

As they walked Ken suddenly blurted out:

"I am… I am God's child..."

The peace and tranquility Daniel felt for days seemed heightened. He stopped and looked at Ken who stopped.

"We all are… we're all children of God."

A tender trance overtook Daniel. A wonderful feeling seemed to caress his lips and warm his eyes. He reasoned that his antidepressant worked extremely well. From the top of his head to the tips of his fingers and toes he felt magical and magnificent, sensational optimistic thoughts cluttered his mind.

"You are… you are… you are the Messiah…" the inner voice kept repeating.

Daniel looked at Ken. He had his eyes closed and hands together as if he were in prayer. The former psychiatric casework II had enough.

"It's a bunch of gibberish," he once again told himself.

"You are…" it said again.

Daniel wanted no part of the charade. He walked on and reminded himself of the psychosocial material he developed regarding intrusive and unwanted thoughts:

"That's a bunch of brain trash." he reasoned silently.

He then decided to repeat the entire psychosocial rehabilitation lesson:

"Our brains are constantly at work, and they send out thousands of messages a day, and sometimes our brains tell us things that are wrong and are just not worth listening to. So, we need to ignore it, and we only pay attention to our brains when it tells us something positive and good or something that is productive and constructive."

Daniel's mind automatically kicked back to a similar lesson he taught kids in school when other kids verbally tried to push their buttons:

"People talk all the time, and we say thousands of words a day, and sometimes some people say things that are just not worth listening to, so we simply ignore it…"

Daniel stopped the recall, took a slow deep breath through his nose and slowly exhaled.

He didn't know what to make of this sudden delivery of brain trash, so he dismissed it again and again and again. Every time it pops up in his mind, he identified it for what he it was:

"Pure and utter gibberish... brain trash... I'm not a Messiah... I'm a guy who's come out of long depression, and I'm happy and grateful for it."

As he continued his stroll down the hallway, he recalled what Bob the recreation therapist had told him days ago:

"You're what's known as a late bloomer."

"A late bloomer... I've bloomed..."

The two children of God walked on silently. Daniel's eyes smiled and he felt a wonderful energy permeate throughout his physical self.

He kept his word; he walked to the ward. two-south's hallways three times a day, from exit door to exit door. Observed on closed circuit monitors and when he marched past the nurse's station, Daniel passed and made no eye contact keeping his mind's focus on his newfound lessons which he knew he needed to learn.

As Daniel strolled, Federal employees maintained a vigil at closed circuit monitors. Surveillance cameras caught one peculiar thing that was noted: Every time Daniel reached an exit door; he touched the blue plastic placard affixed to the alarmed blue door. In particular, he touched the last two words of the sign's warning to staff and visitors: "Thank you."

Chapter 9

When Miller thought about the volatile situation around the world he closed his weary eyes. In his mind World War III surreptitiously started in the Middle East before World War I not to mention World War II. The good doctor could not sleep, and he decided to untangle the knotty problem that has plagued humanity ever since they began processing recollections: Territory.

He scratched his head and started to retrace the territorial confusion. He remembered that in the last decade of the nineteenth century, the region known as The Ancient Near East in the 8th Millennium BCE geographically began from the Sea to the Mediterranean Sea and from the Black Sea to the Persian Gulf and Red Sea. Miller studied the period for his doctorate. The area consisted of Mesopotamia, Caucasus, Anatolia, and Canaan and Egypt.

Miller knew it was an extraordinary thing and the area became even more confusing when geographically, in the 21st Century, the region defined as the Middle East, between where Asia and Africa meet became Kyrgyzstan, Tajikistan, Uzbekistan, Turkmenistan, Afghanistan, Pakistan, Iran, Iraq, Turkey, Syria, Lebanon, Jordan, Saudi Arabia, Kuwait, Bahrain, Qatar, United Arab Emirates, Oman, Yemen, Egypt, Palestine and Israel.

Ergo, five became twenty-two and it all added up to one thing in Miller's mind: He knew that throughout history the blood spilled over the vitally important issue of land was merely humankind's way of being repaid in its own coin.

"It'll never end," he decided.

Miller turned a page in his mind and concentrated on the United States cold war nemesis: The Soviet Union and that region of the planet. He knew because of a Soviet invasion and occupation of Iran which began on September 16, 1941, Mohammad Reza Shah Pahlavi's father was forced to abdicate his throne to his first son of his second wife.

A shiver went up Miller's spine as he recalled that period of history. He never liked the Shah of Iran, and he had little respect for the newly installed young monarch who had several titles. Miller recalled when he was first introduced to the stuck up Iranian. He was ordered to memorize all his titles. At their first meeting at the great palace, he was to bow, kiss the guy's hand and to stay in that position as he referred to him as: "His Imperial Majesty, Emperor, King of King and Head of the Warriors."

The future Shah of Iran was only twenty-two years of age when he was handed the keys to the kingdom. "He was brash, conceited and quite a lady's man," Miller remembered.

Miller closed his eyes and brought back the memory. A feeling of disgust crept through his arteries as the moment's image when he stooped over the newly crowned king kissing his hand. He lifted his head to look the pompous person in the eye and that he got back a healthy dose of arrogance and disgust.

In the studies he read about brain development Miller now knew that the young leader had one really big thing against him besides his other pitfalls: An undeveloped brain, for officially a brain does not fully develop in males until they are twenty-four years old, and in a female the age is twenty-two and a half. Before that, kids are expected to mess up. They are expected to take risks and to be experimental, as well as impulsive.

"The Shah did not disappoint," Miller thought.

The senior gazed across the room to a plate of cookies resting on a table. He stood and he walked toward the day-old chocolate chip delights his cook baked. As he munched down on one, he continued his recollection about that period. He was a young man himself in 1935, when Persia adopted its country's official name: Iran. The future Shah was a mere teenager, and he recalled that the Shah was just two years old when in February 1921 a military commander, Reza Kham, seized power. It is not clear whether the name of the country was changed for ornamental reasons or simply because over the centuries Persia itself and the region were just like a tike's brain: Undeveloped.

From Iran's early existence when the Sasanian dynasty ruled Persia and Zoroastrianism was the dominant religion from 224-651 AD, that period was followed by an all-out conquering Arab invasion which brought it to its end. The newborn again nation gave birth to Islamic edicts which came to the region in 636 AD.

Miller questioned why in the 20th Century when a new prime minister took office in 1950, and about nine-months later was assassinated, succession was led by a nationalist who brought the people the nationalization of the oil industry, which was, up to that time, dominated by the British-owned Anglo-Iranian Oil Company.

He knew that consequently, an embargo and blockade was imposed by Britain, which stopped oil exports and damaged the economy. This mess in Miller's estimation was followed by a tug-of-war for power between the now-wise Shah and his nationalist foe.

For a second Miller had some acid reflux, when the chocolate chip cookie came up his esophagus and he remembered how chaos ensued, and the Shah fled his people and his country in August 1953.

Of course, because of his inability to serve his people, in 1953, the west's favorite Iranian was reinstalled in a coup which was engineered by the United States and British intelligence services.

Chapter 10

When the staff on two-south received notice that Mr. Sherman was one-hundred percent genuine, college degree and all, two-south came to attention. Floors simply mopped were now buffed and polished, and professionally speaking staff appeared to be at their best.

Mrs. Bernstein sought Daniel out and talked to him about programs to help with his PTSD over sexual assaults and one that was in Kansas. The special PTSD facility primarily helped veterans returning from combat in Iraq and Afghanistan who suffered from the illness. The other option was for Daniel to be treated by an expert in the field located in Culver City, California.

Daniel believed all this special treatment was because he had a degree in journalism: "They must think I'm on some undercover assignment for The L.A. Times, or something," he thought. But Daniel told the truth because he had never worked in the field he studied for. Besides his job in the business world after he graduated and except for his two years as a Substitute Teacher, he always worked in mental health. Whatever the reason, to Daniel the staff looked and acted differently.

That morning, he awakened to the sound of Marlene Goodwin, the lead mental health technician. She knocked on patient's doors and announced: "Vital signs." Daniel emerged from his room and soon felt something was different because in Daniel's observation the staff changed their tune. He thought that most professional people amplified their professionalism.

He went through his morning routine like a seasoned NFL player goes through a practice drill. Done a half-hour before the day room opened and breakfast was served, Daniel decided to walk.

He popped a mint through his lips to combat cotton mouth and took off.

Ken wanted to walk with Daniel and so together they went from one exit door on one side of the ward through all the halls to the other side of the ward. Sam saw them and asked if he could join them too and he did.

Daniel's depression was history. He felt wonderful. Anti-depressants don't take away depression, as he knew. They only elevated the mood, and his whole attitude towards life, himself and others had changed. No longer depressed, he felt the beauty of the world in and around him.

After breakfast Daniel, Ken and Sam walked through the halls again. Daniel made a commitment to himself: "I'm going to walk for twenty-minutes, three-times per day, morning, noon and night."

While Daniel walked, he began to think. He had been wrong for so many years about so many things. The resentment he held toward his family, all the anger, all the bitterness, was now addressed in his mind. He understood that he had another chance now to change and this time he knew he couldn't just say that he's changed, he knew he had to show that he had changed. He started with respect for self.

Sam dropped out after a few laps. Daniel and Ken walked in their powder blue no slip slippers up and down the shiny tiled hallways.

At the end of the hallway Ken stopped and asked Daniel if he could tell him something. The young man looked down and softly kicked at the floor. With his facial expression flushed, he looked at Daniel and shyly spoke to him like a young man who just asked his girlfriend if she would go steady.

"Daniel, I… I think I'm the son of God."

Daniel looked at him, turned and started to walk again. Ken quickly caught up and looked at Daniel for his response.

Speechless for a moment, Daniel's face flushed at the coincidence, he too had thoughts which he shared with no one:

"You are the Messiah," said the little voice inside his head.

Daniel dismissed the idea as total gibberish, but the thoughts continued:

"You are…" it said again.

"I am not because that's gibberish," he responded in his mind.

"You are… you are the Messiah."

"I am not," he responded silently.

Emphatically, he added:

"That's totally utter nonsense."

As they walked Ken suddenly blurted out:

"I am… I am God's child..."

The peace and tranquility Daniel felt for days seemed heightened. He stopped and looked at Ken who stopped.

"We all are… we're all children of God."

A tender trance overtook Daniel. A wonderful feeling seemed to caress his lips and warm his eyes. He reasoned that his antidepressant worked extremely well. From the top of his head to the tips of his fingers and toes he felt magical and magnificent, sensational optimistic thoughts cluttered his mind.

"You are… you are… you are the Messiah…" the inner voice kept repeating.

Daniel looked at Ken. He had his eyes closed and hands together as if he were in prayer. The former psychiatric caseworker II had enough.

"It's a bunch of gibberish," he once again told himself.

"You are…" it said again.

Daniel wanted no part of the charade. He walked on and reminded himself of the psychosocial material he developed regarding intrusive and unwanted thoughts:

"That's a bunch of brain trash." he reasoned silently.

He then decided to repeat the entire psychosocial rehabilitation lesson:

"Our brains are constantly at work, and they send out thousands of messages a day, and sometimes our brains tell us things that are wrong and are just not worth hearing. So, we need to ignore it, and we only pay attention to our brains when it tells us something positive and good or something that is productive, constructive, or creative."

Daniel stopped the recall, took a slow deep breath through his nose and slowly exhaled.

He didn't know what to make of this sudden delivery of brain trash, so he dismissed it again and again and again. Every time it pops up in his mind, he identified it for what he it was:

"Pure and utter gibberish... brain trash... I'm not a Messiah. I'm a guy who's come out of long depression, and I'm happy and grateful for it."

As he continued his stroll down the hallway, he recalled what Bob the recreation therapist had told him days ago:

"You're what's known as a late bloomer."

"A late bloomer... I've bloomed..."

The two children of God walked on silently. Daniel's eyes smiled and he felt a wonderful energy permeate throughout his physical being.

He kept his word, he walked through ward two-south's hallways three times a day, from exit door to exit door. Observed on closed circuit monitors and when he marched past the nurse's station, Daniel passed and made no eye contact keeping his mind's focus on his newfound lessons which he knew he needed to learn.

As he strolled, Federal employees maintained a vigil at closed circuit monitors. Surveillance cameras caught one peculiar thing that was noted: Every time Daniel reached an exit door; he touched the blue plastic placard affixed to the alarmed blue door. In particular, he touched the last two words of the sign's warning to staff and visitors: "Thank you."

Chapter 11

In the spring, Daniel left the dusty rural Nevada town he lived in for three years. He moved over the mountain to metropolitan Las Vegas. At first, he was to move in with his father "until I get settled," he told his dad.

Herbert Sherman lived in a small, subsidized apartment complex. He offered to share his bed with Daniel, but the son opted for the sofa.

The two never got along

"Probably since I was born," Daniel recalled.

When Daniel was young, he was against anything his absentee father suggested. If his father recommended a book for his son to read Daniel would passively accept the hardback, but he never saw beyond the front cover of the literary work. If a movie was suggested Daniel dismissed the film in his mind. If his father told him something was good to eat, he passively rejected the foodstuff.

After one night Herbert and Daniel began to have problems. To Daniel, Herbert needed only to wake up and see him motionlessly sitting on his sofa for the battle to begin. The younger Sherman wasn't looking in the newspaper for a place to rent or for a job, Daniel was stuck in a frozen grip unable to move or advocate for himself.

"When are you going to go out a look for a job?"

"I'm going to apply for unemployment. I'm going down to their office today and I can look for a job while I'm there. "

"Well, when the hell or you going? What kind of work are you going to do?"

"Oh, um, I'll go in an hour, or so. I could start applying for a federal position. I get veteran's preference, and I can see the veteran's representative at the unemployment office. I've got my DD-214."

Daniel knew his comeback responses always irritated his father as if he were conning him.

"Do not fucking con me, Daniel Sherman. I can look at your face and I can tell you're lying."

"I'm not lying."

"The hell you're not."

"You fucking think you're just going to sit on this fucking couch all day."

"I understand. I'll get unemployment or disability again."

"The fuck you will. You quit your job, Daniel! You're not going to get unemployment! And you're not getting disability either, not with all the money you have in the bank!"

"Yeah, I can afford a place."

"Who the fuck is going to rent an apartment to a fat, ugly and unemployed deadbeat… And if you think that money's going to last, you're only kidding yourself!"

I'm real sick dad. I can't do anything now."

"Well, if you think you can just sit around on your lazy ass and live life off of me you can forget about that."

Daniel's head was lowered, and his eyes were staring at the floor.

"Look at me when I'm talking to you."

By now, Herbert looked like he was steaming. His face turned red as his son avoided eye contact.

"Why?"

Herbert's eyes seemed to light up with anger as his voice and words delivered the one-two punch.

"Because… I'm your fucking father, that's why!"

Daniel felt nervous. His cage needed only to be rattled for him to want to break free.

"I can't stay here with you."

Daniel stood up and began nervously collecting the few belongings he brought in.

"I'm not going to stay here…"

The dejected offspring made several trips from the apartment to his car, just shoving things in wherever they could fit. On his last round he looked to see if he was leaving anything behind. Daniel looked at Pearl, his little dog.

"I can't care for her anymore," he thought.

"You forgot Pearl," Herbert sarcastically reminded him.

"You'll have to find her a new home. I can't care for her."

Daniel felt suicidal. He contemplated renting a motel room, getting some alcohol and taking every pill, he had. But, as he marched out of the apartment in despair, something brought him back. Maybe what brought him back was his good common sense, which was dormant just like a sleeping volcano. Or maybe it was the guilty feeling he had about leaving Pearl behind. In any event, he turned around and walked back to find the door closed, which wasn't surprising since it was one-hundred and ten degrees outside. He rang the doorbell and Herbert answered.

"I changed my mind," Daniel confessed.

"About what…"

"I'm not leaving Pearl."

With that he moved past his father who made no attempt to physically stop him. He picked up his little poodle and gathered her stuff and huffed out of the apartment with what must have been an exhausted look on his face, as he saw the whole incident.

Daniel was broken in mind, spirit and body. He rented a motel room. The scorched weather in Las Vegas was famous; it never disappointed. The wind swirled around him and the gusts felt like that of a hot hair-blow dryer. He gathered a few things, most importantly his bag with his marijuana and he quickly moved it and Pearl into the room out of the heat.

Daniel knew suicidal thoughts could come and go. He quickly turned on the room's air-conditioner and began to self-medicate. He got relief from that and then he took a two-milligram dose of Xanax and a Lortab, and he felt numb enough to simply exist for the moment, relax and to take his mind from what just happened between him and his father.

For many decades Daniel was ready for the one thing he always seemed to do in a crisis: He called Eve.

His former stepmother always took his call when he called her at work. She ran a small bookstore and had about five employees. Each one of them knew how to forward Daniel's calls to their boss. But Eve was busy, and she did not have time for his nonsense.

"You quit your job and now you'll have to live with it."

"I don't want to live with it."

"Look, Daniel I'm busy here. I've got two people standing at my doorway. I've got a problem with a customer who never got the books he ordered because they were shipped to wrong address…"

"Look, all I need is a place to stay."

"You had a place to stay."

"Yeah, but now I can't stay there… I just can't…"

"Your father called me and said you were about to leave Pearl behind, but that you came back and got her."

Daniel lowered his head again.

"It's hard for me to care for her."

"Listen, I've got to go. Call me in a few hours."

Daniel hung up the phone and began to eat some of the fast food he purchased through the drive-thru before he got to the room.

Drugs and eating always seemed to pacify him, and when he called Eve back a few hours later she had a suggestion for him.

"Bill, this guy who works for me needs someone to move in with him."

So, Daniel rented a room in an apartment for a ridiculously high price. His sickness had him convinced that it was a lucky break to come across an opportunity where he could easily ease into a new living arrangement without questions, references or deposits. Besides that, he reckoned there would be no extra expenses like a security deposit, or a pet deposit or the last month's rent. "Just pay half of the rent and half of the utilities," the soft-spoken oriental man said to Daniel when he arrived.

Daniel had struck a deal over the phone and agreed to move in even before he saw what was described as a luxury room in an upscale apartment complex.

As Daniel saw it, that agreement worked for him and for the guy who worked for his ex-stepmother. Bill's wife recently left him, and he couldn't pay his rent unless he rented out the empty bedroom.

As it turned out the luxury room was nice, the carpet was thick and there was a ceiling fan and a walk-in closet, besides, he had his own bathroom. But, outside his walls, in every conceivable inch of the apartment, the luxury disappeared into what Daniel politely described as a cluttered mess.

Bill's entire former four-bedroom house was squeezed into the apartment like someone who bought one of those storage spaces and filled it up from floor to ceiling. There was even an aquarium with a big snake in it and a crate with a rare desert tortoise which Bill apparently trapped out in the wild, which was illegal.

Daniel moved in, nonetheless. He gathered the strength to unload his car. He bought a new bed and a new recliner and paid for them to be delivered. After he collected the proper tools in which to vegetate with, including marijuana, he sat in the room and vegetated.

For three months he sat in his comfortable burgundy recliner with no cable or local television reception. His day was spent there because there was no other space in which to sit down. Even the messy kitchen was a disaster zone.

Every day he watched the same films repeatedly on his DVD player, mostly old black and white horror films from the 1930s and 40s: Frankenstein, The Bride of Frankenstein, and its four sequels, Lon Chaney Jr. in all his Wolfman films, and his favorite Bella Lugosi as Dracula and the subsequent sequels which were minus Lugosi.

He paid outrageous prices to illegally obtain marijuana to self-medicate, and mixed with Lortabs and Xanax, which were legally prescribed for him. He kept the cluster headaches at bay, but what he was doing to his mind, body and soul went under his radar screen, which was quite fuzzy to begin with.

When Daniel resigned from his position as a Psychiatric Specialist for the State of Nevada, and after a few months of life in clutter city, his depression finally got to him. He repacked the car and embarked on a 12,000-mile journey crossing the country not once, but twice.

He traveled in total silence, never once tuned in to a radio or entertained by a music CD.

With his vehicle packed like the apartment he had just moved out of, Daniel headed off with his clutter and his toy poodle Pearl in the passenger seat. He left Nevada, his last duty station where he served the mentally ill, and on the first leg of the trip he traveled to Reno.

He planned to move to Oregon to live and to be placed on their medical marijuana program. But, on the first day of his trip when he arrived in Reno, he stayed in a hotel and planned to leave the next morning.

He never made it. Psychologically paralyzed by an illness he should have recognized long ago, he could not move forward. He phoned his sister in Pennsylvania, who invited him to return there and to live with her and her family until he got on his feet.

With the best of intentions, he made the 3,000-mile trip across the country only to find everything there was on ice, as well. He was frozen, once again. He was unable to do much at all. This included taking care of his hygiene, which had become a particular problem over the past year, or so.

One day in April, while in Pennsylvania, Daniel accompanied his younger sister Kelly, who had errands to run. A tall pretty woman with slender features, Kelly grew up healthy, proud and popular. She showed little signs of her age. She was younger than Daniel by five years and she and her husband Pete had a lot of friends.

Kelly settled her business in the downtown area and she and Daniel stopped at the Farmer's Market, and they feasted on some rotisserie chicken.

When they got back to the car an impulse suddenly hit Daniel. The impulse was the kind he never questioned, he just went full steam ahead, regardless of the impulses cost or consequences…

He asked his little sister to stop at their mother's home. Uninvited and unannounced, for the first time in ten-years, Daniel just showed up to see the woman who birthed, suckled and raised him.

When Lionel, his stepfather, told his wife who was visiting, she was upstairs resting because she recently had a hernia operation and so she tenderly made it to the top of the staircase and descended the flight with grace and a warm expression on her face.

"Daniel," she said with a lift in her voice tone. I'm so happy to see you. How are you son?"

"I'm okay, Mom… I'm okay…"

This was followed by a sincere hug and they cordially talked for a couple of hours. The misdeeds of both parties drifted away without ever citing their difference. For some reason, Daniel suddenly realized that they just didn't matter anymore. He thought about how his mother had reached out and tried to communicate with him several times during those years, but he was always unable and/or unwilling to reciprocate. And he still didn't understand beyond the fact that before him sat his aging mother.

On the day he and his mother reconciled she was 75 years old. The woman whom he battled as far as his memory could or would take him was in fair health. And, for the first time in Daniel's adult life he had a mature civil conversation with her. Two nights later, he, his sister and his sister's family all arrived once again for dinner at their mother's home, which was prepared especially for Daniel.

"I you're your favorite, son, chicken cacciatore."

Heavy in body, low in mind, and challenged hygienically, Daniel announced toward the end of dinner in the depressed state he lived in: "I'm leaving in the morning," and he told the group gathered for what in his mind was clearly a reunion that he would move to where he thought he needed to be from the time he took off from Nevada in the beginning: Oregon.

There was no surprise outcry from his sister, or her family, and Daniel felt that Lionel cared less. Daniel still owed him seven hundred bucks for one of his other excursions back east that he backed out on. Only his mother reacted. She told Daniel in her sincerest tone:

"Daniel, you've just got here."

Daniel lowered his head.

"I know… I just must… I must," he bemoaned.

They finished their meal and visited with each other for a little while longer, and then Daniel's mother hugged her son, and they said goodbye.

Uncertainty gripped Daniel. That nagging dastard feeling hovered over him like some UFO just waiting to beam up its latest human for experimentation. With great intensity he felt frozen and trapped within this unpleasant paralyzing force. He now gained insight into the fact that he had just displayed to the only people who knew him his highest level of insincerity, which only reinforced his father's notion that he was nothing more than one colossal error.

His father had announced the ugly truth to him once when he was hurling hate balls at his son: "You were a fucking mistake. We never planned to have you. We didn't need another baby, and we didn't want another one either. You're weird. You disgust me, Daniel Sherman."

He remembered his father's words as if they were just played back on a recorder. Those negative connotations were so deeply ingrained inside him it was if gorilla glue was used to paste them to the wall of his memory bank, and no matter what he did he could not break free of them.

Early the next morning daylight broke with a grey overcast sky. Daniel never unloaded his car from his possessions. His sister sighed, but Daniel thought that she had lost no sleep over his decision to leave. He had done this before, many times, in fact. Oh, the cars were different and there was a different dog, but Daniel was still the same as he always was: Unabashedly self-centered and neurotic.

Kelly hugged her older brother and said goodbye. She had her hands full with a chronic alcoholic husband, and two young boys, so Daniel's drama never seemed to him to faze her anymore. She had grown up to expect it, as far as he could tell in his long drive back across the land of the free and the home of the brave. That was part of Daniel's problem: He had too much freedom. He made sure he never got involved in anything that would tie him down, keep him in place, make him feel settled. And as far as being brave. He believed there wasn't a brave bone in his body, an entity of him that he had grown too loath and always treated as such.

The guy who had no respect for himself, arrived in Oregon a week later. His energy level was low. If he were a battery, he would have thrown it away because the energy encased in the cell was totally drained and not rechargeable.

Daniel took hours to perform simple tasks. Even so, he rented an apartment, ordered furniture, and again, with the best of intentions, moved in. Three weeks later, he bowed out, again. He accomplished nothing while he was there. He couldn't even pass the written test to get an Oregon driver's license, which he attempted three times, so he did not join the medical marijuana program, which is why he went there in the first place.

He returned his furniture, and the store refunded his money, minus a restocking fee. Finally, he notified his new landlord of his decision and made up some far-out story on why he had to move back to Nevada.

"I need to move from a wet climate back to an arid one," he claimed.

It was early November and Daniel moved back to the same dusty rural town he left in April with his tail between his legs. He rented a fifth wheel and unloaded his possessions from his car into the type of dwelling he had never even been in, yet alone lived in. The huge trailer was clean, new and immediately caught his eyes.

"I could live in this," he thought.

He paid the landlord the first and last month's rent. Just two-days after he moved in; however, Daniel decided he had to move again.

Southern Nevada's winds are wicked. The force of nature whipped the desert earth through the air at tremendous stinging speeds and add to that the radioactive particles from above ground atomic tests conducted less than fifty miles away from the dusty rural setting in the 1950s, and the environment felt like hell to him, and he convinced himself it was like hell, as well.

Here he was out in the middle of the desert. But Daniel did not feel like he lived in a fifth-wheel trailer out on the great barren desert. Rather, the whole experience felt as if he were on a ship out to sea in very rough waves. As the wind rocked and rolled the tiny fifth wheel around, the force of the gales took shape in his sedated mind, and he just knew that a great wave was coming and with the power of the blustery weather he would be swept away forever and that would solve his little problem as to whether he would kill himself.

The sway and the sound were tremendous at times. The forceful current of air blew through every crack and crevice in the mobile unit and its howl sounded as if he were on a very loud freight train.

He self-medicated but that did not pacify him. He felt sick, seasick and he decided on a plan:

"I must leave here… I can't stay here... I can't load the car up with everything again and I don't want the landlord to know. I'll load the car a little bit at a time over three-days and take off the next morning… where can I go? What can I do?" T

He alienated friendless loner decided:

"I'll go back east again… I won't tell anybody… I won't bother anybody… I'll stay in a motel for a week and find a place to live and a job. Nobody will know I'm there..." he told Pearl.

With his mind set Daniel scratched his smelly ass and remembered he had not taken a shower in a week, but he hated the fifth wheel accommodations. All the maintenance that was required and he never did.

Even the toilet was an issue.

"I can't flush the toilet paper down the toilet after I wipe?" he said candidly to the disabled landlord when he moved in.

"Nope," the round pleasant man replied. "That'll clog her up and then you've opened up a big old can of worms," he added.

Daniel had an abundant stash of marijuana he procured, and he tried to lose himself by self-medicating.

He obtained his precious stash of medical marijuana when he traveled to Ventura, California before he returned to Nevada. Some people he had met through his ex-stepmother years ago resided in the coastal town. They were more than willing to help Daniel obtain what he needed from a medical marijuana dispensary that Gilda belonged to. She was approved of the use of it because of her anorexia and it helped. Her husband used it too. He self-medicated like Daniel.

The couple took Daniel from Ventura to Los Angeles. Once at the dispensary only Gilda could go in and the two men waited in the car. Daniel gave her enough money to buy an ounce of quality buds and ten grams of hashish.

He was supposed to move to Ventura, find a place to live and get a job, another one of his good intentions moves. That very first night he flipped out. He felt awful and those feelings would not go away. The climate was the opposite of the desert and after he saw what his former Las Vegas friends had to live in and what they paid. Daniel quickly decided that he could not stay.

The next morning, without a word to his friends before he left, Daniel and Pearl left the motel they had stayed in that night and headed once again back to the dusty rural town in Nevada.

He believed he would be okay now that he had a good supply of some quality marijuana to help with the cluster headache pain when it came, "and to help me feel better," he rationalized when he used it from morning through night.

He still used Xanax to cut down on the frequency of the "suicide headaches," which a specialist in the field called it one night on CNN's "Larry King Live." Daniel still remembered the doctor who stated: "That's the only type of headache I've ever seen people kill themselves over."

Daniel never opened the "can of worms," but he opened his hatchback in the evenings and slowly over three-days, loaded his car with most of his possessions. He left some items behind: A replica of an old-fashioned radio, a huge wall clock, clothes and containers, some VHS video tapes, a few of his CD's, and non-perishable food he loved to stock up on when there was a sale, to gain what he called: "A consumer victory."

By abandoning some thirty odd cans of Chicken of the Sea salmon, which was "the best" in Daniel's mind, and ridding himself of all his other unwanted possessions only showed that he was still depressed beyond the point of no return. Suicide was on his mind more than Chicken of the Sea.

Besides, he was exhausted and too tired to bother with it all. At one point he was going to leave his RCA thirty-two inch flat-screen HDTV he had bought only a few months ago, but later, he changed his mind and loaded the light object into his small economy car.

Daniel wanted to leave without confrontation. He knew that the landlord made money on him. He did not cheat him in any way. He wrote a note of explanation and put it and the keys in an envelope:

"I cannot stay here. I'm not well and the fifth wheel is too much for me to handle."

The next morning, he departed with Pearl in the passenger seat of the car and his lighter load of possessions, and he took off at the break of dawn and placed the envelope in his landlord's rural mailbox.

He drove east. With clear skies and dry roads, he felt lucky as he took off. He remembered in all his past excursions over the years he had always driven across the country during springtime when the weather was not such an issue. Now, with wintertime rapidly approaching, he felt fortunate the weather was clear, and the roads were dry, as he once again drove another leg of his 12,000-mile journey.

He did not relish the moment or any of the moments during his expedition toward his end of existence, as he saw the whole trip. The ride was nothing more than just back and forth and back and forth until he fizzled out like an Alka-Seltzer.

No, driving was not relaxing or therapeutic or even a casual addiction that he enjoyed. Moving along the interstate's hour after hour and mile after mile, with his butt numb from sitting so much, driving was a chore, a hard chore.

The work was like a major cleaning job, which he knew nothing about because he never spent hours and days cleaning or remodeling or renovating anything, except maybe his brain. The precious organ that brought him all the cluster headache pain was a work in progress.

With mistake after mistake, the errors all added up to one thing in his noodle: Either he was going to do himself in or his mistakes would do him in and save him the burden of his ultimate task: The destruction of self.

Silently he and Pearl drove through Nevada and into Utah. This time he decided to take interstate I-70, which was the pathway through the middle of the country, instead of interstate I-40, which was the southern route which crossed the nation.

Daniel felt fortunate. In the late 1980s and through the 1990s he made good money but lived above his means and gambled. He pissed away so much money that he was highly in debt to credit card companies. Subsequently, he filed for bankruptcy and all the debt was later discharged.

When the new turn of the century came, and his life rebounded after the start of the new millennium he completely changed his ways. Instead of living above his means, he lived below them. He stopped gambling, smoking cigarettes and drinking diet coke, so he saved quite a bit of money, which was a relief because after he resigned from his job, he was not eligible for unemployment insurance, just like his dad, Herbert said.

He and Pearl took a rest-stop in a small town in rural Utah. Daniel decided to call his mother and tell her that he left the dust and the desert, but he did not say where he was going: "I don't want to sound mysterious," he said to his formerly estranged mother. I'll just say that I'm heading east," he told her on his cell phone.

His mother, who still felt ill, and his stepfather were on the phone:

"Daniel… okay, Daniel you do what you think you need to do," his stepfather said with his Philadelphia accent.

"But Daniel you're a Jewish boy," his worried mother pleaded with him over the phone.

"I know, mother," he replied as he recalled how far he transgressed away from the religion he never connected with since he was a teenager. "I'll be okay," he told her to alleviate her concern. "I'll keep in touch," he added.

When Daniel left the dusty rural town and hit the highway he felt as if he only had a few months to live. He had to end it. He went over many plans to commit suicide. None of them appealed to him. He thought about just driving his car into a brick wall, just like when he accidentally drove into the side of that tractor trailer, but the memory of that convinced him not to.

He also thought about getting a gun and killing himself, but he didn't like guns, so that was out.

He even thought about jumping off a building, but he decided that was scary. No, when the time came, he would buy a bottle of vodka and take all the pills he had.

But he didn't want to die in the desert where there was no family to claim his body, which was one rational he used to take yet another trip back east.

He and Pearl were held up by snow in Nebraska, so the journey took him a week to cross the country.

When he finally arrived in the state he had been born and raised in he knew this trip would not be like any other of the fifty or so times he had made the trek. He did not come all this way for a fresh start, or a new beginning, which found him freezing up like a Popsicle, unable to do anything, every time.

No, why was he back made no sense to him when he finally got to where he was going, he did not want to live anymore, he did not want to participate. To him life was like one long bad joke that never ended.

The folly went on and on and at the very end there was the all-important punchline, but no one laughed, especially he who bore the brunt of the silly and nonsensical humor.

The Super 8 motel was the cheapest rate he could find. Daniel set the reservation up and arrived in the dingy dive the day before the last leg of his journey. His final day on what he thought was the long road toward oblivion escaped his senses.

Tall mature trees devoid of green were replaced by some of the most exquisite blend of colors nature produced. The few hundred miles to the Super 8 were lined with dense forests on both sides of the interstate, and unlike the desert southwest, which laid claim to cactus, Joshua trees and beautiful desert scenery, he later reflected that nothing was remotely like Mother Nature's best work, the fall season along the eastern part of the country.

As Daniel drove along, he thought only of him and the terrible feelings and the awful times he had experienced. For a split second he reminded himself how much he loved his work with the mental health populations, especially when he taught psychosocial rehabilitation skills to them, which he never even remotely applied to him. He looked over at Pearl, who lay next to him. She was asleep… ever so the loyal and precious, if it were not for Pearl…

Daniel bought the local newspaper The Kinkaid Daily. Kinkaid was a small and quiet town. Aside from the Pentagon's Army War College located at the

Kinkaid Barracks, U.S. Army Garrison. For one-hundred and ten years the college trained United States military members for their leadership positions as officers. The small community also housed a prestigious liberal arts university.

The town had an early twentieth-century look and feel. Many of its structures were freshly renovated and the fixed up and the freshly painted old habitats brought out the lust and charm of the town and that period.

To Daniel the community scene looked a whole lot better than Las Vegas, who just blew up every building that did not suit the owner of the land the building lay upon and just replaced the structure with something new and monstrous.

Daniel showed up at the Super 8 motel. He reserved a non-smoking room, which he always did since he stopped smoking cigarettes. His use of marijuana was different in his mind. This was permissible if it was smoked clandestinely.

So, he only smoked one-hitters and always in the bathroom. He would lay down towels, so the odor did not escape, and he sprayed Febreze on the towels and into the air. Most importantly, when he lit the one-hit pipe, he deeply inhaled and he kept the carcinogen in his lungs and brain, and when he exhaled it produced very little smoke.

Daniel stayed high. He smoked very early in the morning when he first awoke, and he would smoke every few hours after that. He also masturbated. At this stage as he saw the situation, he would do anything that made him feel better.

But getting high and masturbating stopped producing the stimulations he sought. Nothing worked right in Daniel's system anymore. The use of marijuana brought anxiety, and he would turn to his Xanax, which is a drug normally prescribed as an anti-anxiety medication for mental health consumers. In Daniels case, however, they were to cut down on the frequency of his cluster headaches and they did. But Daniel took more than he was prescribed, and when he masturbated, he would ejaculate, but there was no orgasm. Also, he used Lortabs, an opium-based product prescribed for cluster headache pain if he got one.

Of course, Daniel took them even when he didn't have the pain, and the only reason was to try and kill his psychological pain. As a result of their use Daniel's digestive system failed to function properly, for more than a year, he never had a solid stool.

Room 29 at Super Motel 8 was dank and dismal and Daniel felt even more miserable. The room looked like the kind of place a man would meet a cheap hooker. The bedspread looked dirty and smelled. The pillows lost their fluff ages ago. The old television's reception fits the décor. Nothing was right with Daniel. Even the mirror and the dresser and the little table and chair were unacceptable.

It was the middle of November in the state in which he was born and he easily recalled how dank and dismal November weather could be when he pulled back the unflattering drape which covered the window of his motel room. He noticed the dark gray skies. The dampness had a retched smell.

"Nothing like the Chamber of Commerce weather they have back in Vegas," he reminisced to Pearl.

The red phone never rang. Daniel hoped a call would come through either on the red phone or on his cell phone. Despite his promise to himself, he called and left messages on his mother's and sister's phones when he arrived in the little town which was a short distance from his hometown.

His was an almost lifeless soul which had now spent a week in the lifeless room. After he had done a load of laundry at the motel he called his mother's home.

"Hello," he said.

His stepfather answered. LIONEL BELLMAN, age 78, married his mother when Daniel was fifteen and the two never got along. His was a passive aggressive relationship with his stepfather and they never came to blows or harsh words.

"Hello, Daniel…"

"I called… why hasn't anybody called me?"

"Your mother is not feeling well…"

"Oh… what's the matter?"

"We're not sure. It may be pneumonia… we don't know…"

"Well, has she been to the doctors?"

"Yes, and Dr. Kio isn't sure…"

"Well, can I talk to her?"

"No, she's upstairs and she can't talk now."

"Well, what about Kelly? Why hasn't she called me?"

"She's sick too… she's got the swine flu Pete told me, and she's home sick in bed."

"Oh… okay… Thanks, Lionel..."

"All right, Daniel..."

Daniel closed his cell phone and immediately reopened it. He pushed a couple of buttons and called his sister's house. Pete answered in a froglike voice.

"Hello…"

"Hi, Pete, it's Daniel."

"Hi, Daniel…"

"Lionel told me that Kelly's sick in bed."

Suddenly, Pete coughed as if a ton of mucus was in his esophagus and with a stuffed nasal voice he replied hoarsely:

"Yeah, we're all sick…"

"What's the matter?"

"Well, your sisters in bed with a hundred-and-three temperature… she's very sick… she's got the swine flu. The boys both have colds, and I think I have the flu too…"

"Well, I've been staying in Kinkaid for the past week… I called and left a message… I thought Kelly would call, but I understand why she hasn't…"

"Yeah, she's really bad…"

"Pete, could I come over and help? I'll stay a little while and I can cook and clean and help with the kids…."

"Hold on, I'll ask your sister."

A minute passed and he returned to the phone.

"All right, Daniel… come over and you can help…"

"All right, Pete I'll be right over…"

Daniel checked out of the motel and with his car still loaded with most of his things, he only needed to load Pearl and a couple of items, including his precious stash.

His sister's house at 8973 Shamrock Road nestled itself in the quiet bedroom surroundings alongside many other small middle-class homes. Daniel believed it must have been a nice home in the twentieth century when it was constructed in the 1950s. In the twenty-first century, however, the dwelling looked old and rundown.

"The best option is to gut the place and start all over again," he told himself.

Kelly moved into Pete's childhood home when she married him. Pete's parents sold the home to the newlyweds and retired to a luxury motor home which they traveled in throughout the country.

Pete's father was tall and trim with thick grey hair. He had a diplomatic air about him. Before he retired, he was a General in the Army National Guard. His mother was a sweet plump talkative person with a kind angle to her Pennsylvania Dutch accent. Both had since passed away, his father from alcoholism and cancer, his mother from complications of diabetes.

The history of the home was not clear when the home slipped into disrepair, but hardly a month went by without something going wrong. The single-story home had a finished cellar, half of which was a laundry and storage area. The other half was a 1950s alcoholic's dream.

The area had thick red and black shagged carpet with a huge bar that stretched ten feet in length. Behind the bar were reminders that filled the wood paneled walls. There were many old, framed photos of their family during good times.

There were also numerous bar relics: Budweiser and Michelob signs that lit up. And cute bar relic, which bore the first names of Pete's parents: "Jerry and Pat." There was a drunken hobo standing under a lamp post. There was even a lamp whose base was a giant beer bottle. These relics from bygone days sat amongst dusty old liquor bottles and bar and shot glassware.

Pete was proud of his home and the bar. He and a few of his friends moved in a huge projection television he bought at a garage sale. The furniture scattered throughout the area was also purchased through garage sales.

In fact, except for a new sectional sofa and a new refrigerator the couple bought nothing when they were married, practically everything was obtained second hand, even a beautiful colonial dining room set Pete's parents bought back in the 1950s.

Pete was in his fifties and five years older than Kelly. They met at a bar a mile or so away from his home. He was an average sized guy with a bit of a gut. He had an average face and a full head of thick dirty blonde hair. Coincidentally, Pete and Daniel went to the same high school, but they never knew each other.

When Daniel arrived, his brother-in-law was busy with his morning cigarette and coffee. Pete looked hung over and Daniel greeted him verbally from a short distance away. Plumes of toxic smoke, which repelled Daniel, hovered around Pete like a London fog. Kelly did not smoke and never had. She restricted Pete's smoking to either in one of the two full bathrooms, outside, in the single attached garage, or downstairs in the basement recreation room. Secondhand smoke was prevalent.

Latent clouds of carbon monoxide crept up and down the once white walls which now looked like stained white teeth. The death smoke even discolored the ceiling, which seemed to be crying out for a good paint job.

The couple had two young boys. Michael was twelve and Zack was seven. Both appeared to be smart kids, but they were bound to inherit some of their father's unhealthy lifestyle. The youngest was full of love.

His eyes still held the innocence and wonderment of childhood in them. Both had thick heads of beautiful hair. Michaels was dark brown, which matched his mother, who he resembled.

Zack's hair was strawberry blonde, which matched his dad, and he seemed to have a mix of facial features from both parents. The oldest whined a lot and picked on his little brother.

As to their parenting skills Pete yelled at the kids to gain compliance. He pushed their buttons, and they pushed his buttons. Kelly, however, was more laid back in her approach.

Kelly worked for the State of Pennsylvania while Pete was a stay-at-home dad who worked part time at the legion, tending bar.

Pete crushed out his cigarette, exhaled, and filled the small area of the kitchen with a cloud of smoke. Daniel's eyes followed the plume, and he tried to dodge it.

"You know Daniel I've got to tell you, when I told your sister you were back and wanted to come and stay with us, she said:

"No" he told him.

An uneasy feeling crept through Daniel's central nervous system. He needed a Xanax after his brother in law's remark.

Pete wasn't Jewish, which was a major violation of Daniel and Kelly's mother's edict: "You must marry a Jewish man," she would tell Kelly. And the same message was drilled into Daniel, different gender notwithstanding.

Both of Sarah Bellman's youngest offspring failed to honor their mother's words. Only her eldest Hal lived up to expectations and Sarah Kansky, which was her maiden name, showed extreme pride toward her son and daughter in law, which produced her first three grandchildren and who did well for themselves.

Daniel tried to charm his way back into Kelly and Pete's household. Things he would never do for himself he performed for them. He scrubbed toilets and floors. He swept and loaded the dishwasher every night after dinner. He did load after load of laundry, which he folded and placed on the beds he had made that morning.

Daniel tried to be wanted but he wasn't. When Kelly emerged from her bedroom after three days of high fever she was not in the mood for Daniel.

"Well, you've got to find yourself a place to live and get a job," she said. That was always her message when Daniel showed up. The message never sank in and never happened.

Frozen once again and standing with his back up against a wall the depressed man could not understand why he was not wanted. Why do people leave him feeling unwanted, unloved and un-liked.

Daniel had a long line of people in that department, and nobody was ever in the other line: "No waiting in the wanted, loved and liked line," he always thought. But he never understood. His skull was thick even though his hair had fallen out when he was back in his twenties.

Daniel sighed and agreed to her terms. He looked in the paper's classifieds every day. He searched on the computer and tried to network, but who can network without anybody to network with.

"I've got a lot of good experience working in mental health," he would tell himself.

But the depression stopped him in him like a traffic light that turned red. He could not motivate himself. Whenever he came back to his hometown, for some reason, he always returned to this loser pattern. Daniel felt he was jinxed because of his wicked ways when he was a child and teenager.

He realized the situation was such that he and Pearl would soon be back in the car headed west.

As the boys played with electronic gadgets and Pete smoked outside the front door, Kelly read the newspaper. The television was practically always tuned into a children's program and Daniel just sat there. He looked grumpy and weary.

When the phone rang Kelly continued looking at the paper and Pete ignored it too. After a few rings the little one answered.

"It's Zada Lionel," he told his mother.

Kelly looked perturbed, closed the paper and walked to the phone. She still sounded sick when she answered.

"Hello…"

"Hi, Kelly your mother has just been taken to the hospital by ambulance. She's very sick…"

"What's the matter?"

"Well, we think its pneumonia, but we don't know. They're taking her to the Holy Hospital. I'll call you later and let you know what room she's in…"

"Okay… thanks, Lionel…"

With a worried look on her face she hung up the phone and told everybody the news. The kids went back to their kids' duties as Pete put out his cigarette, opened the storm door and came back into the house. Kelly resumed reading the paper as she answered Pete and Daniel's questions about the phone call.

"When can we go and see her?" Daniel asked.

"He didn't say."

"Your mother hasn't felt well for weeks," Pete told Daniel.

"Months," Kelly added.

"Bubby is in the hospital?" asked one of the kids.

The house fell into the doldrums with each party going their separate ways. Kelly went back to reading the paper, Pete went outside for another cigarette, and the kids went back to being glued to their video games and the television.

Daniel got up and went to his room. He sat on the bed he had just bought, turned on the television to Cartoon Network and clandestinely self-medicated.

Sarah Bellman was ill, very ill, in fact. She had stage-four deep-rooted lung cancer. But that reality never sank into Daniel's mind.

Lionel, his stepfather, refused to allow him to visit his mother, but when his brother and sister-in-law arrived from Israel, he relented. Daniel was obese, smelly and there was a dark cloud of depression, which followed him everywhere he went.

Hal now spoke softly and was kind to his brother, which was not always the case when they were young. Daniel had not communicated with Hal for more than ten years. Hal's wife was a gifted woman. She was smart and she looked to Daniel to be the kind of person who was comfortable with her life.

Their grown kids immediately flew in, as well. Two of them lived in London, but not together. They saw each other about once a month, and Elliot who recently moved to Boston with his new wife.

Daniel thought Hal's kids were awesome.

They looked beautiful and healthy, and they were clean cut and smart. Two of them had their master's degree and one had a doctorate. Any individual could take one look at them, and it was obvious they were on the road toward happiness and success.

His nephew's wife was a genius and was written up in Newsweek.

Sharona Lipsky earned her doctorate as did her spouse, but in a different discipline, and made headlines in the computer software world and a fortune to go with it.

Daniel first met the handsome young Israeli born woman when he traveled to Israel in the late 1990s for Hal's daughter's Bat Mitzvah.

For the most part Hal's kids ignored their fat smelly unkempt uncle. They were cordial and talked with him a little, but Daniel knew they did not come all this way just to see him.

"Who'd want to see me, anyway," he told himself.

Daniel sat at the foot of his mother's hospital bed and recollected the stories he heard about his mom when he was a child.

In the beginning Sarah Kansky led a lower middle-class life. Her parents, both immigrants from Easter Europe, met, married, and moved the family from a small dwelling on Fern Street to a much nicer home on fourth street when Sarah was a mere teen. She was a beautiful girl and grew up and made many friends. Popularly, she went to high school dances and parties, and she graduated. She never went on to college.

At one of the dances she met Herbert Sherman, a young Jewish Frank Sinatra look alike who was introduced to her and they fell for one another. She fell in love. He fell in lust. After they were married, she never worked outside the home, but she worked a great deal inside the family dwelling. She always kept the small row house in impeccably clean conditions as well as her three young children.

Herbert was known around town as "the golden rod." He was a schmoozer and a playboy, and he was unfaithful to his new wife. He never wanted to be a father, because he did not like children. After fourteen years of marriage, he met Eve a young woman twelve years his junior. Herbert divorced Sarah and immediately married the young beauty who was not Jewish.

The late 1960s divorce was unusual at the time. Even though the hippy movement was in full force, it was not commonplace, and after Herbert left Sarah with three young children, he quickly fell behind on his child support payments, and later, he stopped paying all together. There were no State agencies to track down deadbeat dads and make them pay in those days, as Daniel recalled.

Sarah's life changed. She was crushed at first and it led to a brief hospitalization. After a few days in a psychiatric ward, she was discharged against medical advice because she said:

"I've got to get back to my kids."

She picked her life up, got a job as a receptionist and tried very hard to maintain her household. As years passed, she moved from one position to another.

All along she tried to provide for her offspring, and she did the best she could. Her parents lived several blocks away and were very supportive.

They helped tremendously with the kids, especially Daniel. Hal was a junior high student; Daniel was in elementary school and Kelly was still a baby.

Lunches in those days were not served at school, and everybody went home to eat. Daniel hopped skipped and jumped his way to his grandparents' home every day where a great hot lunch and his grandfather's favorite TV show, Hogan's Heroes, which was in syndication at the time.

His grandfather was a rotund man hitting his 60's and he always sat in his recliner and smoked a pipe. Daniel's grandmother was a fantastic person full of love and they both set a good example for Daniel.

Daniel's grandparents originated from Poland where they both immigrated from in the 1930s. They were teenagers after they came to the United States.

They courted, engaged, and married, raising three handsome children. They ran a shoe business which went from flea market to flea market and the business enabled them to put their youngest child through college. They worked Sunday through Thursday and took off Friday and Saturday to observe the Sabbath and attend a Jewish Orthodox Synagogue near their home.

In their shoe business they set up the shoes with one shoe atop each box on display. Each location they went to have a men's, woman's and children's section. "Mo," which is what the grandchildren called her, handled the ladies and their shoes. "Pop" handled the men and their shoes, and both handled the kids and their shoes. When Hal, Daniel or Kelly was old enough they separately came along and helped with the business.

Hal and Kelly and their grown kids were downstairs eating in the hospital cafeteria. Lionel sat silently with his arms folded in a corner chair of the hospital room while Daniel sat in another chair at the foot of his mother's hospital bed. Daniel just sat there silently and stared at her. His mother's beauty was drained from her body.

Oxygen tubes protruded from her nostrils. A stand with an IV bag attached held a second bag, which delivered other medications, intravenously. She looked at Daniel and their eyes met for minutes until Daniel ignorantly said:

"Harold, when she goes home, I want to come and visit her."

Lionel sighed deeply and snapped:

"Daniel, she's not coming home!"

"Maybe that was the moment when reality sank into my brain," which is what he said when he reflected about the whole experience later.

Sarah asked Lionel and Daniel to adjust the foam pillow under her back to make her more comfortable. They both worked with her until the pillow was adjusted just right.

Daniel was at the hospital for a couple of hours that first day he was allowed to see her. When the rest of the family entered the room from their lunch Daniel got up and stood motionless for several minutes and then reported that he had to go back to Kelly's. Privately, he yearned to self-medicate.

Ten days passed and Daniel visited his mother on most of them. These days were surreal to Daniel, and he increased his use of pot, hash, Xanax and Lortabs.

On the tenth day of her hospitalization, in the afternoon, Daniel's cell phone rang. It was Kelly.

"Mom passed away twenty-minutes ago," she sadly reported.

Daniel had felt a sudden pain in his heart about twenty minutes ago, but he never said a word to anyone about the incident. He also never told his mother that he loved her because deep down he knew he did not. He did not love anyone… Not even his dog… Not even self…

The woman he fought with for forty-one out of fifty-one years was gone. Sure, they reconciled in April and Daniel was glad he did that. Even though the reconciliation was never planned, and it just happened it all still baffled Daniel, but he was glad him and his had mom made up.

Throughout most of Daniel's life he showed little respect for the one person who tried her best to provide a stable home with a roof over his head and food in his belly. He took her for granted, which was the same way he took life itself…

All those years Daniel's animosity and disrespect towards his mother stemmed from two incidents when he was ten years old. And in those two moments his life was paved down the path of anger, bitterness, resentment and a great deal of incorrect conditioning and suffering for decades. He never understood a lot about his life. The connection never clicked in his mind. His nearly lifelong depression placed a permanent hold onto the whole matter.

He knew the reason a person's depression goes unrecognized and remains unresolved is because their sickness remains untreated with the proper medication and counseling, and except for the self-medication they regularly use to numb their psychological pain the sickness remains to be a mystery throughout their mind, body and soul.

Daniel knew he was sick, but he was unwilling or unable to do anything about what ailed him. His depression continued in full force.

Even though he removed the word estranged when he talked or thought about his mother and his life with her, they never talked about the roots of their estrangement. He thought he had put it behind him, so he said to himself:

"Here was a strong woman that tried her best to do everything right… It's so sad she had to have a shmuck like me around… She didn't deserve it."

At that moment he cried. He was not clear who he cried for, however, himself or the loss of his mother. He looked for her beauty, but he could not find the image. He felt as if he was out to sea and his life was stranded in a heavy fog. He could find no beauty in anything, especially himself.

Chapter 12

Two days later, was the day of the funeral. The burial took place at the Jewish Orthodox cemetery where Daniel's grandparents, aunts and uncles and cousins were buried. Sarah Ann Bellman was to be laid to rest in their company.

Olev Israel was a huge cemetery. Grey gravestones dotted the landscape as far as could be seen. That day the skies were grey, and no sunshine even contemplated breaking through.

Inside the cemetery's simple structure there was row after row of long brown wooden benches without cushions. The rows were separated by a red carpeted aisle which ran up the center of the structure to the front where a simple lectern stood in the middle. On either side of the lectern were flags: The Stars and Stripes flag of the United States of America and the Star of David flag of Israel.

The air inside the ground level one-story building was neither conditioned during moments of heat nor heated during moments of cold. The whole thing struck Daniel as if God wanted those who grieved to go without any comfort while family and friends rested one of his souls.

Coldness snapped at people's skin like a smoker who was trying to stop flicking at a rubber band around their wrist, the cold bit through the skins surface with a powerful message to their brain.

In Daniel's case the message was still not clear to him at all. Somber and medicated only on Xanax he wore an extra-extra-large white dress shirt, a tie and an old navy-blue sports jacket, which sort of matched his only pair of forty-two-inch dress pants. Underneath, he still had good common sense to wear a pair of sweatpants and a sweatshirt to fight off the cold.

He walked in alone. First, he picked a black yarmulke from a brown wooden box housed outside the entrance of the building.

As he entered, he started to see faces of his past: Relatives, old neighbors, good friends of his mother and friends of his brother and sister…

Daniel slowly moved toward the front of the somber chamber where he could see his family on either side. Along the way he shook hands with a few people. He remained composed until he came across one old face from his past, he could not hold back his emotions. The source of his emotions was simply a man who knew his mother. He was a nice man when Daniel was a boy and on that day the reason for the sudden loss of composure was primarily because only took a simple instance to trigger the great wealth pent-up emotions to surface.

The emotions have been brewing for days, weeks, months, years and decades.

Now the emotions broke through like a runaway train, and to Daniel, they seemed like they were about to run off the track.

Daniel took a seat next to his sister and her family in the front row. On the other side of the aisle sat his brother and his family along with many cousins, aunts and uncles.

Daniel attended only four other funerals in his life: All grandparents. Tense, he said nothing but acknowledged people with somber facial expressions and little head nods.

As the Rabbi entered, he was dressed in a black suit and wore a black hat. The draped casket which bore the Star of David followed. The Rabbi spoke for five minutes and turned the lectern over to the family. Daniel's brother and sister and law were the first to speak. Solemn and concise, they each spoke of the virtues of their mother. Next, Kelly rose and spoke. She delivered words of her mother's strength and attributes. Daniel did not approach the podium and said nothing.

Only twenty minutes passed before they said Kaddish, the prayer for the dead. The closed casket sat atop a wheeled apparatus and was pushed down the center aisle out to the grave site by two men. They were followed by the Rabbi reciting Hebrew verses from the prayer book he held in his hand. The family followed him, which was followed by a large procession of people.

Outside, about ten feet from where her parents were laid to rest decades ago, Sarah met with her resting spot.

The hole had already been dug. There was a great mound of brown earth next to it. There were ten folding metal chairs next to the grave site, and a large green canopy covered the proceeding.

Lionel would later report there were one-hundred and thirty-four guests who signed the condolence book. Daniel Sherman was one of them.

The immediate family took their seats next to the squared oblong hole. The casket was taken from its wheeled devise and the cloak with the Star of

David was removed. Silence permeated the surroundings.

Under dark grey skies only the wind winding its way around the proceedings was evident. A stinging damp mist accompanied it. The casket was placed atop a metal device used to lower it into the burial ground.

The Rabbi continued his prayers in Hebrew and then spoke in English. He invited those under or outside the large green canopy to shovel earth to cover the grave. He said it was a "mitzvah."

The young Orthodox Rabbi pulled the spade from its resting spot in the mound of dirt and was the first to deliver a shovel full of the earth back to where it belonged. Spontaneously Daniel rose up and moved to the front of the grave.

The Rabbi handed him the shovel, and without thought, he delivered shovel load after shovel load after shovel five shovel loads to be exact.

A family member tapped Daniel on the shoulder and signified enough. Perhaps he needed the Mitzvahs. Perhaps he was in a hurry to get away. Whatever the reason, Daniel Sherman delivered the first layer of earth that completely covered the casket which contained the body of his mother.

Daniel made no eye contact with anyone. He sat back down, and he watched as dozens upon dozens of individuals took a shovel full of dirt and returned the soil from whence it came.

There was no tombstone, that would not be presented until the unveiling, which was a ceremony performed about one-year away from death.

Kaddish, the prayer for the dead was recited by the immediate family once again.

Afterwards, people cluttered into little groups and quietly consoled one another. Daniel stood alone as he walked towards his mother's parent's headstone, which was a modest grey tombstone first placed there decades ago.

The tribute to his grandparents exhibited a slight sign of weather decay. Daniel noticed small stones atop it, which were traditionally placed there by family sighting their commemoration. The sick man loved his grandparents. He gazed at their grave for several seconds before he picked up a round smooth stone he spotted nearby on the ground. He wiped the dirt off the pebble, kissed the small rock and gently placed the precious stone on top of the grave.

The groups started to disperse. Daniel walked up the black tarred driveway alongside the building. He looked around and tried to spot his sister and her family. He needed to catch a ride to the Shiva at his mother's and stepfather's home.

Daniel did not see them.

"They must have left from the other side of the cemetery," he thought.

Suddenly, he could hear his brother calling out his name. He and his wife were about to get into the back seat of a sedan, and he motioned for him to come and join them. Daniel waved them off and said:

"I'm going with Kelly."

He found his sister about a block up the street. They drove in virtual silence, but both stated:

"The funeral was a lovely tribute to Mom."

There were no more tears, no more loss of emotions on Daniel's part, because he was exhausted.

Sitting Shiva is a weeklong process for families to pay homage to the dead. Special low folding Shiva chairs and boxes full of prayer books are sent over by the Synagogue. Virtually everyone who attended the funeral, and then some, visits the home at one point or another during the week. Great amounts of food are brought in for breakfast, lunch and dinner.

The weeklong tribute was not somber. Memories resurfaced and stories retold, and old family photo albums are thumbed through again.

The daily ritual that had taken place in millions of Jewish households over thousands of years began around 10 a.m. and stopped around 8 p.m. each day. During that time the immediate family is present as visitors come and go.

On this first day of Shiva as well as on the last day the Rabbi visits the mourners. He offers his knowledge and consoles the family on their loved one's passing, which is part of the cycle of life.

When Daniel arrived at his mother's townhouse, he avoided the great number of people all crowded together throughout the kitchen, dining and living rooms. He headed upstairs and sat in an overstuffed chair. He looked around the room. There was a computer desk and office chair with a personal computer on top, a matching overstuffed sleeper sofa similar in color and style to the chair he was sitting in. The furniture all sat atop thick tan wall to wall carpet.

The room was cluttered with bags and suitcases, and he could tell that this is where his brother, sister-in- law and grown children stayed.

Daniel did not feel well. He lost his tie and took off the sport jacket. His sister-in-law appeared at the doorway, smiled and respectfully asked if he was going to join everyone downstairs.

"Maybe in a little while… I'm exhausted."

A week went by, and Daniel sat through most of the Shiva. A couple of times he made excuses not to show up right away in the morning, but he felt he had paid respect, nonetheless.

Back at Kelly's home life was slowly getting back to normal. About a week after the Shiva ended Daniel could tell from his sister's nonverbal communication that something was up.

As she sat back in her recliner her silence sent a strong message to him. He tried to carry on civil conversations with her, but she was not in any mood to talk or listen.

"You want me to leave," Daniel said.

Kelly did not look at him, but she nodded her head.

"I think it's time..."

Daniel realized that he needed to get a life… Kelly had a life… Hal had a life… But he never had one.

Followed by a cold half-hearted hug on both their parts, Daniel and Pearl took off the next morning.

As he drove through the grey mist of the cold morning on the state's turnpike he was headed west, and the only location that came to mind to proceed to be a place he couldn't fathom. On impulse he decided on: Bakersfield, California.

Chapter 13

Miller greeted the news like a child greeting a report card being issued in school. Anxious trepidation seeped through every pore in his face. He and Allison believed their plan was essential: Keep Daniel Sherman in the hospital. The team needed time. "Besides, he's as fresh as bare baby's bottom," Allison philosophized

Normally, someone with depression would be in a psychiatric facility for five days, at the most. They managed to keep DANIEL for fourteen days behind the guise of weaning him from Xanax, something 3G's medical consultant reported: "The amount of Xanax he was on was an extremely high dose. I wouldn't give six milligrams a day to anyone, ever, but when he gets down below two milligrams the cluster headaches will return."

The team of elders did not like that prospect either. But they had more important issues to hand. Ignoring the obvious would be foolish for the officials believed radical Islamic fundamentalists and other zealots would twist the world back toward a moment in time good common-sense people would never want to see, but Kushner doubted the solution.

Forcefully, Miller put down his pen and asked:

"Do we want this world to return to the stone-age?"

"… and you think Mr. Sherman is going to have some kind of impact?" Kushner asked.

Miller nodded and gently picked up his pen.

"I do, he can appeal to the vast majority of the world who sit in the middle of this mess, and we can only hope that they can curb the zealotry of their fringes."

"He's been a substitute teacher, and he's taught skills to people with mental illness. He's no diplomat," Kushner argued.

"We don't need a diplomat... We don't want a diplomat…" Miller shot back.

"So, you think Mr. Sherman is simply going to walk on water and that's going to work?" Kushner asked sarcastically.

Allison cleared his throat, and he was prepared to speak. "Even before he was treated for depression this guy had good skills. He reached people who are hard to reach. Just think how he'll be now that he's not depressed."

"What if people don't believe in what he has to say? What if people don't like him? You read Dr. Sanchez's report from LA," Kushner retorted.

"We're keeping a close watch on him. He's returning to Bakersfield today, and let's just wait and see how he does and what he does," Dr. Allison reported.

"Tom, I really don't think we have much to go on. With all the audio and visual surveillance recorded we don't have one shred of evidence that he even knows or believes, for the matter."

Miller pulled a stapled report from a folder. He handed the document to

Allison as he pointed out, "We have interviewed his old neighbors and a few childhood friends of his sister and his father. There was nothing but basic anecdotal information we're already aware of."

Allison seemed intrigued at what he was reading as Miller went on:

"When our people interviewed his former stepmother, Eve Sherman, we reached Daniel's one and only confidant. Why even after she divorced his father, Daniel's kept in close contact with her. She's been his confidant for forty-two years. He talks with her just about every day and she is the one and only person we've identified who he talks to confidentially…"

"She may know something, but how can she know everything? We don't even think Daniel knows everything," Allison replied.

"He cries on her shoulder. He shares secrets with her. He bothers her, sometimes several times a day. She's described him as an insecure person, you know, and she has no idea what our interest in Daniel was all about." Miller said.

"And…" Kushner remarked.

"And she's been a treasure trove of information."

"I still don't see any concrete evidence which points to him as the Messiah, the Second Coming, or the Birth of Armageddon," Kushner recounted.

Allison reached for his reading glasses and said: "We have him talking with another psychiatric patient: Ken Post…" Miller interrupted and said: "…who thought he was the Son of God…"

"Yes, and Sherman said nothing to him about it except we are all God's children," Kushner rebutted.

"Did you see the look in his eyes?" Miller demanded.

"We have him touching 'thank you' all the time when he walked the halls and reached an exit door. What do you think that was all about?" Allison asked.

"I don't know, maybe he was thankful just coming out of his depression," Kushner reasoned.

"Roland, Eve Sherman reported that Mr. Sherman walked into a classroom each day as a stranger and he doesn't know the kids and they don't know him. In a matter of minutes, he's able to gain the complete cooperation of children who by all accounts eat up substitutes like they would cherry pie…" Miller told them.

"Yes," Allison added, "and she found his assignment notebook detailing every school and teacher he substituted for. There are over five-hundred entries, and our field agents have identified teachers who still remembered him."

"Yes, but comparing children to religious zealots is a bit of a stretch Tom…" Kushner answered.

"Yes, I understand, but we can see the beginnings of something different here… something brand new. What he said was not taught to him. He didn't get it out of some book… He's harbored a philosophy inside his mind that has been brewing somewhere in this universe for more than a thousand years…" Miller debated.

"…and you think that Mr. Sherman is the one chosen to deliver these words," Kushner said.

"Remember Roland, he fits all the criteria perfectly, even down to the one we missed in our initial report: Tattoos and piercings: None, Roland, none."

Kushner leans back in his chair sighs and runs his hand through his thick silver hair, as Miller excitedly picks up another report.

"Look, we have a report here that at one school a young girl had her desk pushed up against the chalk board away from the other students because she was so destructive and disruptive to the class that the teacher wrote a letter about her behaviors and warned the substitute, who turned out to be Mr. Sherman. Quote, the substitute is instructed to press the emergency button and notify the school office that will dispatch the principle and the vice-principle immediately..."

Miller smiled as he pushed his chair back and folded his legs.

"The report states that this child pulls her hair out and has violent tantrums in the classroom... the button to the office was never pushed that day, Roland. Do you know why it wasn't pushed?"

Kushner appeared un-enthused.

"I know, Mr. Sherman..."

"Yes, Mr. Sherman in five minutes was able to speak the words that changed this problem child's life and that is when he was depressed, although he was self-medicating in the evenings, Eve Sherman reported to us."

As Miller and Kushner continued their debate, Allison picked up his copy of the report and read it in more detail.

The report read: "February 20, 2010, Subject: Sherman, Daniel H. Interviewee: Sherman, Eve M."

Allison's bright blue eyes scanned the page until he reached the section of the report that spoke of the young girl:

"...Subject Daniel Sherman returned to said school a few weeks later for a different assignment. He was a monitor during recess. The little girl: Allison Moore, told our field agent that she ran up to Mr. Sherman and told him: "Thank you, Mr. Sherman you taught me how to be good."

Allison took his eyes off the report as Miller told Kushner:

"...Daniel's under our umbrella. He's set up with the VA for his medical and psychiatric services which are good."

"Kevin, you said he's like a newborn kitten, what do you mean?" Kushner asked.

"If Mr. Sherman is who we think he is this whole phenomenon will unfold over time, it won't happen overnight," Allison replied.

"Tell our people I want daily updates. We need to know what he's always doing. We need to know who he knows and where he goes. We need a full accounting of his every minute," Miller insisted.

Allison reached for a copy of The New York Times a headline for an article on the front page read: "Arab Leaders Urged U.S. to Stop Iran."

"I concur with observation, but the findings should be filtered through the analysis section, as well. Mr. Sherman's father reported there are two upcoming family events scheduled for the fall," Allison said.

"What about them?" Miller asked.

Allison read another report:

"Father reported subject's nephew's Bar Mitzvah scheduled for the end of September. Subject's mother's unveiling takes place on the next day…"

"How can we be sure he'll go? Kushner asked.

"He showed up for everything when he was at his lowest point of depression. Logically, he'll attend…" Miller figured.

"He was back east at the time, of course he showed up," Kushner charged.

Miller watched the eyes of Doctor Kushner and said:

"He didn't have to, Roland… and we know from our interviews Daniel Sherman has a habit of making up excuses when he doesn't want to do something… he even sat Shiva…"

Dr. Kushner looked perplexed, because he did not relish his position as an antagonist, but, nevertheless, he knew there was still enough room for reasonable doubt.

"Our subject's appointments with the VA are set for next month. He has money so he won't be in any hurry to get a job. Logically, he'll be looking for one and we must see to it that he remains unemployed, at least until after the family events…"

Allison nodded as Miller made a note of an idea he had.

"We also need to consider interviewing his Israeli connections. I suggest we start with his brother and sister-in-law in Israel…" Allison said.

"Are we going to conduct them in the fall sometime around the family events?" Kushner inquired.

"No, it's a perfect opportunity for us to observe Daniel and his interactions with his family, because they haven't exactly gotten along over the years. In fact, as an adult, the only person who he ever kept consistent contact with him is his ex-stepmother, Eve. We'll keep staff abreast as to who we want to interview, when and where…"

Dr. Allison sat back in his chair, scratched his chin and concentrated on a portrait of Thomas Jefferson that hung on a nearby wall. Dr. Miller relaxed and poured a glass of water for himself from the pitcher. Dr. Kushner took a couple of slow deep breaths.

Each senior intelligence official realized that over the next six months they would once again become students, which was something they have not had to do since the days of Franklin D. Roosevelt.

And to do this, which would be unbeknownst to their subject, Miller and his team made the decision ten days before Daniel was discharged from the hospital that digital surveillance needed to be planted everywhere.

There were six set-ups in Daniel's studio apartment and several in the common areas of the apartment complex which captured every movement and moment. There were also three planted in his car which grabbed the view from the front, as well as from the back and the side.

Allison studiously watched his colleagues' faces for they told a story. Kushner looked ambiguous and doubtful, while Allison knew his face matched

Miller's, which was complicated, because they each knew that their subject, Daniel Howard Sherman, was to be placed under a microscope and Lord knows what they'd find.

Chapter 14

Daniel usually didn't think much about trees. But at this moment, they seemed to be very important. He let the thoughts pass. During winter months some trees looked saddened. Their heavy bark layered thick strong trunks with solid roots engraved upon soil, which supported bare naked branches that were patiently picturesque against a solid grey sky. They were all seemingly frozen at a point in time. With their living branches unmasked they revealed the tree's true beauty. God's monuments were devoid of their vibrant green occupants and disengaged multi-colored foliage which scattered through whirls of wind toward an ultimate destiny: These creatures of the forest remained patient and awaited readjustment, which was so certain to arrive.

As he boarded the VA bus to Bakersfield, Daniel thought about Jones and the man's terrible saga. The sick soul had to learn his lessons the hard way. Daniel felt a new appreciation for his world.

"That could have well been me," he thought to himself.

The chartered bus arrived in Bakersfield. Daniel noticed dozens of thorny rose bushes scattered throughout the grounds of the illuminated VA Outpatient Clinic. He thought they waited good-naturedly for their moment to bloom.

The one-story clinic was closed. Darkness fell minutes after the dark grey sky turned in for the day. Permission was granted to those wanting to go inside to make a phone call for a ride home. A security guard stood by the building's entrance and allowed people with their VA identification cards to enter. Daniel had an ID card, but he had no one to call. He thought about calling for a taxi but decided against it.

"I'll just walk home," he thought.

He was not sure how far away he lived, and he did not even know which direction to go in. He knew California Avenue would lead him home. He asked the bus driver who pointed toward one direction. Daniel slung his overnight bag around his heavy hooded pale green jacket and started walking.

When he reached a major intersection, he hesitated and looked around. He had walked for twenty minutes, and he believed he was lost. He noticed a small convenience store and decided to ask in there. Daniel emerged knowing that he walked in the wrong direction.

He retraced his steps through underpasses, over bridges and against heavy traffic. When he reached Oak Street, he was told to make a right, and several blocks up would be California Avenue.

Daniel took his cell phone out, turned the device on and called Eve.

"Hi, Eve…"

"Well, hello…"

"I got off the bus from Los Angeles and I'm in the process of walking home because I didn't want to take a taxi."

"Where are you?"

Daniel strained his eyes to make out the street sign.

"I'm on Oak and 25th Street… I need to get to California Avenue."

Her brain's automatic reflex kicked in as her slender fingertips quickly moved across the keyboard, not unlike a great concert pianist beginning her concerto. The computer savvy female brought up directions from the laptop in front of her. As the high-tech tool once again proved the computer's invaluable contribution to mankind, she looked around her "tin can," as she described her home.

Her dwelling was a mobile home, and her tin palace was concretely planted into the earth of a large senior's only mobile home park in Las Vegas.

Built in the early 1970s, her double-wide and kitchen area, one big bedroom and two smaller rooms.

"You're about six blocks away from California Avenue…"

"So, how's it going?"

"Oh, I'm doing fine. I discharged around eleven this morning. I ate some lunch, and I got onboard a VA bus which brought me back to Bakersfield. We had to stop in Sepulveda, but I'm here."

Eve could hear Daniel as he breathed, and even though she had not physically seen him for nearly a year, she talked to him almost every day and she knew he was way out of shape.

Her memory kicked back to the interview with the radiant Federal Field Officer Ethel Braveman who just showed up at her door last week asking about her former stepson.

"He's been out of shape for about eight-years now… The last time Daniel was physically in good shape was just after the turn of the century. With Daniel being in shape physically doesn't last too long when he's out of shape mentally," she explained tactfully.

She remembered when he was just ten and the first time, she ever met him: "He was a cute kid with a nose for trouble. He was always pushing his dad's buttons. I liked him, but his father was very impatient with him because he was impatient with people in general, especially with kids."

"Why did you marry him?"

Eve hesitated with her answer and whispered:

"I wanted to get out of that run down little town I was living in. That's where we met."

"Please, tell me about it."

"There's not much to tell, really… I made my way to this bar, and he was there… I found him rather handsome, and we liked each other… You see Daniel's father was a traveling salesman for a vacuum cleaner company. He serviced department stores that carried the product, and his territory included my dingy town and that's how he happened to be there that night."

"So, you had an affair with him?"

"We dated… he came up about once or twice a month and I was in college and living with a couple of girlfriends, so we'd just go out."

"Did you know that he was a married man?"

"Not a first."

"Tell me about the first time you met Daniel. Where were you and what was he like?"

She refolded her bare feet beneath her torso as she rearranged her bottom on the cushioned couch. The ex-stepmother reached for her pack of cigarettes and matches and selected one of each. The astute agent moved the sleeve back on her grey tweed jacket and glanced at her watch.

"Do you mind if I smoke,"

"Actually, I do…"

Eve was caught off guard. She never asked a visitor if they minded before. She quickly concluded the courtesy would be the last time she would ever ask. Befuddled, she looked at Ethel Braveman and then at the cigarette held inches below her mouth.

"Oh…"

Braveman smiled at her and she smiled back.

"I first met Daniel when he was ten. He was a precocious child. Anything he wanted to do his father opposed, and anything his father wanted him to do he opposed. We were living in an apartment, and Daniel came during his

Christmas break from school to visit for a week. Herbert that's his father… Herbert and I bought a Christmas tree, and we put the lights on the pretty little thing. We saved the balls and tinsel so that Daniel could enjoy helping. When we came into the apartment Daniel immediately questioned why there was a Christmas tree. "We're Jewish," he said… "We don't put up Christmas trees."

His father tried to explain the tree's purpose in the only way he knew how: Loudly and impatiently:

"I paid those sons a bitch $15 for this goddamn tree. I'm your father and that means you're going to like whatever the hell I tell you to like… understand?"

"Daniel froze when his father talked to him in that tone. I later explained to him that I was not Jewish and that the tree was really for me. Daniel and I seemed to hit it off from the beginning. We played board games together and I played my guitar and sang a few Peter, Paul and Mary songs which he seemed to like and enjoy."

"What about the tree?" Braveman asked.

"Oh, we finished decorating the tree and his father bought him a nice gift, a clarinet, but Daniel never really learned to play the instrument. I tried to cook for him, but he didn't particularly like my menus. I'm not much of a cook… anyway, his father had that attitude at the dinner table and demanded that Daniel eat every bite on his plate, I made pork chops the little guy never ate pork chops before…"

The interview went on for over an hour and Eve provided a lot of background on her former stepson, whom she mentored throughout his life. She was only twelve years older than Daniel at the time she married his thirty-six-year-old father. She gladly gave Braveman permission to contact her again if she needed to, "anything I can do to help…" she said believing the interview was for its said purpose, a routine VA background check.

"But he never asked me about Daniel's military service," she confessed to herself as Daniel told her that he would talk to her later.

Daniel thought about how the VA had gone through his wallet. The wallet was relinquished upon his arrival, and all the cards had been taken out, rearranged and were put back haphazardly.

As he marched up California Avenue with his bag strapped around his torso, he decided that issue was not important and to keep his mind occupied with other issues during his walk home, so he processed his two-week experience in Los Angeles.

With his commitment to always show self the utmost respect he decided that the single most important thing he learned is to keep self-healthy and clean, and that would start tomorrow, he promised to self.

"First, I'll pick-up Pearl from the doggie hotel and take her home and get her situated. Then I'll drive up the street and see if I can find a gym to join. I'll go every day," he professed.

He reached a busy intersection, which indicated he had about four or five blocks until he got home. Perspiration soaked his upper body inside his winter jacket, and he quickly made his way across the street.

While doing so he recalled how important personal hygiene was and that he showers every day, which he did along with other critical hygiene routines while a patient on two-south.

"I will have a fresh towel every day after I shower," he insisted.

He realized he only owned one towel, and he used it multiple times before he put it in his dirty laundry. He recalled, however, he would go without a shower for days and he would wear the same clothes, underwear and socks numerous times. He washed the towel with his clothes about once a month he recollected. His sheets and pillowcases were stripped and washed just about three times a year.

"This will not do," he confided to self. As he walked, he thought:

"Tomorrow I will go to Big-Mart, and I will buy six towels and along with the one I already have, I will have a fresh towel every morning after I come home from the gym and shower. Starting tomorrow I will strip my bed, and I will wash my sheets and pillowcases along with my clothes at least once a week, and I will never wear the same underwear or socks more than once. Also, I will never wear the same clothes more than once, except jeans, those I can wear two or three times…"

There was one more important matter that came to mind: The mirror. Daniel decided that the best thing for him not to do was to look in the mirror. He was very emphatic about it:

"My appearance doesn't matter, as long as I can say every day that I did my best to keep self-healthy, clean and safe."

Daniel reached the street where his apartment complex was on. When he reached his door, he ceremoniously pulled out his key, took a slow deep breath, and he stuck the key into the keyhole, turned the piece of metal and exhaled as he softly pushed the door open.

Chapter 15

His world started anew the next day. First, he picked up Pearl and paid her hotel bill.

"She's the cutest dog… you better keep an eye on her, somebody would snatch her in a heartbeat," the doggie hotel clerk claimed.

Pearl looked happy to be home. Daniel gave her fresh food, water and a crunchy bone. He hopped over to Big-Mart and bought six towels and a pack of underwear, as he remembered he only had three pairs that still fit.

Bakersfield seemed different somehow. A large variety of strong mature trees dotted the landscape. But, somehow, the people were different. Everywhere he went people were pleasant, kind and polite. Hispanics, mostly Mexican Americans, were the majority population in Bakersfield. That was fine with him. He liked them because they were pleasant, they worked hard, and they were good family people. He always thought that they were a very handsome race and full of rich culture and strong community pride.

As he drove in the direction someone told him he would find a gym, Daniel's eyes wandered. The undepressed state of mind he found himself in was rich and fantastic. He not only felt different, but he really was also different.

When he left the apartment that morning, he sensed change. He felt he was going in the right direction, but everything felt new, as if he did whatever he was doing for the first time.

He walked slower because even that felt very different and new to him. When he started his car and backed the vehicle out of the parking space, he did it slowly and deliberately because driving felt very unusual and new to him. And as he drove the car, driving felt like a first-time experience. His mind felt as if his body were in motion.

Daniel felt pleased. The fresh face strived toward meeting his inner-self's responsibilities that day. The errands were all in keeping self-healthy, clean, and safe.

On his first day he did not look in the mirror even when he shaved. He avoided looking into his eyes. He sensed they were different because anyone he encountered stared at them.

Eerily and coincidentally wherever he went people were still nice and kind and friendly. But even so he was curious and asked himself:

"What are they seeing?"

He considered it a major violation if he looked, even once, like he'd turn into a pillar of salt:

"What I look like is not important or relevant, and that goes for Daniel or anybody else's physical looks. If the inner self follows our top three responsibilities, then that is all that matters. What matters is how we feel, because we look how we feel: If we feel good – we look good. If we feel happy - we look happy. If we feel angry -we look angry. If we feel sad - we look sad. If we feel bad - we look bad," he reinforced to himself.

When he reached the Veteran's Outreach Center, he entered what would normally be an agitated, fruitless and tedious experience to the disheartened character he used to be.

As he saw the situation, outside his down in the dump's environment, powerful heart-filled moments now crammed his mind with warm memories to paste into his new personal album, his scrapbook of love.

The Veterans Outreach center was a beehive of professionalism, and the queen bee wore a cell phone in her ear as she guided five or six worker bees, who were really, work study students attending college fulltime under their country's GI Bill which they so deservedly earned.

Daniel stood in line behind other veterans in need of assistance. They were accessing veteran benefits for everything from education to a service-connected disability. Daniel required use of the Resource Room, which was a computer lab equipped with five high-speed computers and an Information Technology professional. He diagnosed and fixed computer glitches and assisted veterans with their resume and job searching.

Daniel checked in and sat in the waiting area. The line of padded chairs was filled with veterans and their dependents. A brown door buzzed, and an employee pushed the door open and entered. The Vet Center was busy operation. There were constant phone calls, and a slew of veterans waiting to be checked in. There were files to pull, and the queen bee, a small friendly lady with round cheeks and short brown hair kept it buzzing.

Kayla oversaw the entire operation, and she saw to the undertaking that not only were veterans, and their dependents served, but they were to be served in the most professional manner humans could possibly muster.

The brown door swiftly swung open, and Jake McHenry propped the entry open with his backside because the door automatically closed very quickly.

He had a sheet of paper in his hand. The nearly bald veteran with some grey hair on the sides and back of his head looked kind. He was from the 60's NO APOSTROPHE generation. "Daniel Sherman," he called out. Daniel stood and walked toward Jake, and the two rotund veterans shook hands and greeted each other.

Once again, Daniel knew his eyes were communicating something good and he reasoned that his old vacant face now looked occupied. They walked back past a series of offices where Veteran Representatives or Vet Reps were busy helping those in need.

When the two got to the first resource room, Jake stopped.

"I want you to meet James. He's our resource director and conducts special classes on resume building and job searches."

James was a tall, handsome and well-built man. He had a light brown complexion which was complimented by his rosy cheeks.

As he sat at a computer and typed, the thirty-something man suddenly stopped turned his body and looked at Daniel. Jake slowly stood up and smiled. His eyes were affixed to the newcomer. The former Marine, now retired, served twenty years in the service and reached the rank of master sergeant. He and Daniel shook hands firmly.

"If there's anything you need, I'm here to help you."

"Thank you."

The two veterans stood silently for a second as their eyes studied each other's.

"Um, well, Mr. Sherman… our room is down the hall," Jake said.

"Thanks, James… I'm sure I'll be seeing you."

"Anytime… anytime…"

"We're back here," Jake said over his shoulder.

They entered the computer room which was lined with five stations. Each station had a comfortably padded office chair in front of the personal computer, all of which were occupied at the time.

Jake had a desk at the head of the room with a personal computer. Only he was the master computer, and he could look at whatever happened on any of the other five computers. Jake sat in his office chair at his desk. Daniel was motioned to sit in the chair beside the desk.

"The first thing you must know is that no veteran can be in the hallway unaccompanied. The reason is due to confidentiality, so you must be always escorted, even to use the restroom," Jake politely commanded.

The former marine looked like Daniel's mother's brother. They talked for an hour and Jake asked a lot of questions of Daniel. What branch of the service was he in? What rank did he achieve while serving? What was his MOS (his job title while he served)? What kind of work was he looking for? How did he find out about the resource room, which he referred to as:

"The best kept secret in town?"

Fresh as the day, Daniel answered the questions. He was in the army from 1976 through 1979. He earned the rank of Specialist-five just after two years of service. His MOS or job title: 75B – Administration: company clerk. He wanted to pursue a job back in his career field of mental health. Daniel confidentially told Jake that he learned about the resource room while he was hospitalized.

With Jake's interest sparked he wanted to learn more, and he did overtime. Jake liked gossip, especially the juicy stuff and he got a lot of juice out of Daniel at first. But Daniel quickly recalled his levels of discloser skills and gradually implemented them with Jake and others at the Vet Center.

Daniel gradually got around to doing a lot of things. The antidepressant medication was so effective and so powerful that he had to get used to the realization that he now lived in a whole new world. A good world he dearly loved. He knew he had received a priceless gift, but he had to be patient, however, there was a lot to learn, and he did not expect to learn what he had to learn all in a day.

"Are you coming tomorrow?" Jake asked.

"Yes, I'm coming every day."

"Good, well then tomorrow we'll start with completing your master application which will be helpful to you when you're doing your resumes and when you need to fill out job applications."

James showed up at the resource room doorway. The battle tested marine had his hand over his heart. He looked squarely at Daniel, took a deep breath and exhaled.

"Daniel, right…"

"Yeah, Daniel…"

"If you want to join my class on resume building and job interviewing, I'm starting a new one on Monday," he said as he kept his hand over his heart and gave Daniel eye contact.

Daniel drove to his home that afternoon with questions on his mind. He slid a new CD into his car's player which was Elton John's Number One's: Rocket Man.

As the music started a powerful surge of emotion swept over him like a wave. Tears of happiness and love flowed uncontrollably through his eyes. He shook his head as "Your Song" played. "No, it's not true… It's all gibberish…" he insisted.

It took him a minute to regain his composure. He knew unwanted intrusive thoughts had to be addressed, immediately. Especially the one he just had. He decided to turn the music down and he concentrated on the road.

A wonderful hypnotic state enveloped him but allowed him to drive. The feeling filled him with a joyful and loving numbness and the feeling convinced him that self-medicating with drugs or alcohol was for losers.

"There's no better high… It's so pure and wonderful I feel so alive."

When he arrived back home Pearl looked happy to see him. Daniel held the little nine-pound poodle and petted her. He leaned back into the recliner and Pearl sat on his heavy torso. He had not even the slightest urge to do anything that was not in self's best interest. He took from his experiences today that there are people who naturally feel great, and that a power operates inside them that is so powerful, so wonderful, and so beautiful that they and everything around them are affected.

"Do I have the feeling?" he silently wondered.

He reasoned that the energy is not delivered using drugs, alcohol or treating self or others as a sex object. To master it takes an effort, a strong effort to first straighten out or readjust the mind and then to feed the proper information into the brain, ergo to become reconditioned.

Reconditioning is not necessarily religious information.

"Although if that leads one to the energy and that's what works for them then that is a good," he thought. "Any way people got there was good. To get there and to stay there is all that matters."

Daniel believed he was on path and headed in the right direction to begin his journey towards the greatest place in his mind, where body and soul live in harmony as one, the path toward freedom.

Chapter 16

Daniel woke up and got out of bed. Rested, he recalled his first day at In-Shape. He met Juan at the appointed time and place. The young Hispanic male with a face and body Madison Avenue would love showed the new member a few exercise tricks. One was to be in the push-up position. But, instead of Daniel's hands on the mat, he was to have his elbows on the slab of foam.

Juan demonstrated from that position how to get up on the hands and then back down on the elbows. Daniel was never good at push-ups, period. Juan waived the get to your hands part and just wanted Daniel to stay on his elbows, again, in the push up position. Sweat poured out of the overweight tub and his body quivered after just thirty-seconds.

"Breath…" Juan encouraged.

Daniel was holding his breath, not on purpose, so he took a breath. His quivered arms, legs, head and torso rattled like a building in Tokyo during a massive earthquake.

"Come on, you can do it," Juan said, motivationally.

Daniel's mass collapsed on the mat.

"Whew… whew… I'm out of breath," the out of shape exerciser said. He breathed heavily.

Juan had him go through a few other routines and Daniel's sweat saturated his white T-shirt, as he noticed that more than enough emanated from him to water a plant.

"I'm worn out, Juan," Daniel admitted.

"Okay, do you know how long you exercised today?"

"Um, three years…"

"…eight minutes…"

"Eight minutes!"

Daniel found humor in the memory as he fought against the early morning darkness. It was 5 a.m. and Pearl was still asleep when he reached sightlessly for his sweatpants his brother gave him as hand-me-downs when he was back east. They had belonged to Hal's son, and they bore the logo of the school the grown-up young man attended when he was a kid and lived in Israel.

Daniel felt warm. He had not had even the hint of a cluster headache in almost seven months. He was overjoyed at the thought, as he blindly made his way to the little closet area and reached along the wall for the light. He flipped the switch, and the silent light illuminated the small area and threw off enough light to do whatever he had to do in the bathroom without having to turn on that light, which triggered an exhaust fan that sounded like a Harley Davidson motorcycle.

He avoided looking at himself as he passed the double mirrored sliding closet door. He always did that. Every day for six months he avoided all mirrors, and he had no idea what he looked like. He did not want to know. He had no idea how much he weighed. The number did not matter. What mattered was what he asked himself "…am I healthy and clean?" And each day he reflected on his hospital discharge six months ago, he verified his findings that he was.

His health was his priority, and he never socialized at the gym, except once.

The day started typically as he finished his sit-up routine. He noticed two young Hispanic men using a piece of equipment that he was curious about. He initiated a short conversation with them and asked how the equipment worked. One of the men who wore a sweatband smiled and showed him while the other who had a shaved head asked.

"Do you come here every day?"

Daniel looked at him.

"Yes, it's a nice way to start out the day on the right foot."

The young male with the shaved head was taken aback by the statement for whatever reason, which Daniel did not know. The other surveyed Daniel with a smile. Daniel smiled back but he felt socially awkward and stated:

"Well, thanks I appreciate the help."

They parted company that day, and when Daniel occasionally ran into them at the gym, they would exchange greetings.

The seasonal time of the year was early summer, and the veteran exerciser and military veteran finished the first half of his daily morning work-out at In-Shape. Daniel went through a series of seven or eight pieces of exercise equipment, which worked on different muscle groups.

He started the morning with Juan's elbow push up, but he never went up to his hands like his trainer did. He just tried to hold his body and elbows in the push-up position for the length of a song which played on the gym intercom system. Once he completed Juan's exercise and the muscle equipment, he did his cardio work out on the treadmill, and he walked vigorously for thirty minutes.

While he walked, he concentrated his focus on one point in eye's view: A sticker on another piece of exercise equipment in front of him. The sticker bore the name of the gym and a request: "Please wipe down equipment after use." Before the name of the facility on the sticker, however, was the gym's large logo: "IS" with the "I" stand erect and "S" seductively rubbing up against the other letter.

Daniel remembered the first time he ever noticed the sticker.

On the daylight of his second day at In-Shape as he stared intently at the "IS" logo he thought about the two-letters as he walked with a purpose that day.

During the early morning as sweat drenched his t-shirt, suddenly, he looked down at the navy-blue pair of sweatpants with grey stripes on each side that his brother had given him as hand-me-downs. On the right thigh of the work-out sweatpants there too was a logo and in three inch lettering the printing read: "IS," which were the initials of the school his nephew and nieces once attended. He found humor in the coincidence: The gym's logo was "IS" and his sweatpants logo was "IS." He facetiously thought: "It proves that I'm in the right place."

Instantaneously, Daniel's mind dealt him a blow, because when he looked further below the three-inch "IS" logo on his sweatpants, the sight brought on tremendous emotions, which he fought back. Nevertheless, tears welled up in his eyes as if they were a river ready to swell over its banks. And then, suddenly and uncontrollably, he burst into tears as he read the name that was printed below the logo: "Israel."

With more determination he walked even more briskly. His hands swiftly moved to his eyes to wipe away and block the onslaught. He wanted no one to see him in his current emotional state. He straightened his posture and shook his head a few times to get back to a controlled state of mind.

As he moved through his treadmill routine, he required a touch of readjustment to stay composed again after his brain rekindled that moment yet again.

"It's gibberish… It's all gibberish…" he repeated silently as he felt his emotions toying with his eyes.

As his sweat met up and merged with the flow of tears which ran out the corners of his eyes and down his cheeks, Daniel looked up at the eye in the sky and then quickly down again.

He remembered the large color monitor situated at the front desk when he comes in every morning. There were nine six-inch squares on the monitor, which captured the goings-on around the facility.

He reassured himself that the video surveillance was just taping, so no one saw him, he reasoned that he shouldn't feel embarrassed by his emotional outburst, especially because he regained his composure rather quickly and he believed no one around him was near enough to see.

But what Daniel did not know and did not have even the slightest inkling of was that the whole incident was immediately observed and reported up the chain of intelligence back to the overseers in Washington, especially the details about the sweatpants he wore every day to exercise in, which was reported from the very first day he stated at In-Shape.

Daniel wondered why in the middle of his exercise routine memories, feelings and thoughts often tried to intrude their way in to his mind. Some of those intrusions were important, but a lot was total gibberish. So, what he tried to concentrate on and thought about was what he had worked out in his head over a period of days.

The experience was just like his good-side speech he always gave the kids every morning when he was a substitute teacher.

Insight did not develop in a day. That work required months of effort and continuous practice. And constant adjustments and readjustments were necessary before he got the repertoire just right, and by then, he knew the piece so well, he could recite the poetic prose backward if need be.

He knew that this formulation would take an even greater amount of time, effort, sweat and tears.

As he briskly pushed himself on the treadmill, the idea of incorporating the old material into his new material, which he shared with no one, was easily decided upon.

Developed overtime Daniel created his mantra, which was a series of good common-sense rules that helped keep an awareness of who he was and what he was all about. These words were to become the values and principles which he would follow and live by.

What he composed started as a few words, and over days more words were added, and within a month the structure really took shape. So, within a few months, his song was complete, and he repeated it numerous times a day, but always in his mind. He not only repeated it during his cardio routine, but he also repeated it in grocery stores while he shopped, or when he drove his car, or as he sat on the toilet and even while seated in the dentist's chair as he underwent a root canal.

He became so proficient at the mantra it was as if the words were tattooed into his brain. The mantra became a part of him which he sincerely promised self that he would never want to lose sight of.

His mantra became his guiding light. They were words not only to divert his attention while he exercised or performed or endured life's other type of "let's get it over with" experiences.

He took the words and what they meant and stored them in the most precious location of his human soul: His heart.

The words were simple, and he repeated them ritualistically the same way every day and every time.

With his increased heart rate his legs and arms moving briskly as he deeply concentrated on the gym's "IS" logo and with heartfelt sincerity silently stated:

"My name is Daniel Sherman, and I understand something about self:

"(1) Keep self-healthy and clean and safe."

His eyes flickered as in rote he continued:

"(2) ARECK, which stands for self-awareness, self-respect, self-esteem, self-confidence, self-celibacy and self-kindness. All of which is maintained and controlled with my highest level of conscious awareness: HCA on ARECK, with my highest level of concentration: HC on ARECK and with my highest level of self-discipline: HSD on ARECK."

He wiped sweat from his forehead and continued:

(3) RFGLUCKHCS, which stands for what is taken to heart, reflects to my mind, body and soul and through my eyes it's projected on to others. This is my highest respect toward self and toward others, my highest friendship toward self and toward others, my highest goodness toward self and toward others, my highest love toward self and toward others, my highest understanding toward self and toward others, my highest compassion toward self and toward others, my highest celibacy toward self and toward others, my highest kindness toward self and toward others, all of which is delivered with humility, confidence and strength, and which is all maintained and controlled with my highest level of conscious awareness: HCA on RFGLUCKHCS,

with my highest level of concentration: HC on RFGLUCKHCS, and with my highest level of self-discipline: HSD on RFGLUCKHCS."

Daniel's eye concentration broke when one of his sneaker laces started to entangle. He pushed the pause button, and the treadmill stopped. He bent over and tightly tied the lace once again, after which, he pushed the restart button and the treadmill picked up where it left off, and so did Daniel, and he knew the next part so well he could already recite the prose forward or backward.

The words were about the good side and what he used to say to hundreds and hundreds of kids over the years he was a substitute teacher. And because he knew that part so perfectly, he felt he needed only to repeat the headlines of the knowledge and leave the meat of the philosophy alone, until the details were needed for whatever occasion or reason.

"I also understand some things about the good-side, including, the good-side opening, the good-side family and home, the good-side and work, school, play, the bike and the remote control and the good-side conclusion, which is all maintained and controlled with my highest level of conscious awareness: HCA on the good-side. With my highest level of concentration: HC on the good-side and with my highest level of self-discipline: HSD on the good-side."

He took a deep breath through his nose and exhaled through his mouth as he continued.

"I also understand that I am a voluntary member of the WWOC and NASOTD, which respectfully stand for the wonderful world of celibacy and nobody's a sex object to Daniel, especially self. Which is maintained and controlled with my highest level of conscious awareness: HCA on the WWOC and NASOTD, which is on, and the incorrect conditioning is off and there is no leering, and RFGLUCKHCS is engaged in my heart. With my highest level of concentration: HC on the WWOC and NSOTD which is on, and the incorrect conditioning is off, and there's no leering, and RFGLUCKHCS is engaged in my heart. And, with my highest self-discipline: HSD on the WWOC and NASOTD which is on, and the incorrect conditioning is off, and there's no leering. And RFGLUCKHCS is engaged in my heart."

Daniel's vision was distracted by someone walking in front of him. But he picked right up where he left off.

"I also understand my six factors: (1) Vince: Professionalism positively does matter, all the time. (2) Merrick: Looks positively do not matter, mine or theirs. (3) McDaniel: Perceptions and orientations positively do not matter, mine or theirs. (4) Jake: Verbalizations, positively does matter – so, no monologues, no derogatory comments, no swearing and no gibberish, verbally or non-verbally. (5) Dave: Levels of disclosure. I'm to maintain a level of discloser file on everybody I meet. I need to ask questions, and I need to give compliments. And I need to mind my own business. (6) Lena: EM=C squared, which stands for emotional maturity equals controlled calmness."

Daniel was so happy with his mantra because it included his good-side speech, and he knew that part by rote.

As for the celibacy part, when he decided on becoming a voluntary member of the WWOC and a permanent member of NASOTD. The reason, he believed, was to correct forty-two years' worth of incorrect conditioning, until true love found him or he found it, and he would continue his voluntary membership in the WWOC until that time and then he would respectfully resign from the organization in his mind.

As for NASOTD, in love or not, he would never look upon self or others as a sexual object. He thought:

"Self and others are human beings who deserve to be always treated with the utmost dignity and respect. Self is not a sexual object to anyone, especially Daniel, and nobody's else's self is a sexual object to Daniel, because the most important aspect of our being is what we have on the inside not the outside."

Daniel's song factors were formed based on his recent experiences, as well.

Vince was dedicated to a very professional individual he met while going to the Vet Center.

As for Merrick, that part was dedicated to Joseph Merrick: "The Elephant Man," a real man who lived in the 19th century. A movie was made about his life in 1980, but the film was not a totally true representation of Mr. Merrick's life. In the motion picture his first name was John, but his actual name was really Joseph. Also, he was not physically abused, and he voluntarily entered the side-show business because that was the only way he could make a living.

Mr. Merrick had multiple cavernous hemangioma tumors that protruded, which resulted in him being known as "The Elephant Man," because of his disfigured appearance. The tumor was the one connection Daniel felt he had to a man who taught him that looks do not matter. Daniel remembered through his research on The Elephant Man that Mr. Joseph Merrick often quoted a poem:

> "This is true my form is something odd,
>
> But blaming me is blaming God,
>
> Could I create myself anew
>
> I would not fail in pleasing you.
>
> If I could reach from pole to pole
>
> Or grasp the ocean with a span,
>
> I would be measured by the soul,
>
> The mind's the standard of the man."

After his admission into the psychiatric hospital where he first learned about his brain tumor and that he was born with the growth and the fact that Mr. Merrick had the same tumor, according to Dr. McDaniel, that prompted Daniel to cut out a small photo of the famous man and the poem Mr. Merrick often quoted. He laminated the image and poem on a plastic card and kept the keepsake in his wallet, so that he could always be reminded of the lesson Mr. Merrick taught him.

Daniel's body showed signs of progress and others noticed. He only knew his old clothes were too big on him and if no one said anything he simply thanked them. He never revealed he refused to look in a mirror. He held this issue at his highest level of self-discloser.

Before he headed to the vet center for the day, he stopped at the Salvation Army Thrift Store. He needed t-shirts, shorts, jeans and dress pants, and over the period since his discharge from the hospital, he visited the store several times and inexpensively rebuilt a handsome wardrobe, which fit him. All these details were noted and reported back to Braveman, the three wise men's connection to the world.

Daniel went to the resource room at the Vet Outreach Center for many months. He networked daily with Jake and James, as well as with a tough woman who was a former marine with Hispanic heritage who worked down the hall, Lisa.

In the beginning, after he returned from two-south in West Los Angeles when everything felt new, the experience was no different at Vet Center.

When he typed on the computer keyboard his fingers did not glide over the keyboard as they used to. Typing felt new and he was slow. He found that when he spelled words recalling the spelling felt new and he could not remember how to spell many of the words he once knew. His thoughts slowed, as well, and he noticed that his short-term recall was affected.

The mental aspect impacted his ability to write a resume and with constant adjustments the task took him a good month to finish one. He received invaluable help from Jake who would critique what he wrote, and when he could not get all his job history on one-page for a functional resume, Lisa helped him. She had dark brown hair on her shoulders, chubby cheeks and a great attitude. The former marine who rode a motorcycle to work sat by him and coached the veteran through the functional resume process.

After the resume' was good enough Daniel sent the work out. He looked on websites and identified many social service positions in mental health. He sent out dozens of them with cover letters, some were emailed, some faxed and some by mail.

About a month after he started, one agency called him and set up an interview. Daniel was not ready, really, and he did not do well in the interview. He was complimented on his resume, but the agency sent him a letter and said they found someone more qualified for the Rehabilitation Specialist position than he was.

Disappointment set in for a day, but he continued his routines unabashedly. Unexpectedly, he got a bright idea: Look for a job in Hawaii. He always wanted to go there in fact he was supposed to go there when he volunteered to join the army.

After he selected the type of job he wanted to do in the military, the recruiter asked him where he would like to go for his duty station:

"Hawaii," Daniel said, enthusiastically.

But when he finished with basic training and job training, he was given orders to go to Germany, which freaked his mother out.

As to the reason he did not go to Hawaii:

"It's not in the contract you signed. It must be in the in writing and in the contract," he was later told.

So, the idea of going to Hawaii appealed to him as he sat in the resource room at the Vet Center, which was always monitored by one of Braveman's team.

What also appealed to him were the numerous job vacancies with the State of Hawaii, which he was qualified for. After weeks of precious time, he completed five long and detailed State applications, and he was found qualified for three of them. Alas, one interviewed him, and no one selected him.

His morale was not affected, however, he built muscle and got in shape, and he never felt healthier. His mind slowly started to come back and his ability to spell returned as well.

ARECK was completely engaged, as was RFGLUCKHCS, the Good Side, WWOC and NASOTD and his six factors: Vince, Merrick, McDaniel, Jake, Dave and Lena, and his mantra was operating well inside of him, as well as, what he projected to the others and the outside world around him.

One of the first things Jake suggested to Daniel after he finished his resume was to apply for Federal employment. USJOBS was the United States Government's official web site and as Jake put it:

"The toughest job application you'll ever fill out."

With those words Daniel shied away from the suggestion at first.

Jake was contracted to work in the resource room at the vet center for nine months. Then he was required to take off for two months (with no pay) before he could submit another application for the county contracted position. While Jake was away, James took over the duties for him.

The extremely disciplined and well-mannered former Marine Master Sergeant was friendly, outgoing and his professionalism was so impressive that the younger man became a role model to Daniel.

Daniel still remembered his second day in the resource room. James entered and when he saw Daniel he put his hands over his heart again.

"It's nice to see your face," he told Daniel.

He and Daniel shook hands that day, and they shook hands every day. Daniel relished James' kindness.

"Thanks, it's always nice to see you. How have you been?"

"I feel blessed," James announced as he looked Daniel in the eyes with his hand still over his heart.

With encouragement from James, Daniel decided to investigate a position called "Rehabilitation Counseling Therapist" with the Veterans Administration.

The job was an important position in Vet Centers and there were vacancies all over the country. The nature of the work was to assist veterans who returned from armed conflict in Iraq and Afghanistan. The job description detailed that the work was intense and required a great deal of knowledge, skills and abilities in mental health.

Daniel met the criteria for the required educational level, even though his bachelor's degree was not in a related field. But, most of all, what qualified him was his twelve years of mental health experience.

He applied for the position all over the nation. He told James: "I'll go to wherever the job is, and it doesn't matter where it is."

He spent months carefully completing the tedious mostly narrative application. In all, he applied for one-hundred and eleven vacancies from Florida to Maine from New Hampshire to California. He knew getting responses back would take a few months. He would have to wait to find out if he qualified and interviewed.

"You just have to be patient," James said.

Daniel made friends with many veterans in the resource room. Besides their common interest in having served in the military, most were not employed and were searching. A lot of them were much younger than him. There were a few his age and some a bit older.

Daniel met Harry who looked kind and was very soft-spoken. The older veteran was bald up top, he had white hair on the sides and back of his head. Daniel knew he was an ex-felon recently released from Federal Prison, but he never asked him what he did wrong. Again, the reason was one of those "that's none of my business" moments.

Harry came to the resource room every day and once another person asked him what his crime was when he told the fellow he was an ex-felon:

"I tried to destroy an abortion clinic in Fresno. I didn't want to hurt anybody."

The fifteen years behind bars showed on his face that he had learned his lesson about that episode in his life.

There were many other vets with long criminal history who utilized the computers in the resource room. One fellow had twenty-nine misdemeanors. Another was arrested sixty-seven times, he claimed, which Daniel thought might be true because the guy was booted out of the resource room because he looked at pornographic websites.

Daniel's routine went on unabated. He never missed the gym. He never missed a shower, and he never missed using a fresh towel. And Monday through Fridays from about 9 a.m. to about 4 p.m. he never missed the resource room at the vet center.

His mind felt sharp, and he knew he appeared sharp just from people's attitudes toward him. The antidepressant proved to be an intricate part of his progress.

His moods, his thinking patterns, his attitudes and demeanor all benefited. He still dealt with gibberish from time to time, but he was on top of that with one recent analyst.

One night, Eve phoned him and confirmed that Daniel planned on coming to Las Vegas for his father's birthday.

"Can you do me a favor," she asked.

"Uh, huh…"

"Will you go to the dispensary for me?"

Daniel hesitated because he had not gone to the cannabis dispensary since before his hospital stay.

"Well, I guess so…"

"I just want a quarter. How much would that be?"

"Um, forty-five…"

"Do you mind?"

"Well, no I wouldn't be going there for myself… It's for you, so that's different… I can do it…"

Daniel knew he had to be at the VA in the afternoon and Vegas tomorrow. He decided to stop by the dispensary after spending the morning at the Vet Center.

When he got inside the dispensary the first person, he encountered a man known as Benny who bellowed jubilantly:

"Long time no see."

Daniel felt cautious.

"Yes, it's been a long time."

He passed Benny who removed his black baseball cap and scratched his shaved head for a second at the queer encounter.

Daniel signed in and walked back to the counter. No one was in line. A tall slender white man who looked uneasy was there to wait on him.

"What can I get for you?"

"A quarter of the California Cannabis," Daniel replied.

As the man removed the jar of buds from one of the glass shelves, Marco entered through a doorway and approached the worker, and the significance of the very handsome young man, Marco, never escaped the former consumer who was waiting for his order to be filled.

Marco looked at Daniel and the customer broke eye contact from him, as well as, from the man who waited on him. The two medical marijuana men had issues with each other.

Daniel took just a split second to recall that Marco was the person Daniel remembered who guided him to the dispensary the very first time from the doctor's office.

"Look, Marco I'm forty-one years old and I think…" the worker said to his apparent boss.

Marco interrupted, walked to the counter and stood beside the employee who was waiting on Daniel.

"You can be replaced, you know…"

Daniel stood there silently in his wonderful hypnotic state as his eyes averted the exchange.

"I could find someone right now," Marco said as he looked at Daniel and they locked on to each other's eyes.

"What about this fellow right here," Marco said as he pointed at Daniel.

Daniel just stood there and said nothing.

"No, I guess…" the employee mumbled.

Marco looked at Daniel. The medical marijuana dealer held amazement in his eyes, and before the purchaser completed his transaction and left the counter he asked:

"What's your ID number?"

Daniel paused for a second.

"9857."

As Daniel left the counter Marco quickly moved in front of the computer and typed on the keyboard. Daniel did not understand. He took possession of the small brown paper bag and departed with the bag's content intact.

Little did the subject, and the entire operation know that it was being monitored by three Federal agencies, including the intelligence team.

Later that day Daniel had his fifth appointment at the Veterans Outpatient Clinic in the mental health department, and for him the powerful and wonderful feelings he held were as much a part of his life as they had ever been. There was no lull in that department. He entered the building and checked in with the receptionist.

He sat and waited. He was half an hour early for his appointment. He did not want to watch the TV, so he began to process some more of his experiences.

Was his interview with the recreation therapist, Bob while Daniel was in the hospital and his reference to the patient as being a "late bloomer."

Daniel wondered about blooming and thought: "Who determines when we are to bloom? Do we determine if and why we bloom? What kind of bloomers are there?

"Early bloomers… Late bloomers… and non-bloomers…"

The man with the new mind reasoned that no one can shove blooming down their throat and all the sudden they begin to bloom. And no one else can shove it down a person's throat and the phenomenon will take place.

"You have to be in the right place in your mind at the right time," he thought.

He went on to reason:

"You have to be willing to donate a lot of time, effort and energy into the process."

He concluded that:

"Love equals respect and respect equals love, and when we show the utmost respect toward self and toward others, we are showing love toward self and toward others. When we verbally or non-verbally swear or verbally or non-verbally make a derogatory remark we are not showing respect toward self or toward others, and when we do not verbally or non-verbally swear or make derogatory remarks, we do show the utmost respect toward self and toward other."

Daniel was fascinated by philosophy, but he was not well read on the subject, or on any subject, although he knew that good common sense (GCS) was the fountain from which knowledge flowed.

He recalled to himself that from the age of ten to the age of forty-two in all of his fifty-two years, self was neglected, sedated, emotionally, physically and sexually abused by him and others.

For the remaining years, however, his philosophy helped to turn his life around.

Self was to receive the opposite treatment from the soul now that he had an awareness of self. Daniel, who had inhabited this life form from the moment of this being's birth and who will continue doing so until the life cycle ends, and when that moment of his life form's last breath comes, which eventually comes to all, he pledged with highest determination that he will always treat self with the utmost respect.

"Fate plays an important role," he believed.

Fate determines a great deal of our life process:

"Fate delivers us life. Fate delivers safety and luck. Fate delivers friendship and love. Fate delivers danger and harm." And, as he looked deeper in to himself he said: "Fate delivers us death."

His brilliant hypnotic gaze was interrupted by a young man who wore a white medical jacket along with his VA identification badge.

"Mr. Sherman," he said.

The young oriental man had a small frame and wore wire rimmed glasses which sat on his tiny nose which was attached to his smooth youthful unblemished complexion. Dr. Chu, a doctor in residency from UCLA served veterans for a short work-study period.

His mannerism was tender and polite. The student doctor used a computer to ask a long list of questions to the out-patient veteran as they went along.

Once he introduced himself Daniel answered his questions, and included in the highly personal psychiatric quiz was a question about psychiatric ward two-south in West Los Angeles. He wanted to know about Xanax and whether Daniel had completely weaned it off.

"No."

Daniel went on to explain the day he went to 1 ½ milligram symptoms of the cluster headaches returned.

"My left nasal passage blocked up disabling oxygen from getting to the back of the brain and the left side of my brain was tender to the touch," he demonstrated with gestures.

"I also sensed the change in my breathing pattern. These two steps are tell-tale signs that indicate a full-blown cluster headache is coming. I believed that if I didn't intervene at that point, I would soon have one. Immediately, I went up to 2 milligrams per day and that was back in March and for seven-months, I've been on that dosage and there hasn't been even the hint of one," he said with great relief.

Dr. Chu typed quickly and wondered:

"We are not prescribing Xanax… I don't understand."

Daniel explained that he did not want to get into any debate about Xanax.

"I've had these headaches for seventeen-years now and in the 90s the VA tried everything. From sixteen tanks of oxygen, which were delivered to my door one day, to the medications I shot up my nose, put under my tongue, and all the oral medications. Nothing worked."

Dr. Chu's body orientation moved away from the computer to Daniel as he swiveled on the little round seat, and he gave Daniel direct eye contact.

"I was prescribed Xanax for the cluster headaches six-years ago, by my primary care physician. Before that the cluster headaches had the upper hand, and the episodes of pain were bad. I was in misery. After I was started on Xanax, the frequency of the headaches has cut down tremendously."

Dr. Chu looked at Daniel and to the patient the doctor seemed intrigued.

"So, you are not totally weaned."

Daniel nodded affirmatively.

"I was not about to get into a long-winded debate with the VA, frankly. I know what works and I'm not going to be a guinea pig anymore. I'm still being seen by my doctor twice a year in the dusty rural town I used to live in, and he writes me the prescriptions."

Dr. Chu swiveled back around and rapidly finessed the keyboard. He asked about sexual assaults.

"I don't want to talk about those," the veteran replied.

"Fine, we can move on. You don't have to answer if you don't want to."

He read another question off the computer monitor.

"Do you go to church?"

"No."

Dr. Chu swiveled back toward Daniel and looked directly in to his patient's eyes.

"You don't go to church?"

"No."

Dr. Chu paused for a second as his eyes scanned Daniel's.

"But you are spiritual."

"Well, yes."

Dr. Chu paused another second before he swiveled back to the screen and typed.

"Okay, so you believe in God?"

"Yes."

"But you follow no religion?"

"None. I was raised Jewish if that's of any help."

Dr. Chu asked more questions and Daniel felt pleased because he answered concisely, and he did not divulge too much information. He spoke directly to the point without long drawn-out monologues, except for the Xanax question, and he believed he had to defend his actions with a full explanation regardless of how the question was phrased.

Daniel showed he learned how to control Daniel and in turn self. He felt emotionally mature, and that self-assured feeling entered his psyche, which he felt in mind, body and soul. Highly personal topics were kept at the highest level, between GCS, Daniel and self.

As a result, Daniel grew inside and self-benefited from the development. He felt connected.

And so, on that day, the military veteran made great strides. He cemented and united the two entities: body and soul as one. The two were together and worked hand in hand in harmony.

"United we stand... divided we fall…" Daniel remembered.

He felt amazed by the direction his life was taking and by the simplicity of the words and how everything had changed in his world.

He drove to Las Vegas the next day with Pearl in the passenger seat and he played music all the way.

He ate dinner with his father and Eve. She kept in friendly contact with Herbert Sherman, as well as keeping the Sherman last name, which was a far cry from her maiden name: Stiegelmeier.

Herbert, who turned seventy-eight that day, looked good for his age. The two older adults were very happy to see Daniel looking so healthy. They both complimented him enthusiastically.

"What do you weigh?" Herbert asked.

"I don't know… It doesn't matter," Daniel replied.

Afterwards, he went to his car and presented his father with a gift. He also presented Eve with a brown paper bag.

"Oh, good, I've got your mail," she said. She reached into her purse and handed Daniel an envelope.

Chapter 17

Kushner's fingers were entwined in his thick grey hair as if he were prepared to pull it out. "This report is incredible," he fathomed. Allison's face wrinkled as Miller read over his copy with trepidation. The three men were engrossed as they read a nine-month synopsis on their subject movements before and after his hospitalization.

"He just happened to go back east twice in a seven-month period, after he'd not been there for ten-years! And he drove his old car packed up with his possessions" Kushner exclaimed.

Miller and Allison looked at each other.

"And without any forethought he stays in a motel for a week. There he calls his mother's and his sister's home, who are both sick and unable to speak and unexplainably weaves his way out of the motel and lands at exactly at the right spot at the right time to be witness to the family drama which unfolded. It's all fantastic," Kushner conceded.

"Fate," Allison said.

"I'm glad we set up surveillances in advance because we're getting a great deal out of the monitoring. What we have here, gentlemen, is either a very strong effort by a man to rearrange his life to a point that he's never been at before, according to our accounts, or a great effort by a great man to correct an incorrect life, by making a complete overhaul in every aspect of it. There are so many things I could say about this guy."

"Yes, I'm in agreement," Allison alluded as Kushner's jaw was frozen in the dropped position.

Miller stood up and paced the floor in back of his chair.

"Just think of it, gentlemen, we have a mental health professional who is struck down, not once, but twice. The first time, with crippling cluster headaches, which some people commit suicide over, and he still gets them, but he endures and bounces back. And that was during the decade before the turn of the century."

Kushner follows Miller's movement with his eyes.

"And then at the start of the new Millennium he's well enough to become a teacher and then a mental health professional again."

"Inconceivable," Allison added.

"Coincidentally, we see that he slowly spirals downward again and this time he is completely struck down, and instead of doing himself in, he roams the country and according to our reports he had no plans, he just goes everywhere on a whim, and, somehow, he ends back up back east in his hometown again."

"And then he leaves there and continues destroying himself, and once again, on another whim, he reaches out. Why? It's downright stranger than fiction…"

"Which truth often is," Allison adds.

Kushner looks at Allison and raises his eyebrows to their highest point.

"So, gentlemen, Mr. Sherman ends up in our lap with the VA in Los Angeles, and somehow, through all this he totally bounces back again, and this time stronger than ever. How can this be? What is at work here? I'll tell you what I think is at work here. It's all the doings of the Highest, I'm telling you, the purveyor of savant and of souls. God is at work here…" Miller said.

Kushner stood and walked behind his chair and to some extent recanted.

"I'll admit it all has a strange connotation to it, but we can't say assuredly, with one-hundred percent accuracy."

Allison stood, pushed his chair back and stood motionless.

"That's why it's imperative that we push forward and continue with our surveillance. We're slowly finding out what's on his mind," Allison insisted.

"This morning, he went to the mental health clinic at the VA in Bakersfield. Our people have watched and listened to every second of feed every day since he's left West LA, but all the report said was that he does not go to church. We know that" Miller said.

"There's so much surveillance on this guy that we're liable to trip over it," Kushner admits.

All three men stood behind their high-back red leather chairs with their hands on top of the seats as Kushner began to elaborate.

"I saw the report. Tell me, why are we just feeding questions through a doctor in residency. And why did our people ask him about church, when it should have said synagogue? We need to have better control over this, Tom.

Why don't we send a team of experts to grill him? Why aren't they seeing him every week at the VA? Why isn't he in therapy? We know he went to the medical cannabis dispensary and made a purchase: $45 for one-quarter ounce of California Cannabis. He's using again…"

"Roland, number one he's still legally permitted to purchase marijuana. We have no reports of him relapsing, and he went to Las Vegas the day after he went to the dispensary, so we know he bought that for Eve Sherman because he did hand her a small brown paper bag in the restaurant parking lot."

"Well, I say we should have taken him in, or we should have taken her in. We could be learning more from him if we put the pressure on," Kushner pushed.

"That's not going to help us. As to your other inquiries, we don't want to scare him. We know he's not affiliated or that he attends any religious services."

The ringing of the fax machine interrupted their thought patterns.

As it started spitting out pieces of paper like an uncontrollable old fashioned Wall Street ticker tape, and all three men's focus became redirected for a second. When the fax stopped, they returned to their discussion. Miller walked over and retrieved the documents and started reading them, they were, of course, all about their subject.

"Besides his regular routine haunts, he never goes out, not even to eat. How can he watch the same films over and over? He's must have watched The Invisible Man a hundred times, and what's with his fascination with the Sherlock Holmes series from the 40s? I do not understand," Miller said has he laid the pages on the conference table.

Allison walked over and picked up the pages.

"I'm amazed. The guy never looks at himself in a mirror, and he never masturbates. He doesn't smoke. He doesn't drink. And he doesn't use drugs. And he's using his prescription medication responsibly, whereas before, he abused the hell out of them. This guy doesn't even have a tattoo or piercing on him. Now, I'm dumbfounded, because that also meets with the initial criteria which wasn't mentioned in the original analysis."

"That's just one more for the confirmation theory," Miller sounded off.

"How can he live such an isolated life and still seem content and make all this personal progress?" Allison wondered out loud.

Kushner walked around and picked up a few pages.

"It must be due to Pearl. We ought to order surveillance on her while he's out. I still say we ought to grill him at the VA during one of his appointments."

"Oh, don't be silly, Roland, we're trying to be subtle about this remember. We want it to play out naturally. We've got the best surveillance, and if we send a team to grill this guy he's smart enough and experienced enough in mental health to know this is not the way it works," Miller insisted.

"That is where the All Powerful was smart: Setting up someone with a twenty-year background in the field, only to spring him in. Remember gentlemen, as we speak, right now all over this country, and all over this world there are people who believe and readily admit that they are the Messiah, the Second Coming, and they may say it and believe it, but we don't, however, because we know better. But Daniel Howard Sherman has never uttered a word about this in more than nine months now," Miller said, passionately.

"He admitted that he was spiritual," Allison pointed out.

"Yes, but that's of no help, but there's one other important side issue that is significant: Money," Miller articulated.

Kushner continued reading as Miller explains his rationale.

"In the decade before the century turned, he lived above his means, gambled a lot and went bankrupt. Now, all the sudden, after the turn of the century and the new Millennium, he's suddenly very responsible. He doesn't gamble at all. He lives below his means and, has no debt and he conveniently saves upwards of $50,000… and then he falls apart and has the funds to sustain himself for a couple of years."

"What are we to make of that?" Allison asked.

"Oh, that can be attributed to maturity," Kushner answers. "How are we dealing with his employment?"

Miller motions to Allison, who had oversight of that issue.

"There's good news and bad because practically every resume he's sent out has been intercepted and handled. We missed one and he was interviewed, but we were able to quash that one, too, however. He sent several resumes to Hawaii that he received notices of qualification for, but only one set up an interview. I decided to let them go ahead and we learned some tidbits of his philosophy, and it's a little different from when he was a substitute teacher and a caseworker, so there is something new there."

Miller sat down as did his colleagues as Allison offered more information.

"Recently, however, Mr. Sherman's new angle has been quite a challenge for us. He's submitted one-hundred and eleven federal applications for employment with the VA, and they were all for the same position: Readjustment Counseling Therapist."

Kushner looked shocked.

"We were unable to stop the qualification process because it's so quick these days, and there was miscommunication between our agencies. Our southern region was not able to stop the VA workers in Georgia from referring him."

"Which isn't a bad thing, actually," Miller squeezed in.

"No, because you want him grilled, Roland, well the VA can do that for us, under the guise of a job interview, because as a result Mr. Sherman was found to be qualified for all one-hundred and eleven vacancies he applied to, and with seventy-one notices he ranked high enough to be referred to the hiring authority, but, with the other forty he did not rank high enough and so his name was not referred for consideration."

"Interesting," Miller noted.

"We've managed to get with every one of them, and we stopped all but ten. I thought it prudent to allow them, because when they set up telephonic interviews with him, they will help supply more information."

Kushner read off the page he was examining.

"Our people are working with the Veteran Outreach Centers on the scripted questions."

"Do we have a copy of his narrative in answer to the application questions?" Miller asked.

"We do, Tom and you'll find this interesting," Allison said.

He reached through the pile of reports in front of him on the conference table. He hands Kushner and Miller a copy, beside him a separate report marked: "CLASSIFIED: GOD."

"Please note this particular narrative to question one which I believe gives us great insight," Allison stated. The two men began to read the poorly written writings of Daniel Sherman:

"As a Psychiatric Case Worker II, Teaching Parent Relief, Mental Health Technician I, Therapeutic Recreation Coordinator, and even as a Substitute Teacher, I bring to the table 14 years of direct care experience.

Some examples of the different populations I serve and different community settings in which they occur covers the full spectrum of the mental health field from a locked in-patient psychiatric ward, to a residential treatment home, and community outpatient clinics, young and old, veterans and nonveterans, male and female, my experiences dealing with various client populations include providing services to psychiatric, substance abuse, and clients involved in legal difficulties with a diagnosed psychiatric disorder.

First and foremost, I teach skills. It's a process whereby I assist the client in reconnecting with him or herself. I focus on teaching skills that empower the client in their understanding related to self-awareness, self-respect, self-esteem, self-confidence, self-kindness, and self-discipline.

This enables the client to understand self-better, and it also allows the client to understand that we all have a physical self that we can see on the outside, and that it is totally under the control of our inner self which occupies it.

Sometimes we have control over what we do to self, what we put self through. But sometimes we don't.

For example, someone serving their country in an armed conflict or someone caught up in a natural disaster.

If it was beyond our control, we must process what the inner self and the physical self-experienced. Understand that serving our country is the noblest act someone can perform. The mission, the sacrifice, is such that one can go no higher.

And if it was caused by Mother Nature, then it is also beyond our control, and we must dust ourselves off, understand, and move on with our lives.

These two entities, inner-self and physical self must act in harmony. They must stand together, and we must be aware of it and always keep in mind. And once we are aware, and we keep it in mind, we stop self-medicating or punishing self, because we are now complete.

If there is awareness, then self becomes the most precious thing that one can ever possess. It's priceless. There is nothing in our lives that can even come close to it. We (our inner self) are the caretakers of self. We must care for self as if we were providing care for our most fragile and delicate possession. We must respect self. We must be kind to self. We must understand self. We must stand by self. We must be strong for self. And we must do our utmost to defend self and our country. Finally, we must keep self as healthy and clean as we possibly can.

And, so, when we reconnect with self, as a result, our inner self then wants to make it up to our physical self. And, also as a result, by using our good common sense, we come to the realization that we'd never do anything that's harmful to self or is not in self's best interest, on the contrary, we begin to have the utmost respect for self, and in turn we show that same respect for others. If we don't show respect for self, how can we ever show proper respect for others?

Subsequently, our inner self even feels a little pity towards what our physical self has gone through, and then we want to make it up to ourselves.

Our inner self wants to provide the best care we possibly can to our physical self. It's time to heal, time to make up. It's time to adjust, and to recondition our minds.

Example 1:

Adjusting/reconditioning - working through issues:

I ask a client(s) to repeat two words in their mind(s). They need not ever utter these words out loud; they are strictly for them and them alone. I want them to say, "SHOW RESPECT, SHOW RESPECT, SHOW RESPECT," and I ask them to keep silently repeating these words in their mind(s) repeatedly, and as much as they need to.

I want them to keep repeating these words often, and believe these words, feel their meaning, and keep applying these words to self, and to others who they encounter.

Continue repeating these words. Now repeat the words so loudly in your mind, drawing them out as long as they can.

Begin to silently shout these words to self without moving your lips.

Now, imagine shouting these words from the tallest rooftop, atop the highest mountain, from sea to shining sea. Keep shouting these words to yourself, say them a thousand times a day if you need to, and keep imagining that you're on the rooftop, atop the mountain, or on the shore, as if you are shouting the words from one end of your country to the other.

Once we continuously say it, believe it, feel it, and we are constantly aware of it, we then begin the process whereby we can come together as one. We understand. We have the utmost respect for self and others, we reunite with self.

This is particularly important to those who have PTSD, having served in armed conflict. The brain was adjusted/conditioned one way, to be a soldier. Now it is time to readjust/recondition another way to work through the horrors they've encountered.

It will require work, an effort over days, weeks, and months. But keep continuing, because a little effort everyday can go a long way.

And sometimes self-discipline must take over because our brain is telling us something that's just not worth listening to. Using our good common sense, we know better, and we must dismiss the impulse or thought because as grown-ups we know right from wrong, and we know that unwanted memory, unwanted thought, or impulse is not in the best interest of self.

This leads to self-awareness, self-respect, improved self-esteem, self-confidence, and to a drastic change in attitude which results in us wanting to be kinder to self.

Example 2:

The first exercise is to write 3 things down that we love. I love my wife. I love my kids. I love my mother.

If we take the word myself, it's just one word. I live by myself. I don't like myself. I don't care about myself. I can't help myself. What happens if we split that word up and make it two words? It then communicates a different meaning; I love the self that encapsulates it. I respect the self that encapsulates it. I honor and cherish the self that encapsulates it..

We can then begin to treat self with respect, a different attitude. Our mind and our thinking can then move in a different direction.

You begin to see that self belongs to you, it's yours. You are the owner. You are the caretaker. You are the producer and director, and your physical self simply distributes it.

And, sometimes, those unwanted thoughts and impulses can be wrong. When our brains are fully developed, and we use our good common sense, we know the difference between right and wrong, we know what is good and what is bad. So, we now can begin to look at things from a different perspective.

We then begin to appreciate our past and what we did or did not do to ourselves; was it something we had control over? If we had no control of what the inner and physical self-experienced it's time to understand and reconnect.

And if there are other issues, psychiatrics, substance abuse, etc., we now possess a keen awareness of what we've put through. We try our hardest or better put, we give our all, and we want to make it up to self and to correct all the discrepancies.

Since, the invention of the MRI, experts in the field of brain development have conducted studies which determined that the frontal part of the brain, the part that knows right from wrong, and what's good or bad does not fully develop in a female until they are 22 1/2 years old. In a male the age is 24. Before that young people are expected to mess up. They are expected to be impulsive, take risks, and to be experimental. That's why grown-ups are here, so that they can set a good example. And when we are grown-up and we look back at our youth, most of the time we can say to the self that encapsulates me we would never do what we did when we were younger.

Through maturity our inner self grows, and our awareness and knowledge of things sharpen. Knowledge is power, so, the more knowledge we have the more power, respect, and confidence we can then possess.

If someone is facing legal difficulties, or they are involved in self-destructive acts, they must figure out what went wrong and how they would do it differently the next time, so that they don't repeat the same mistake. If they repeat the same mistake then they have not learned their lesson, and they continue to digress into their old patterns.

But if they do learn, and they don't repeat their mistake, then they can recognize that they've grown a little inside, whereby they should give themselves a little pat on the back.

Why do we make mistakes? It's so we can learn lessons. When we are younger, school supplies us with many lessons, reading, math, science, etc.

But we also have life lessons to learn, and every day we face lessons in life. And because we are not perfect, we can make mistakes at any time.

Example 3:

I point out that everybody has a good side to them and a bad side.

What is our good side? It's when we are nice, kind, considerate, helpful, friendly, respectful, courteous, and polite etc.

So, we don't want to build up and show our bad side, because it's only there to teach us lessons. We want to do our utmost to build up and show our good side, and show it as often as we can, because that's the only side that serves us."

"Very good Kevin… Roland does this help?" Miller asked.

Dr. Kushner put down the copy of the report and readjusted himself in his chair.

"Let's just continue with our surveillance and our wait and see approach," Kushner said.

Chapter 18

One Saturday night Daniel's loneliness got to him. Coupled with the fact that he could not find a job, the self-pity led him in the direction of having a couple of drinks at a bar. He ordered one screwdriver and later another. They made him feel nice. The nice feeling only led to the desire to have some more nice feelings, alone.

Daniel knew he was wrong and when he showed up at the dispensary the next morning to purchase some cannabis, he realized he was walking across a bridge in a direction he did not want or need to go in. But, nevertheless, he continued his mistaken journey.

Benny greeted Daniel and the "long time, no see" member signed in.

"Where've you been?" Benny asked.

Good old Benny still wore his black baseball cap.

"I'm just not using as much."

Daniel headed for the counter. The person behind the counter was Marco who waited on customers. Daniel was about fifth in line and when Marco caught Daniel's eye, Marco's affect brightened, and he waved to him. Daniel curiously grinned and gestured his acknowledgement.

When he reached the counter Daniel told Marco he wanted a quarter of "California Cannabis."

While he waited on his customer the medical marijuana man started a little conversation just like a bartender may do while tending bar.

"You work out every day, don't you?"

Marco placed buds on the electronic scale. Daniel looked at the buds on the scale and the handsome Marco. His body obviously answered the next question, but the question came anyway.

"Yes, I do… do you work out?"

"Yeah, I do…"

Daniel felt uncomfortable where he was, and he felt even more uneasy about why he was there. A conflict between his core and self-ensued, and the befuddled contradiction played with his mind.

"Oh, where…"

Marco paused and filled the small plastic bag with its content.

"In-Shape..."

Daniel was puzzled and taken aback. He did not want to think about what he just heard. He had more important self-destructive plans on his mind.

Daniel said no more. He went home, got buzzed and drank alcohol, too. He could not account for his actions. Sure, he felt the pressure of being lonely and unemployed.

"My savings are being eaten up… I applied for so many positions, and no one has offered me a job," he rationalized.

Be it, whatever, the bottom line: Daniel slipped. The next day he woke up to reality and he discarded the alcohol and threw away the pot. He came to his senses because yesterday he knew he had failed. He remembered his pledge to self and to his GCS.

"I will get a job. I'm not going back to the incorrect conditioning because I know better," he said aloud.

He thought about his GCS.

"I need to use GCS, obey and follow GCS unconditionally. GCS is the power behind the goodness I show toward self and toward others. I, Daniel, didn't use a speck of GCS yesterday. I've let the self that encapsulates me down. I have no excuses. I was wrong."

Sure, he felt guilty and ashamed because he slipped. But the slip was not self's guilt or shame. The slip was Daniel's, the proprietor, the caretaker, the entity who promised never to do anything that contributed to the destruction of self. Self was the innocent bystander in all of this, and self-did nothing wrong. Self-had no say.

"Self just follows instructions and carries out what Daniel wants," he thought.

The philosophy maven dove deep into his heart and served an eviction notice: Self-pity was the negative feeling to be replaced. He got a pencil and paper out and reorganized his thoughts and remembered:

"Replace the bad with the good. Understand what happened. Why do I make mistakes? I make mistakes so I can learn lessons. What lessons did I learn? How could I do it differently the next time, so it won't happen again? I must understand, forgive and move on, immediately."

He continued his sober argument:

"My emotional drive has an enormous appetite. If my emotional drive doesn't get what it wants, namely a job or some companionship in this case, my drive seeks out other avenues to feed on in sorrow. Most, if not all the time these are self-destructive avenues: Drugs, alcohol, excessive amounts of food, and those only consume self, which ultimately make me, Daniel, an unfeeling, unrecognizable heap of no-good trash, again."

And the innocent victim is always the self who bears the brunt of the damage. Self deserves much better. Daniel serves, provides and takes special tender loving care of self. Daniel decided he will not jeopardize his most precious and priceless gift. "I will never take self for granted, again."

Daniel acknowledged his sensitivity. How easily swayed he was, one way or another.

"When I'm sensitive to heat, I turn on the fan, I turn on the air conditioner or jump in the water," he said. "When I'm sensitive to cold, I turn on the heat, I light a fire, or put on more clothes," he added. "When my nerves are sensitive to pain, I take Tylenol," he observed. "My feelings are sensitive to insults and criticism and rejection as well, but that's only if I invite those feelings in," he deciphered. "I can always adjust and readjustments for heat and cold and pain, and insults, hate, rejection and criticism should be no different. I must adjust and readjust when these emotional upheavals happen."

He recalled two-south, and that life is all about making the right adjustments and readjustments until the fine tuning is tuned in just the way the station should be, so one can clearly hear it and/or see it. Nobody wants to listen to a radio station which is incorrectly tuned in. Then he recalled what is referred to as the "idiot box" by some, before there was cable, and people had those awful rabbit ears to pick up reception. And he recalled that nobody wanted to watch a television station that wasn't tuned in so the picture and sound wasn't as clear as it could be.

"Nobody's perfect, not even a radio or television stations, so adjustments and readjustments are a never-ending part of life," he concluded.

Math never was Daniel's best subject and as a result he never understood geometry or algebra, yet alone calculus. But he did know how to add, subtract, multiply and divide.

One day when Daniel entered In-Shape a few weeks later, he went right to work as normal. He recognized he slipped almost a month ago and thought about the fact that sometimes one must take two steps backward to take a step forward.

And he realized that it was some old cliché, but even so, the cliché that was an anomaly, a blip, and now he felt back on track. He completed the first leg of his routine on the second level of the gym and walked downstairs.

As he walked into the area to go through to the exercise equipment the two nice young Hispanic males who had taught him about a piece of exercise equipment many months ago were there. There was the one who wore his headband all the time and the other with the shaved head.

"Hey," the shaved headed one said.

"Hi, how's it going?" Daniel responded.

Suddenly, the handsome one with the headband reached out and shook Daniel's hand, and the other with the shaved head followed suit. Daniel felt good because the gesture was nice, kind, and friendly. He wanted to make friends, and he needed to.

But, quickly, today's encounter with the two young men all this time caught up with him as he performed the exercise on the piece of equipment, because they both reeked from the odor of marijuana.

Daniel waved to them after he was done.

"See you later."

"Have a nice workout," one replied.

"Take care," said the other.

Daniel moved toward the open area and thought about the two young men, and after nine months he finally put two and two together.

These nice young Hispanic males who he unknowingly sought out to show him how to use a piece of exercise equipment and he befriended at the gym many months ago, were two people he knew: The one who always wore a sweat headband and the other with the shaved head. Suddenly, their identities came to him: They were really Benny and Marco.

"Of course," he said out loud with shocked certainty. "The headband and the shaved head threw me off. After I came out of my depression, and I started coming here I never went to the dispensary. When I met them here, one always wore the headband and the other always had a shaved head… That's what threw me, because I went to the dispensary twice: Once for Eve and then just a few weeks ago when I was a fool, and I just never took notice: The one with the headband at In Shape, was Marco, and he never wore a headband when I encountered him at the doctor's office that first day or at the dispensary, or any other time when I saw him there, and the one with the shaved head, Benny, he always wore his black baseball cap when I saw him at his work."

Daniel's realization made him feel foolish. But the realization also gave him an idea:

"If I don't find a job in the next six-months, I'll take Marco up on the offer he made the day I went to the dispensary for Eve, and I'll ask him if I can work for him."

But then he realized. He knew going to work in a medical marijuana dispensary was a crazy idea and he doubted he would ever actually ask Marco.

"You know I never put two and two together," he walked back to say to them anyway. "You're the two guys from the dispensary," he added.

Marco and Benny smiled and nodded.

"Yeah, that's right," Marco said.

"Yeah man," Benny piped in.

"Wow, I never realized it until just now."

They all found humor in the mix-up.

"Well, I understand now," Daniel said as Benny added his observations.

"Yeah, man you've taken off a lot of weight. I remember when you first came into the shop about a year ago and you are sure different now. You carry yourself so differently, too."

"Oh, thanks."

Daniel went back to routine, as did his new friends. The handsome Marco and funny Benny smiled and shook hands with Daniel every time they encountered him at the gym. But they never saw him again at the dispensary because Daniel allowed his approval certificate to use medical cannabis to expire.

That date was one year ago from that day at the doctor's office when he first met Marco. And, ever since his stay in the hospital, where the depression lifted, and with not one cluster headache, he believed he had the antidepressant and the small dose of Xanax to thank for that.

So, he had no further use for something that only worked toward the destruction of self in his case. Oh, he realized medical marijuana is an important medication for some: People undergoing chemotherapy for cancer or an AIDS patient, but he acknowledged that he was not a kid anymore and he was not in his experimental stages of life. He was a grown up and he thought:

"It's high time I started thinking and acting like one."

Chapter 19

The grey-haired man watched as an envoy of the Ambassador of The United States of America to Israel phoned apartment 748, in Tel Aviv. She appeared professionally confident and comfortable. She was impeccably dressed in a smart grey business suit, and Susan Kaplan's long golden hair and sensuously curved body fit her distinguished facial features perfectly, he thought.

The man knew that the forty-two-year-old diplomatic envoy spoke on a telephone line that was not secure, and security was a top priority inside the diplomatic walls.

Her phone call to a civilian in Israel was not the same as a phone call over secured connections with Washington, because any conversation of that nature was monitored, recorded, studied and analyzed by the best in the business and her every move outside the United States Embassy in Tel Aviv was shadowed, as well. All these actions came with the territory, he thought.

Apartment 748 was a work of art. The spacious living quarters were two levels of elegance. All that luxury was accented by a head-to-toe glorious spectacle, which was a beautiful wall of glass that provided a breathtaking view of the Mediterranean Sea from the twenty-seventh floor of one of Israel's most prestigious residential structures.

Hal and Becky Sherman recently remodeled their kitchen, which took three months, and they appeared comfortable among its smart interior design and contents. Purchased a couple of years ago, the couple had lived in Israel for several years before, and now they were back.

Daniel crisscrossed America sick and in despair. He felt he was a tarnished vagabond. Hal and Becky crisscrossed the world enriched, entranced and in class. Their success was due to the couple's determined efforts to create a telecommunications company which turned out to be very successful and was later sold for a fortune.

Becky's consistently warm and inviting facial expression, which was a portrayal of human art, motioned and leaned toward a sprawled breakfast bar made of finely polished grey granite speckled in grey and white. The kitchen luxury was a smoothed uncluttered surface which was enhanced by a spectacular crystal bowl filled with fresh fruit.

The curious but tenuous reaction reflected in Becky's big bright brown eyes prompted Hal to glance away from the article he started reading when the telephone rang. His forehead wrinkled as he momentarily stared out over a copy of the Jerusalem Post at his wife of thirty-years.

"Who… Yes…" Becky replied innocuously.

Hal put down his paper and with strong inquisitiveness he scanned his elegant wife's body language. Becky turned and gestured an "I don't know," with her hands, arms and shoulders to her husband.

"Hang, up…" Hal said. Becky shooed away her husband's comment with a hand gesture and a wrinkled face.

"Yes, that's right, Mrs. Sherman, I am calling on behalf of the United States Ambassador to Israel, and we are extending a special invitation to you and your husband, which will be arriving by special courier very soon," Ms. Kaplan said as the grey-haired man watched her body language.

"It's on Thursday, the 29th… that's right, and our Ambassador will be hosting a presentation to honor the anniversary of the Yad Vashem Museum. Our government recognizes the historic museums critical importance to Israel and to the world. We hope you will accept the Ambassador's personal invitation to be with us on that evening." Ms. Kaplan added.

"Yes, we'd be honored to attend of course, but why may I ask are you inviting us?"

"Your names were forwarded to us by your friend, Noah Krevsky, who is the curator of Israel's Metropolitan Museum of Modern Art, as you know."

"Yes, I see, of course."

"This diplomatic event is open to a small number of invited guests, and we hope you will join us."

Becky looked at Hal who halfway went back to his article minutes ago.

"Ms. Kaplan it would be our honor because Yad Vashem is a museum which deeply touches us all."

"Hmm…" Hal said through his newspaper.

Rebecca Sherman tenderly returned the cordless phone to its cradle and hypnotically said: "That was a call from an envoy to the U.S. Ambassador to Israel. We are invited to a diplomatic affair this Thursday at Yad Vashem."

Suddenly, the doorbell rang from the lobby of their impressive residence and Hal got up and answered.

"Shalom," Hal said into the devise.

"Yes, shalom, Mr. Sherman we have a special courier from the United States Embassy in the lobby. He is required to deliver a message to you and Mrs. Sherman in person. Would you like me to send him up?" A lobby security official asked.

"Yes, please do."

After Hal signed for the message from the courier he opened and read the message.

"What's this all about," he asked.

"I don't know Hal, why don't you call Noah, maybe he'll know."

Noah was not there. Nevertheless, the couple planned to attend the affair.

"After all, it's the United States Ambassador…" Becky softly uttered as her mind drifted elsewhere.

The old grey-haired man knew that horror unleashed in mind and heart rarely, if ever, elicited pity toward a sick perpetrator yet alone its dreadful and repulsive source: the deep dark crevasses of a sick soul.

For victims, families and friends' forgiveness can only be unimaginably understood and delivered through clenched teeth and quivered lips at the mere thought of its utterance because innocuous eyes attempted to shield emotional pain, stress, anger and despair, and in the end, forgiveness merely managed to make good common sense soul sick.

His thick grey hair began to show streaks of white as he pursued his thoughts. Cruelty from wicked and sinful hands gashed deeply in mind and heart and left unyielding unhealed psychological scars. Before, ultimately, the greatest life stressor of humankind psychologically and or physically killed those possessed by the devilish deed's sheer immorality.

Acts of barbarism were impossible to lend even a speck of pity to, yet alone sorrowful eyes, for they portrayed the worst in a senseless and unclean mind, which he knew was the twisted root and offshoot of utter evil, the devil inside us all.

But he sighed, because ever since man's first breath on earth, he knew masked evil originated in mind so devoid of love and sanity that the psychosis drifted like a small and lifeless plank of wood atop the surface a great ocean, whereby the sickness rolled and shifted until any remnant of the mental illness was lost forever among the vastness of the rising and falling and never ending foamed waves, because he knew that and old adage rang loudly in all sensible minds: Truth is stranger than fiction and horror transcends tall tales.

He made his way in his best attire to the steps of the great museum. To say Yad Vashem is a memorial would be a vast understatement, he thought. Yad Vashem is a historical icon, a relic, a possession of mankind's soul that must live on into infinity. As he opened the glass door, he saw his two friends and he remembered the quote from the great museum's own words: "A decade in the making, the Holocaust History Museum combines the best of Yad Vashem's expertise, resources and state-of-the-art exhibits to take Holocaust remembrance well into the 21st century."

The grey-haired man was calm and comfortable as he entered and gazed at the infinitesimal, but handsomely attired group gathered under the great dome bearing the eyes of Shoah victims.

As living and breathing eyes looked upward and gazed all around into the eyes of people once alive and healthy, they were forced to reflect and remind them of the torture, pain and horror those black and white eyes held witnesses too. The physical and emotional burden they bore, every second of hell, every minute of misery, every hour of anguish, every day of torment, until finally, these souls took their merciless dying breath.

The United States Ambassador to Israel was Leonard Bloom. His eyes were not fixed on any text or focused on the small group that gathered in front of him. His eyes roamed the eyes circled above him as he carefully chose his words to begin the proceedings.

"America comes here today to express our nations never ending love toward Israel and to the people of Israel and to the eyes that surround us. For we in this modern world owe this tribute to our children and to their children and to history that these eyes that surround us shall never fade from our memories."

Silence filled the room as the grey-haired Dr. Miller, Dr. Allison and Dr. Kushner stood and listened.

"People who live and act with hatred and malice toward their fellow man, especially those who are different from themselves, are not showing respect toward self. They are not showing respect toward others. And they are not showing respect toward God. Their acts show disrespect toward themselves. Disrespect toward others. And disrespect toward God, because people with hatred in their hearts are showing their utmost respect, but that virtue is reserved exclusively for the devil."

Once the Ambassador's remarks concluded the three men decided the other day that amongst them it was Dr. Kushner who would approach Becky and Hal Sherman.

The command distinction in his face, voice and attire attracted immediate attention and focus.

His mission was to arrange a meeting. The three senior intelligence officials caught the eye of Israeli intelligence officials before they left the ground in the United States.

Miller learned of the Ambassador's upcoming event by happenstance. A brief paragraph appeared in the daily intelligence briefing synopsis, and that is when they decided that their attendance at the museum would be a respectable way of connecting with the Shermans to discuss the issues which pressed so on their minds.

"I'm Dr. Roland Kushner Mr. and Mrs. Sherman," he said as he shook hands with each of them.

As every eye in the sky watched and covertly recorded what was said, Dr. Kushner knew he had to be discreet.

"I serve a small part of our government that is interested in a subject that resonates. I must say that I would appreciate your opinions. I was hoping we could meet later today, perhaps this evening. We could have a private dinner at the embassy."

Becky and Hal were mystified. Dr. Kushner's eyes, facial expression and gestures made the moment seem as if the invitation was no big deal.

"We just want to talk. It's nothing really. There are questions which you may or may not be able to help us answer," he said.

"What kind of questions?" Becky inquired.

"Questions which a successful American couple living in Israel could possible offer us some insight to," Kushner admitted sheepishly.

Dr. Miller noticed the exchange and he motioned for Dr. Allison and the two left the dome area.

Israeli intelligence understood that the three men from Washington came to their country for a reason, and they believed the purpose was tied to the Iranian nuclear weapons conflict because Dr. Miller, Dr. Allison and Dr. Kushner dossiers indicated that they served that section of intelligence within the Federal Government.

That was the cover story, but talking with a civilian couple sent up red flags because something was up, and they were faced with a dilemma because The U.S. Embassy in Tel Aviv was impenetrable. The Israeli government had informers within its walls, but they could only report on the comings and goings because when the United States wanted to conduct a secure meeting, they did.

On the evening of the dinner the table was round and immaculate with an elegant white tablecloth, sterling silver cutlery, cloth napkins and crystal glassware which all glistened under a remarkable crystal chandelier which delivered soft light to the faces, table and high-back black velvet chairs guests of the embassy sat on. The group of five dined alone. The Ambassador offered him and his wife regrets for not being able to join them because of a previous engagement.

The group dined on a delectable portion of five-cheese lasagna with grilled asparagus and grilled red potatoes because Becky and Hal Sherman were vegetarians. Light delicacies allowed light conversation to flourish through each pallet and mind during the appetizer.

The dinner went on for more than two hours. The appetizer began with stuffed baked artichokes filled with creamy spinach coated in a crisp flakey outer shell and topped with sweet corn salsa, which Dr. Miller explained:

"There's a chunky blend of corn, tomatoes, red bell peppers and jalapenos."

The main course followed, and each face reflected its approval and pleasure.

Later, they all chuckled as they dug their silver spoons into a short fresh strawberry cake which was the meal's grand finale.

They retired to a smaller chamber. Miller noticed that Becky's and Hal's wide eyes glistened with astonishment at the grandeur of it all. They stood upon a deep blue colored carpet piled so thickly its texture softly cushioned their ever step.

Miller watched as the couple looked around the surroundings which were so austere in relics and furnishings the room looked surreal, and Miller, Allison and Kushner knew that their company was so mysterious that the whole caboodle made them look like they were in a Hollywood movie, and they were the stars.

The circle of seats comforted each body. Miller looked at Kushner and Allison before he began. His eyes concentrated on the young couple, and his serious expression shifted from the lighthearted dinner and table conversation to a more enlightened and serious one before he began to speak. Hal and Becky searched each other for answers, but there were none.

"What's this all about?" asked Becky.

Hal's eyes inquisitively widened as he looked at each of them for answers, but he found none.

"Mr. and Mrs. Sherman… Hal and Becky, if I may… We asked you both here today in the hope that we can go beyond the information we've obtained up until now because you may just have some answers that will help us."

Dr. Kushner shifted into his chair as Dr. Allison gauged Hal and Becky's reactions.

"Gentleman, we don't have any information that could possibly be of any use to you," Becky said.

"Does this concern our telecommunications company, because if it does…" Hal added before Miller chimed in.

"No, let us say we're interested in the weather,"

"The weather…" Hal exclaimed.

"I do not understand Dr. Miller," Becky added.

Dr. Miller broke eye contact with his guests, the Sherman's. He glanced at Kushner who looked intense and at Allison who was hunched over with his elbows on his knees as if he watched a passionate basketball game and awaited his team to reach the basket and score the game's winning points.

Miller looked at Hal.

"I must tell you, first of all, that this is a delicate issue, and it specifically involves a member of your immediate family, Mr. Sherman."

In a flash, Hal was taken aback.

"Who?"

Becky scanned every eye in the room and looked dumbfounded. Dr. Miller paused and lowered his head to his hands.

"Let us review your immediate family, if I may, for a moment Hal."

Hal's forehead displayed every wrinkle possible as his mouth slowly opened more and more with each person Miller mentioned.

"We know that your mother passed away about a year ago, our sincere condolences to you and your family. Her name from her second marriage was Sarah Bellman and her maiden name being Klansky. She married Herbert Sherman in 1953, and they were divorced with three children in 1968. You have a younger sister, Kelly, who is married with two young sons, and you have a younger brother, Daniel.

You were close to your mother and to your sister, but you haven't spoken to your father in 35 years. First, Hal, if I may, why haven't you communicated with your father in all that time, may I ask?"

"Dr. Miller this whole thing is very perplexing. We are invited to a diplomatic affair at Yad Vashem, and we don't know why. Then you approached us and invited us here. Before I answer your question, will you answer mine? Why…?"

"Because my boy we needed to speak with you and your wife. Frankly, we live stateside, and we flew here when we learned of the diplomatic affair and arranged to invite you as guests so that we could, first, meet you and secondly, as I said, to see if we can find out any additional information that could help us."

Hal looked at Becky and then at the elders in the room.

"Help you… help you with what?" Hal asked politely.

"We are not diplomats as you were told when we were introduced earlier today. I'm sort of a detective and along with my colleagues, Dr. Kushner and Dr. Allison, are trying to get to the bottom of something that is highly important. In fact, it's classified."

Hal sighed and shrugged his shoulders.

"Classified? Classified what?" he asked.

"What about your father," Hal?

"Okay my father was a deadbeat dad who left my mother for another woman and who has never been a part of my life. It's as simple as that."

"And you've never spoken since he left?" Miller asked.

Hal looked at Dr. Kushner and Dr. Allison who studied him intensely.

"He was at my sister's wedding about 12 years ago, or so, and I was polite. I said hello and that was it. He also sent me an email several years ago wanting me to forgive him. I wrote back and told him that I forgave him but that I didn't want to reestablish any dialogue with him."

"Okay, thank you Hal. That answers that," Miller said.

Dr. Kushner cleared his throat.

"Can you tell us about your brother?"

"Daniel…"

"Yes, Daniel…"

"Why, what's the matter with him now?"

Becky shifted in her chair to the topic.

"We just want to know about him." Kushner replied.

"Well, he's always been troubled. He's had moments in his life when he did okay, but every five years, or so, it seems, he's falling apart. He bounces around the country, and he just doesn't do well. But he's always been like that,"

"Why did you stop all communications with him? When did that start and why?" Allison asked.

Hal and Becky shifted their attention to Dr. Allison.

"Ah, he… ah, he quit his job, and he was bouncing all over the country because he says he's got these bad headaches and um, suddenly his life rebounded and Becky and I heard that he turned his life around, and that was in the late 90s when our daughter Bessie was having her Bat Mitzvah. So, we invited him to Israel, and we paid his expenses, and he comes but the only thing he really turned around was his weight because he was still miserable, depressed and he complained a lot, especially about the headaches."

Miller looked at Allison, who looked at Kushner looked back at Miller again.

"Anyway, when he returned to the States, he writes me an email and wants to borrow $300 so he can go and have a weekend in San Diego."

Hal looked at Becky and took her hand.

"We already loaned him money back in the 90s. I think it was $900 to help him move to Florida to be with a childhood friend…"

"Which friend and where," Kushner asked.

"Ah, it was his friend Lenny in, oh… I forget," he said.

"It was his friend Lenny who lives in Fort Lauderdale, and it was $1000… and we lent him another $800 so he could file for bankruptcy," Becky reminded her husband.

"Oh, yeah… anyway when he asked to borrow more money, I just cut him off and we did not speak until last November, when he was back in our hometown when our mother passed away."

"How was he then," Miller inquired.

"Oh, he was a wreck," Becky interjected.

"Yes, he was," Hal concurred.

"He smelled… he was really obese… he asked for advice… he saved money while he was a caseworker, but just like always, he was doing okay and then his life took a nosedive," Hal explained.

"Where was he living when your mother passed away," Miller asked?

"I think Oregon or no, maybe it was California… no… no… he was living in a trailer out in the middle of the Nevada desert, my stepfather Harold told me… but just about two-weeks before she was rushed to the hospital there he was back east in Keansburg, again, so I think he was technically homeless and I heard he was staying in a motel nearby." Hal said with shrugged shoulders.

"So did he stay in Keansburg?" asked Miller.

"No, after the funeral… and he did sit Shiva with the family… then he moved to Bakersfield, California of all places."

"What did he do there?" Miller wondered.

"He did it again. He turned his life completely around and we saw him a few weeks ago when we were back in the States for my sister's son Bar Mitzvah and my mother's unveiling," Hal said.

"Has Daniel done something wrong?" Becky asked.

"Excuse me Becky, Hal how was Daniel when you saw him last?" Kushner wondered.

"He was the best I've ever seen him… he was clean, in shape, sociable… never heard one complaint out of him… he not only looked great, but he wasn't depressed anymore.

He spent some time in a psychiatric hospital in Los Angeles after our mother died. I called him there to offer our support because he was very depressed," Hal remembered.

"And, when he got out of the hospital, he paid us back half the money he owed us, with the promise that he'd pay the other half when he landed a job," Becky added.

I never thought he'd ever pay us back.

Dr. Kushner wanted to press forward.

"Is your brother religious Hal?"

"Daniel… no he never… he isn't religious at all."

"He did send that odd holiday card, Hal," Becky reminded him.

Hal looked at Becky and remembered.

"Tell me about that, would you," Miller said.

"Well, Daniel has been cut-off not just from us but from everybody… he's a real loner. We were with him in September like I said… and I must admit I was really impressed on his remarkable transformation. His eyes looked lively, and he was not depressed anymore… all the sudden in December we get what looks like a Christmas card in the mail," Hal said.

"It didn't say Christmas on its Hal," Becky reminded him.

"No, but it was a picture of adobe like villas under palm trees out in the desert and such… inside the printed message was something like "Peace on Earth," Hal tried to recall.

"No, it said "May God Bring Peace on Earth, Love and Happiness to All," Becky said.

"Yes, and then he signed it, Love, Daniel and Pearl."

"Pearl's his little dog," Becky said.

"Did he write the inscription: "May God…" Allison asked.

"Oh, no… that was the already printed inside the card… he just signed it… but the funny thing was he never ever said "love" before to us. Becky and I talked about it, and we never remember him saying he loved anyone," Hal stated.

Miller, Kushner and Allison looked at one another in response to the last answer. Their eyes showed that they knew Hal's last answer was tell-tale.

"Dr. Miller we've answered a lot of your questions. Can you please tell us what this is about?" Becky pleaded.

"We, um… Mrs. Sherman, we'd like to," Miller said.

Kushner motioned Miller to go ahead.

"Tom, we need their help. We need to know what they think. Is it possible?" Kushner implored.

"Becky… Hal… there was a specific reason we chose Yad Vashem to introduce ourselves. It was a ghastly crime against humanity," Miller said.

Heads nodded in agreement as each set of eyes concentrated on the speaker.

"Did you know that Hitler was consumed by the occult?" Miller asked.

Becky and Hal looked at each other.

"Why, I've read about that somewhere at some time, I think," Becky answered.

"He was… he was nuts… he was a drug addict and was addicted to methamphetamine, and all types of opium-based narcotics…" Miller said.

Yes, and his breath was said to smell worse than a sewer. And his feces were grey," Allison added.

"He had the German military running on amphetamines, and he rose to power because he put free beer in the stomachs of his population. Even when World War II was going full force, he had massive underground beer distilleries churning out thousands and thousands of gallons for his people," Allison added.

"Germany went psychotic," Kushner added.

"Yes, they did. And it's in their genes for generations to come," Becky said.

"They wanted the world to believe their propaganda, that they meant no harm to Jews. When at the same time they were rounding up putting up ghettos and ultimately transporting them to concentration camps… you know the rest," Miller said as he lowered his head.

"It's all very sick and it's still awful," Hal said.

"But what is believable is what we have on this monstrosity Hitler. Yes, he hated Jews. He hated gypsies. He hated homosexuals. He hated the physically and mentally disabled," Miller said.

"But he had a gypsy fortune teller by his side at all times," Allison said.

"He had a so-called expert on the zodiac that read the stars and predicted his horoscope every day among his circle of advisors," Kushner added.

"We have tons of documentation on his fixation with the occult and how he operated his life and the German people's lives around it," Allison said.

"And our analysts at the time believed there was one more driving motivation about his mad obsessive compulsive disorder he had with Jewry," Miller admitted softly.

"What was that doctor?" Becky asked.

"He believed that there was a Jew who would rise to become the Messiah and destroy his thousand-year Reich," Miller said.

"You see Mr. and Mrs. Sherman, Hitler believed he was the Messiah. He believed that he was the Second Coming. And so, he implemented a policy to wipe out any possible competition that could possibly get in his way," Kushner said.

"In his psychotic mind he believed, and our analysis showed at the time that he could stop it."

"Stop what," Hal asked?

"Stop the Second Coming, which is how non-Jews put it," Miller stated.

Hal and Becky were flabbergasted at the twist and turn of the discussion.

"What does my brother Daniel have to do with all of that?" Hal asked curiously.

Miller sighed as Kushner and Allison took deep slow breaths and slowly exhaled while Miller dropped the bombshell.

"We think your brother is the one. We think he is the Messiah."

For several seconds silence takes a leave of absence and astonishment reigned.

"You've got to be out of your mind!" Hal exclaimed.

"Daniel Sherman, the Messiah!" Becky echoed in exclamation.

"It can't be Dr. Miller. Daniel Sherman is not very bright. He works with the mentally ill, and I give him credit for that, but he's never written, spoken or joined anything that I know of," Hal said.

"We don't even know if he's a republican or a democrat," Becky added.

"No, you have the wrong person. He can't be…" Hal said in a soft voice.

"He meets all our criteria," Kushner added as a converted believer.

"If you know all that, then why didn't the US do something about it," Becky questioned.

"We know some things, but the United States hands were tied. We were with the Allied forces whose only mission was to crush and defeat the Nazis. The occult component was based on an analysis of intelligence reports and one team of analysts who had a hunch, just a hunch at the time" Allison said.

"But we've been tracking this ever since then and we've had hundreds of thousands of possibilities, but they all were ruled out by different factors, until your brother entered the hospital." Kushner said.

"We never expected that the person we were looking for would have a background like your brother's. It fooled us for decades, but we are certain…" Miller stated.

"Right now, all over this world there are people with the Messiah Complex as it is called. They act, speak, think and say that they are the one," Allison said.

"Your brother, Hal has never uttered a word and we've been watching him closely for months. Even at the Bar Mitzvah," Kushner said as Miller looked at him.

"He acts different from the way he did before his hospitalization. Your recollection of the holiday greeting card is really the first piece of evidence we must show what he may be thinking, besides job interviews and applications he filled out. This all tends to lead us in the direction…" Miller said.

Miller pulled out a couple of reports from his briefcase.

"Because your brother has been a mental health professional since the 1980s, he's only been applying for positions in that field. In interviews he's asked about his philosophy, and when asked to reveal how he would handle certain scenarios. What would he say? What would he do?" Miller said.

"We recorded each interview he's given, and we've received copies of his narratives in response to his application questions, in fact we've recorded his whole life since he entered the hospital in Los Angeles," Kushner told the startled couple.

"Just as an example, here's what he says about a person being a danger to themselves or others:

"When there's no other way in mind, but to kill self. With self so despised, hated and tedious to its occupier, the cheap way out is to slowly destroy self over the seconds, minutes, hours, days, week, months, years and decades, slowly and eventually disintegrating right in front of the eyes who encounter the being. But the blame can only fall at the feet of the soul, who is the inhabitant of self, because self is the innocent party in all of this. Self is the innocent bystander, and self has endured the brunt of the life the soul orders or better put wishes. Self is never to blame. Self does not judge, and self does not talk back. Self does or does not make us do anything because self is just hanging on for the ride."

In another interview he said:

"Self does not want to do bad to it or others, because self is forced into doing what is done, by self's occupant. Self has no say in matters, whatsoever."

Then there is this line of thinking that he wrote in a narrative:

"Our word is not just what we say and claim to live by. Rather, our word is what we follow, and our word is maintained and controlled by our Conscious Awareness (CA), by our Concentration (C), and by our Self Discipline (SD)."

We checked what he was saying out and when he facilitated mental health groups before he quit, and he was only talking about the "Good Side." Now, his whole attitude and philosophy have been supplemented with this distinction between the inner self and the physical self. Listen to this one, we have it on tape:

"Self is the most important entity we will ever come in to contact with. Respect self and its maker. Honor self and its maker. Treating self with tenderness and love, for self is priceless and the most precious gift one will ever receive. But be aware, self does not belong to us because self is just on loan, a rental or lease, if you may. Self is not ours to abuse, use or destroy, because we are merely self's caretaker, and we have to answer for what we did to self and others when life is all said and done."

Listen to this next comment:

"We don't own self we have merely taken temporary possession of it. Self was handed to us in its purest form, to keep healthy, clean, and safe. Self is to represent us among others. Self is not a beauty contest to see who has the most beautiful self. The beauty contest is about who has the most beautiful soul. Self is our vehicle for life, our vehicle toward change, in order to discover ours and others real beauty, our inner beauty, the beauty comes from the heart and what is taken to heart, which is reflected to the mind, body, and soul and through the eyes, projected on to others."

Miller refocused his attention on the couple.

"Hal… can you give us a reason that your brother would be thinking in these terms? Why does he speak of soul and particularly self in I think just about every job interview he's had and every application he's submitted? Help us understand your brother. Is this the Daniel Sherman you know?"

"You don't know what a relief it is to hear something as positive as what was read, and to know that this is Daniel speaking. This is not the Daniel Sherman I grew up with."

Hal looks at Becky who meets his eyes.

"And I don't think Becky would say that either. Daniel was a troubled child and an even more troubled adult. He announced he was gay in the 1990s, but as far as I can tell he's never had a relationship with a man, or even a woman, for that matter. The Daniel Sherman I know left Keansburg after the Shiva for our mother a broken man."

"I remember him saying that Hal has a life, and that Kelly has a life, and that he knew that he needed to get a life. I remember him saying that when we were saying goodbye. Don't you Hal?"

Hal took his wife's hand.

"Yes, I do, and I also remember that when I think of Daniel, a question comes to mind. Has Daniel finally found himself, and that is what this is all about? You don't know him Dr. Miller, he's roamed the country a few times over the decades, and I always saw it that he was trying to run away from himself."

Miller nodded and looked at Kushner and Allison who were listening intently.

"Hal, did you know that your brother was sexually assaulted twice within a three-week period when he served in the Army," Allison said.

Hal and Becky exchanged expressions which implied that they did not know.

"Both times it was the same man. Your brother sought help, but he stopped after a couple of sessions," Miller added.

Hal exchanged eye contact with each doctor.

"Gentleman, I think my brother is a very ordinary man. I think he came out of his depression. I think he found himself and that explains a lot of these writings and theories he's professing. But, again, Becky and I know him, and we hardly think he could be the Messiah. I'll bet you he doesn't think that."

"That's what we're trying to get bottom of this. Hal your brother's life is unexplainable. His finances, as you said, completely turned around from the 90s and now, all the sudden, he's Mr. Responsible with enough savings to not only start paying his debts to family members but to have enough to travel, rent apartments, buy new furniture.

Allison included: And we know that these were honest dollars, which were all earned while he worked for the State of Nevada.

And, then he bounces back and forth around the country. How is it that he always ends up in the right place at the right time? We firmly believe that you brother is being guided, maybe not consciously but there is something that is driving him in the direction he's going," Miller asked.

"Hal and Becky, you've been of help to us, and I hope we can continue our dialogue. We respect your opinions and sincerely appreciate your candor," Miller said.

"And let me assure you Hal, your brother is not in any trouble, so there's no reason to tell him or anybody about our meeting, if you please. We'd like to remain in contact with you, to exchange emails and news, if you would," Miller said.

"I think you both did your best to help us. Thank you very much," Kushner told them.

"Yes, thank you, and it was nice to meet you both," Miller said.

Dr. Miller walked the couple to the door. Dr. Allison walked behind them, cleared his throat and said:

"Excuse me, Hal could I see you privately for a minute."

While Dr. Miller kept Becky busy with small talk about Tel Aviv, Hal listened carefully to Dr. Allison and Becky could see her husband nod his head in concurrence with whatever the good doctor said.

Hal rejoined Becky and at first neither responded verbally, but non-verbally Hal seemed dazed and confounded, and Becky appeared to be in a hypnotic trance.

Allison escorted Hal and Becky to the door, "Thank you again, Mr. and Mrs. Sherman," he told them.

The couple left the elegant room escorted by a U.S. Marine in his dress blues.

They silently followed the Marine and exited the embassy.

Always in good taste, Becky was the first to speak up as they had a moment of privacy outside the embassy gates where a car and its driver waited to take them home.

"Hal… Becky uttered softly in a whisper so she thought no one could hear her but her spouse.

Hal stopped and looked into his wife's eyes, which were filled with sheer amazement.

"You know your brother better is such a thing possible?"

Hal looked down and searched for answers as he sighed and whispered back.

"I can't see it, Becky. I just can't even fathom the possibility. But, before today, I couldn't even fathom the possibility of what just went on here or at the museum. Seriously, I always pegged Daniel as a loser. He just seemed to fit the part. I mean every time I've had contact with him, I can't think of one instance that could rationalize what we were just told. So, it doesn't register with me. This whole scenario is odd. But I don't know…"

"Messiah… that's as far-fetched as saying he's the president of the United States of America," Becky said with amazed giddy eyes and a lilt of laughter in her soft voice tone.

Becky and Hal walked over to the car where the driver waited.

Hal suddenly stopped and looked at his wife and said: "And to think, I once told him he was spiritually impoverished."

Chapter 20

Miller rested his bare feet on a small foot stool as he leaned back and relaxed from his exhausting trip. He noticed a bunion on one of his toes and he wiggled the toe a little, after which he cracked his knuckles before he leaned forward a rolled his shoulders a few times. After all, he thought a man at his age shouldn't be hop-scotching the globe at all hours of the day and night.

But his recent visit to Israel and a few other Middle Eastern nations sent shivers up his well-used spine as he couldn't help but to think about the mess the world found itself in and how the trouble effected the interests of the United States.

He was to meet with the President tomorrow, a task he did not look forward to. As he rested his head against the back of the high back chair, he rubbed his eyebrows and noticed a little dust which emanated from them and swirled around in the air around his eyes under the warm glow of a beautiful and magnificent floor lamp.

He was tired, but he couldn't help but analyze his and his colleague's findings about the state of the world, Daniel Sherman aside, because he knew that a built-in component of every civilized nation was law and order. The men and women who carried out the mission had a deep seeded desire, which was that the bad guys must be caught because they wanted to see justice and when laws had been violated the guilty party must be held accountable.

He admired some of the dedicated men and women he met over the years. Miller always studied and he couldn't help but to think about the detectives who were assisted by forensic teams and uniformed police officers who scoured their territory for wrong doers. Their call meant they would have sacrificed their most priceless possession if they could as they hunted and tracked down the bad guy, the enemy, the person or persons responsible for the wrongdoing, which must be corralled into the pen of the law.

Even decades after a capitol violation, he believed that a crime, an injustice, must be pursued and that the fine professionals he's met over the years were steadfast in their determination to right a wrong.

These people continued and moved on relentlessly. They foamed at the mouth just like Pavlov's dog when any clue was uncovered, or any search bore even the remotest speck of evidence that would lead them to their culprits.

These non-trusting souls bore hatred, but good hatred… Hatred of the crime… Hatred of the criminal who carried out the misdeed and a deep satisfaction was only attained, and their righteous minds would only rest when the day came when they saw that justice was carried out and the criminal or criminals got what they so richly deserved from the arm of the law.

Miller realized that the world was like a giant kitchen concocting one huge meal and that the enemy was like a bunch of cockroaches whose numbers rose into the thousands, millions, and they only showed themselves when they could sneak around when the day was dark and nobody could see them.

Miller sighed as he thought about the wretched mess left behind by these no-good insects, he had to deal with over the decades. They came from all nationalities out of each corner and crevice of the globe. Miller wondered about Daniel and how he could use a good soul like his to drive the insects into oblivion. But, to do this he would open the man up to all sorts of danger.

Again, he was drawn to the tireless work of law enforcement and the good people of the intelligent world who have averted, without headlines and fanfare, a few notable accomplishments. He remembered in the early part of the twentieth century when they averted a meltdown after World War II and the world finally settled in for a period.

When that day happened, they felt vindicated and victorious because there was deep satisfaction which rose within them. They rested easier and knew they were responsible for bringing the violators to justice. They were on the side of what was right and what was good. They knew what was right and what was wrong, and their good common sense told them, and they saw themselves ultimately as the only ones who could have tracked down and carried out justice and to build a case and put the lawbreakers away, hopefully for good.

These were carriers of the law, crime fighters who were no different from fire fighters, in Miller's mind. They each rushed to a scene, investigated and drew conclusions forensically that would lead toward the solution of what happened, when it happened, why it happened, where it happened and how it happened. They were the recorders and reporters of justice, and they spoke to mankind's ultimate authority because they felt kinship with the law because the side of good was just and fair, and because they knew they were on the side of good.

Miller believed that people who hated enjoyed their misguided feelings even if their hatred was bad hatred. They reveled in hate and grudge. Their hunger was satisfied by malice. Hate gave them power and a sense of superiority. They felt aggressive satisfaction that heightened like a narcotic that flowed through their bloodstream. The feeling was hated-high, and although powerful, their devilish deeds were the opposite of a natural enlightened height. They were aggrieved and were taught hate from an early age to allow for the proper pure-hatred development which was essential toward meeting their hatred-goals.

He thought about how the purveyors of disdain pursued pure-anger, pure-resentment, pure-hostility, pure-bitterness, pure-hostility, pure-hatred, pure-animosity, pure- jealousy, pure-contempt, pure-resentment, pure-greed, pure-gluttony, pure-arrogance, pure-vengeance, pure-loathing, pure-superiority, which were all essential seeds that had to be planted, and had to be frequently tended to for pure-hatred to blossom from within them.

Miller drank a glass of water and laid the crystal back on the cherry wood side table as he delved further into thought because he was certain that the mindset of a person who lacked good common sense clearly made up for any deficits.

They used their inner strength and a great deal of their energy as they harassed, singled-out, bullied and persecuted those they deemed worthy of their scorn and hatred. They discriminated against their loathed enemy with pent up anger which was flushed through their system and gushed out through their eyes and from their heart and mind as a natural reflex in their narrow-minded brains.

In their mind hatred was righteous and always correct. Miller contended that their hatred merited distinction because their animosity was a priority, number one on the top forty playlist in their head, in the forefront of their minds, and their hatred merited disapproval because in their thought process, good action demanded ruthless action be taken toward their disgusted nemesis.

All consideration and generosity generated was a reinforcement of their ultimate detestation which was that the aggrieved party deserved every second of malice they were served by their first-class heart-filled enemies who were pumped up with so much hatred they were like a person who exudes enormously large muscles due to their use of steroids, and Miller knew that they were the downright biggest phonies ever to consume oxygen.

Haters have a good time as they hated because hate made them feel alive and they were happy in their hate-filled world because they were stimulated by the notion that if somebody does something wrong to you, you do something wrong back to them, ten times the amount. They felt that inner power and prospered by the wave of negative energy as they crookedly grew not toward the beautiful garden of humanity's greatest and most celebrated achievements, rather toward the abysmal world of the worst in mankind's most notorious and ugliest moments during its most shameful days of life on earth.

Miller jotted down a note to himself based on his thoughts in the wee hours of the early morning when the birds outside his tall well-framed glass of his study had yet to sing their morning songs. "Hatred intelligence takes effort and determination because intelligent haters used hatred to rally the weak-minded, the simpletons whose minds chewed on TV and fast-food. They filled the seats in a theater and watched bloody horror movies while they continuously and mindlessly munched on a large bucket of hot-buttered popcorn, which sat atop their large laps along with their super-sized soda nestled in a cup holder or on the floor beneath their feet."

He rose out of his chair and stretched his arms and torso. He not only was getting old, but he also fathomed he was old. But until his dying breath he pledged he would help Daniel Sherman so that the world could once again settle in.

He knew his goal was achievable. If the world could get over Hitler and his goofy Nazi world then the planet could meet out this one as well.

But he recalled haters have a great deal of confidence in their hatred. He reasoned that their hatred, they think, is positively one-hundred percent accurate and justified and that their hatred excited them. With their hatred they felt in-charge and superior to others and the hated were at the mercy of them by proclamation. They targeted their hate and zeroed in on it as if they were a fly swatter and the hated were the flies.

"For many thousands of years, the Middle East has thrived on hatred. Many factions made hatred a built-in component of their uncivilized nation.

Their law and order were twisted and distorted. The men and women who carried out missions of hatred on behalf of the aggrieved had a deep seeded desire, which was that the hated must be caught and they must be punished and destroyed, and that they must be wiped clean from the face of the earth.

Hatred-experts demanded their kind of justice and their consorted hatred-filled laws, which to them had been violated, meant that the guilty party must be held accountable," he thought.

A moment of clarity rose within his mind when he thought that the hatred specialists assisted by their hatred teams and sympathizers and financiers scoured their territory for their hated, the wrong-doers and they would sacrifice their most priceless possession to achieve what they saw as the victory they were due.

They hunted and tracked down the bad guys, the enemy, the person or persons responsible for the misery they perceived.

Miller knew that over many centuries, what they perceived to be a capitol violation of their rights and privileges, a crime, an injustice toward them or their ancestors or their ancestor's ancestor left these people and their offspring and their offspring's offspring to carry on as they continued, relentlessly.

Generations later, they too foamed at the mouth, just like Pavlov's dog when any clue was uncovered, or any search bore even the remotest speck of evidence that would lead them to their culprits for retaliation.

These non-trusted souls were filled with hatred and their hatred transcended all barriers of time and space because their hatred toward their life-long enemy who carried out the misdeed against them deserved their retribution and distrainment. And, their actions left a deep satisfaction, which would only be attained, and their minds would only rest when the day they saw that justice was carried out and the criminal or criminals got what they so richly deserved, destruction and death.

Miller knew the type so well, oh, so well, he clicked in his mind to himself. He knew they reasoned if that day happened they would be victorious and vindicated and a deep satisfaction would surface from their depths of despair and in their mind their aggrieved history of what they perceived as injustices toward them and their people which took place sometimes centuries ago, and what they carried out as a result would bear them out in their distorted way of thinking.

"Then and only then," Miller spoke into his small hand-held recorder, "could we rest easier because by then we'd know that we were responsible for bringing the violators to justice. We are on the side of what is right and what is good. We know what is right and what is wrong. And we see ourselves ultimately as the only ones who track down and carry out justice in the name of honor for aggrieved people, everywhere.

We must build a case against these mongrels and their distorted brains that will put them away, permanently."

"Because" he mused, "my enemies are merely carriers of hatred," he said about the subject as if they were carriers of some contagious and deadly disease.

"They are fighters who are no different from any other fighter because they rush to crush, and to investigate and draw their self-righteous conclusions that will lead toward their one and only goal which is victory and the defeat and death of another, which is so richly deserved in their pattern of thought."

"No," Miller argued to himself, "they were the reporters of justice in their distorted way of thinking. They speak to mankind's ultimate authority, and they feel kinship with their actions because their cause is just and because they know they are on the side of good and what is right and that the opposition, their opposing group, is the lowest form of vermin that ever-inhabited space or took a breath of life."

Miller couldn't help but pull out a large manila envelope and as he pulled the 8x11 glossy surveillance photos of Daniel out. He came across some of his subject's photos taken when he was just a boy, which he obtained through Hal. Miller smiled at the innocence depicted in that face he looked upon and he knew that he must solicit the help of this child who was now a man.

"After all," he went back to his theory of reason, "my enemy believes that they are servants of God in their minds and that they determine who lives and who dies for God, who they see as being on their side of what is right and who is wrong.

Miller paused and looked out the window as rain pelted the glass.

"And this type of competition built into mankind's soul has always existed, for the rivalry existed between races and the antagonism existed between religions as the war existed between nations and the clash existed between communities and the battle existed between brothers."

Miller believed that this kind of competition was a test, and that the test was a test to see who gave in to their bitter hatred or who could rise above revulsion and overcome their extreme dislike, ultimately to a time and place where they got along with their rivals and lived in peace.

Ultimately, they recognized and dwelled on possible common interests with their newfound peaceful neighbors and most importantly the love brought peace and harmony, and differences were put to rest because they served no one.

Miller remembered one of his professors, Dr. Lee, when he was a student way back in the last century now. He said, "Once oral or written history is understood, processed and rectified through a mutual consideration for each side to exist, they did.

They got along better, they traded with each other, they respected themselves more for their good deeds and they equally respected their one-time foe for their good deeds, for their dignity was reserved and served as a part of their commonality.

And there was room for all to compromise because the theory that the strongest in sheer physical might will prevail gave in to the strongest in sheer inner-might will prevail and they sacrificed, but only in a way that was toward the betterment of mankind and not toward its demise."

Miller knew that many parties in the Middle East throughout their oral and written history had grievances. "It's the most complicated area in the world."

This was all over land and their differences over religion, race and creed which only heartened them and justified their steadfast positions, which cemented their feet into a thick concrete, which stood solidly for many,

many generations over thousands and thousands of years.

Miller thought about the fact that decades ago The United States of America developed and used a nuclear weapon against its bitter rival, Japan, to flex its muscle and to put an end to armed conflict. Logically they would have used the same technology to crush the Nazis, if they had not already defeated them on the battlefield.

The Communists of the Soviet Union developed nuclear weapons to flex its muscle against their bitter rival, capitalism and both nations tested nuclear weapons, but they stopped out of good common sense.

Miller reminded himself that since then, India developed nuclear weapons and tested them to flex its muscle against their bitter rival, Pakistan. Pakistan in turn developed nuclear weapons and tested them to flex its muscle to their bitter rival, India.

Iraq under Saddam Hussein would have developed and tested nuclear weapons to flex its muscle if they were not all brawn and very little brain. Iran wants nuclear weapons to flex their muscle against their perceived bitter rival, Israel.

And a country with brains and brawn, Israel had secretly developed their arsenal of nuclear weapons to ward off their enemies if the tiny nation were ever to come to the brink of destruction.

Palestinians weakened in brain and brawn strapped crude home-made bombs to the torsos of young men, woman and children who blew themselves up to make their point known to their bitter and hated rival, Israel.

Miller wondered if Daniel could make them see the obvious and he asked himself: "When will good common sense prevail and when will strength be measured by the goodness in mankind's soul?"

Miller sat back down and propped up his bare feet on his footstool. He wiggled all his toes as he giggled like a little boy. Oh, how he reminisced about when he was so young and vibrant.

He looked at the photos of Daniel when he was a boy and he hoped and prayed that the fabric of hatred and the battles over land which wove its way through the centuries when men squared off with swords and then guns and artillery and then tanks, airplanes, guns, bombs, artillery and chemical weapons and now tanks, guns, advanced aircraft, bombs, chemical weapons and nuclear and hydrogen bombs would somehow finally end.

Miller reminisced for a moment about what Gerald O'Hara portrayed by Thomas Mitchell said to his daughter Scarlett O'Hara portrayed by Vivien Leigh in the film version of *Gone With The Wind*, as they shared a peaceful moment outside on the family's plantation, Tara before the start of The American Civil War in the 19th Century.

"… You mean to tell me Katie Scarlett O'Hara that land doesn't mean anything to you. Why land's the only thing in the world worth working for, worth fighting for, worth dying for because it's the only thing that lasts."

"Oh, Pa you talk like an Irishman," Scarlett pouted.

"It's proud I am that I'm Irish and don't you be forgetting that you're half Irish too. And to anyone with a drop of Irish blood in them why the land they live on is like their mother… Oh, but there, there why you're just a child, it will come to you, this love of the land, there's no getting away from it if you're Irish…"

Miller's mind recalled that there they stood on small hillside at dusk overlooking a breathtaking view of the heavens and earth with magnificent shades of orange and white and blue above them and far ahead off into the distance over lush green grassy pastures and fields was Tara, their plantation's mansion, which seemed dwarfed by it all.

And he remembered as the theme music sounded and the camera panned back to reveal the full scope of the scene, behind them stood a triumphant mammoth tree with a strong trunk and thick brown bark which supported strong muscled branches which were stretched to their limits and which bore leaves.

Chapter 21

The phone call came at 9 a.m. Daniel awakened several hours before, but he was at In-Shape doing his workout when his cell phone rang, so the message went to voice mail.

"Yes, hello, this call is for Daniel Sherman… I'm calling from Care Start a non-profit organization. I received your resume and I'm calling to schedule an interview. Could you please call and ask for me, James Henderson, I'm the coordinator of the program. Thank you very much."

Daniel followed his workout routine, and his heart rate climbed, as usual, during his cardio exercises and when he got home and heard the message on his voice mail, his heart rate climbed again. He found that an increase in cardiac rhythm always rose when someone called and wanted to interview him for a potential job.

He had gotten a lot of calls like that, twelve to be exact. But Daniel was tired of being interviewed by now because none of them ever offered him a job.

The period that went by hand, by now, has been nearly two years since he resigned voluntarily from his last position and the money, he saved slowly drained away from his bank account. Daniel was frugal, although he knew he wasted thousands of dollars as he bounced around the country, as well as all the money he spent self-medicating on marijuana, both legally and illegally.

He was not worried. He felt fortunate he had savings which kept him afloat all these many months, and even though he tried a second time to collect unemployment insurance, his request was denied:

"…You voluntarily resigned for medical reasons and you're not eligible," he was told both times.

His t-shirt was soaked with sweat but before his shower he picked up his cell phone and called the prospective employer. The interview is scheduled to take place in three days. The job opening was for a Program Assistant, which was a position he was over-qualified for.

"Well, Pearl I've got another interview this week," he told his pet.

Pearl moved her little head from side to side whenever Daniel spoke to her, and she started jumping up on her hind legs and whimpered as if Daniel just said something she wanted to hear.

"No, Pearl we're not going to the park," he told her.

Daniel prepared to be interviewed, and he wrote numerous notes because the notes he believed reminded him of what he needed to say. But then he thought that his notations were a distraction:

"And if I just let go and allowed my mind to take over, the words will flow freely," he thought.

Many of the mental health positions he interviewed for were conducted over the phone because they were outside the state of California. When he interviewed via the phone, notes were spread all over the kitchen and they covered every inch of surface.

Most of the phone interviews were for the Readjustment Counseling Therapist positions with the Veterans Administration and the vacancies were scattered throughout the country. Daniel told each interviewer he would be willing to relocate if he was selected.

The calls he awaited never came. Maine, New Hampshire, New York, Massachusetts, Idaho, Pennsylvania, Ohio, California, Wyoming, Arizona, New Mexico and Florida never made that second call after they interviewed him.

As his hopes dwindled, he stopped looking for federal positions with the VA and he turned his attention to the non-profit sector.

There were many opportunities with non-profit organizations all over the country and he sent dozens resumes; however, most did not respond, but when they did, he interviewed. Each time he was not selected.

He questioned his tactics and analyzed his approach:

"What could I possibly be doing wrong?" he asked himself.

A few of the interviews were local or within a reasonable driving distance so they were conducted face to face. He dressed and presented a professional demeanor. He answered questions as concisely as possible. Sometimes, however, he slipped and said things which demonstrated he needed enrichment in that department.

During one interview an interviewer asked him what his last supervisor might say he needed to improve on. Daniel thought for a moment and then stupidly said:

"…She would say that I talk too much. You see I tend to go beyond the direct point. For example, some people ask what time it is look at their watch and then they say it's ten-o'clock and that's the end of it. When someone asks me what time it is, I tend to tell them about the make of the watch and how it works, before I get around to answering the heart of the question."

He was not offered the job.

The fact he goofed in the last interview did not mean he always messed up because many times he felt he did very well, but, again, the phone never rang twice.

Nevertheless, he moved on. This time he did not slip and feel sorry for himself, so he did not use drugs or alcohol. He processed and understood what he did wrong in the last interview and tried harder.

"I will get a job," he believed in his heart and added to his song during his morning ritual workout.

As Pearl sat at his feet, he logged onto his laptop and hooked up with a wireless network to access the internet. He checked his email and saw that there was another email from Hal. The two agreed to exchange emails when they were together months ago. Lately, Hal wrote to him a lot.

Two people who had never spoken to one another for ten years were now in almost daily contact. He liked the fact that he and his brother communicated with one another. But his big brother's emails started taking a political slant a couple of weeks ago, or so, and Daniel loathed politics.

One email was a video in which Daniel's laptop had trouble playing. Daniel wrote back and asked Hal to summarize what the video said. Hal wrote back and stated:

"Dear Daniel,

In the video the congressman said that the world/USA needs to be very serious about Muslim extremists...every single incident is unacceptable... he feels Israel needs to be supported .... He spoke well and in a very direct way. Love, Hal."

Daniel wrote back: "Well, I understand…"

In another email Hal wrote:

"Dear Daniel,

I thought you would like to listen to this… Love, Hal."

The email video showed portions of a BBC television program where a man was honored for having saved over six-hundred children from Nazi death camps during World War II. The modest elderly man was reunited with more than a dozen lives he saved as he unknowingly sat among them during the television show. Tears flowed through many eyes.

Daniel wrote back and told Hal: "Thank You."

There were several other similar emails which all touched on the politics of Israel and the Middle East crisis.

These thoughts filled his head as the important day arrived and Daniel kept his two most important promises: He worked out at the gym and showered afterward, which meant he kept himself healthy and clean which was a practice he did not miss even once since he admitted himself into the hospital nearly a year ago.

After he got dressed for his interview, he looked in the mirror to ensure that he was color coordinated. Satisfied, he told Pearl to be a good girl and left.

The distance to the interview was a short ride and in the early daylight hours fog hugged Bakersfield like a mother hugged her child, closely.

Care Start was a non-profit organization that served the severely mentally ill in Bakersfield. They provided psychiatric services, individual and group therapy, medications and case management.

Daniel always insisted he would be willing to take on any job and do anything, but he was overqualified for the Care Start position, which was for a Mental Health Program Assistant.

However, after he thought about the potential job, he decided things could be worse. He remembered when he read a sweeping saga by James Michener and how much he began to appreciate his fellow man and the hard back breaking labor they performed and the tireless hours they worked just to put a simple roof over their head and simple food in their stomachs.

"I've got to get over my setbacks because life is not just about me, it just is not. I must be willing and able to go anywhere and do anything at any time, if it's legal and good," he thought.

Escorted into a briefing room with a small conference table, chairs and one-way observation window, Daniel believed the room was a space most likely to have been used to conduct therapy at one time.

Daniel pulled one of the padded chairs from beneath the table which faced the special glass window. He placed an envelope on top of the table and sat down. Self-conscious he looked away from the reflective pane and pulled out documents from the envelope in front of him on the table.

He brought an extra copy of his resume, a copy of his college transcripts and his three references, who were people he worked for in the field and still maintained contact with people who were all from the same rural Northern Nevada clinic he worked at for two years before he started another one of his downward journeys.

Five minutes went by, he looked over his list of references. Just in case someone was watching him. Slowly he inhaled a deep breath through his nose and slowly he exhaled through his mouth.

Daniel looked at the closed door in the room he was led in to for his interview. He stared for a moment at the doors round knob as if he expected the thing to turn any second.

He looked at the clock on the wall and it had been about ten minutes now since he sat down. He wondered for a second what kept them but then realized in the mental health field things could change a minute.

With the sound of a muffled voice outside the door Daniel concentrated on his focus back to the moment. The knob turned and through the door walked an average sized man with short brown hair and a gentle face.

"Daniel, I'm James Henderson."

The prospective employee rose from his chair to shake hands.

"Mr. Henderson, it's a pleasure to meet you."

"Please, take a seat."

Daniel readjusted his body and his mind to the matter at hand as the man spoke.

"Let me tell you about us… we are a non-profit organization serving the severely mentally ill population of Bakersfield. We've been around since the 1980s, and we provide services to roughly three-hundred special needs clients in our community."

Daniel's eye contact and body orientation were completely attentive and keened on the speaker.

"I looked at your resume and you're overqualified for this position. You know it pays minimum wage, which is $8.25 per hour, and it would really be an on-call position at first, but eventually it will become full-time, but I can't speak to when. Can you tell me why you want this job?"

Daniel looked above Mr. Henderson's head for a second and then he looked down for another second and then delivered eye contact and his response as he folded his hands together.

"Well, sir, my desire is to get back into my career field and when I saw your announcement on the internet, I thought this would be a place where I can be of service to your organization and the population you serve. I understand I'm overqualified, but I thought with the knowledge skills and abilities that I have I would be looked upon as an asset."

Daniel swallowed because he knew his answer was not one of his most articulate ones.

"Very good, Daniel…"

Henderson looked at his handsome wristwatch.

"We do things a little differently around here. I'm going to leave you now and there will be a knock on the door. Here is the client's history.

Henderson stood, went to the door, and walked out.

Daniel deeply sighed and took his vision away from the door and for a brief second, he looked at his reflection in the one-way observation window. He again wondered if people were watching him.

"May Jenkins is a black 34-year-old chronically mentally ill women. She's never married, and she lives alone. Her depression began back in her 20's and she had a substance abuse problem with alcohol. She is overweight and she never graduated high school. She has a 13-year-old son who lives in town, but he's living with his grandmother because "Mom's a nut." She is frequently hospitalized due to her tendency to harm herself. She's also attempted suicide twice: The first time by cutting on her wrist which was 15 years ago, and the second time was a year ago when she swallowed all her medications at once. She receives Social Security Disability; food stamps and she resided in a small, subsidized apartment."

Daniel's attention is gained by a knock on the door. May Jenkins entered and she scanned Daniel up and down.

"Uh, hum."

"Please, take a seat, Ms. Jenkins."

"Oh, you can call me May, that's all right…"

"May, I'm Daniel. What brings you here today?"

"Oh, you know why I'm here, uh, hum…,"

"Well, actually I'm new here and I don't know exactly why you're here…"

Daniel gave her unconditional attention. May looked away and pretended to cry. She had smooth dark brown skin and a neat appearance, which did not surprise Daniel because he knew she was just playing a part.

"Because I want to kill myself, that's why."

Daniel looked at her compassionately.

"Well why would you want to do a thing like that?"

"Because I hate myself and I like to cut on myself, see."

She held out her forearm. Daniel noticed some reddish lines were drawn onto her skin.

"Now May, why would you ever want to do that? I read here that you have a son…"

"Yeah, and he don't want nothing to do with me. He called me a "nut."

Daniel looked deeper into her eyes.

"But May, he just doesn't like that side of you, and you don't like that side of you because your attempts at suicide and when you do things to hurt yourself prove that. But there is a good side to you as well. We all have our good side and a bad side, and we need to learn about our good side. We need to become aware that it's there, because our good side is a very important part of us, and we need to bring it out and use it."

May's deep dark eyes fixated on Daniel.

"May, when we show our good side, good things happen to us. But, when we show our bad side, bad things happen to us. May, you are a good person. I can take one look at you and it's very clear to me that you have a lot of goodness inside of you. You just need to show it. You need to show it to everyone. But, more importantly, you need to show it to yourself."

May folded her hands and continued to concentrate on Daniel's face and words.

"You've got to start learning some skills that will help bring that goodness out for you and everybody to see, instead of keeping it deep down inside you."

May's face softened as she listened to.

"What do you see when you look at my nose, a part of my physical self-right? What do you see when you look at my arms, legs, head or ears? Again, they're parts of my physical self. Now, what do you see when you look into my eyes? Is that a part of the physical self?

May raised her dark eyebrows and she had a "where is he going with this" look in her eyes.

"The eyeball and the retina are a part of the physical's self-hardware but what's projected through the pupil, which is that little brown part of our eye is what is in our soul because the pupil is the porthole into the soul.

You know what I mean?"

May shook her head because she did not know.

"A porthole is a big round circle the size of a medium pizza and it's a window on a ship like a cruise ship and people peer out to look at the ocean. Our portholes allow others to peer into our soul as well because our eyes project what has been taken to heart. What we hold closely to heart. What is guiding our heart? If we were abused physically, emotionally or sexually those traumas have been taken to heart. If someone treats us disrespectfully and hatefully or insults us that emotional trauma is often taken to heart.

Daniel noticed May's eyes moving to the lower left as if she was processing the information.

"Then we have anger, resentment, bitterness, hate and a lot of other negative things filling up our heart, instead of good things like love, friendship, goodness and respect filling us up like it should."

May had a genuine tear drop down her cheek as her eyes welled up.

"And May, if there's one thing you remember from meeting with me today it's what we take to heart is reflected to our mind, body, and soul and through our eyes it's projected onto others."

May remained silent and showed respect to Daniel, which was apparent in her eyes and body posture.

"Your son's only seen the worst in you. Now you need to show him the best that's inside you. And you can't just tell him that you're going to do your best, you've got to show him! But, first, as I said to you earlier, you've got to start showing your goodness to yourself. May, you're here on earth as a caretaker, a protector and provider for self. When our souls are presented to this world they are matched with a body, and they are connected and united. When we grow up life has a way of separating soul from self and then there is conflict and division from within," he thought.

Daniel's voice went to its softest level.

"May, the soul and self-need to be together. Remember that saying: "United We Stand, Divided We Fall?"

May nodded affirmatively.

"Well, that just doesn't apply to countries and communities, those words apply to us as well. Soul and self-need to unite, and they need to stand together and work in harmony as one. May needs to connect with self and then you will begin to build your inner strength. You will have an awareness of self. You will show respect for self. You will have better self-esteem, self-confidence and self-kindness."

May looked down at her folded hands.

"However, many years you're here occupying self, and you're only expected to try your best. Don't be mean to self. Don't punish self. Don't cut on self. And never do anything that could lead toward the destruction of self. We don't like it when others treat us badly. That's not okay and we do something about what they're saying or doing. Why is self-different? If treating self badly is not okay when others do it, then treating self badly is not okay when our own is the one doing it."

May smiled at Daniel.

"Treat self with the utmost dignity and respect, and you'll do just fine. Are you still drinking?"

"Sometimes…"

"Well, it's time to join up with a group and learn how to stop. You can do it. You don't want to destroy self. Self should be your best friend. Self stands by you silently and never makes a fuss. Doesn't self-deserve the best treatment from you?"

"Yes…"

"Okay, reaching a goal takes a step at a time, as they say, and today is your first step. I want to see you climb all the way to the top, okay?"

"I'd like to meet with you again so we can talk more about this."

Daniel looked at an imaginary appointment book.

"How about next Tuesday afternoon at three o'clock…"

May was taken aback because of the way Daniel spoke to her just as if she were a client.

"Sure, Mr. Daniel… I'll see you again."

They both rose and shook hands.

May left and Daniel wrote a D.A.P. case note: (D) Description (A) Assessment (P) Plan.

D) "Client appeared alert and her hygiene and casual attire appeared neat and clean, as well. A) Client discussed some concerns with her life and appeared to listen attentively to some feedback. Also, it appears that clients need to obtain Psychosocial Rehabilitation skills to improve their self-awareness, self-confidence, self-respect and self-esteem. P) Pursue PSR group attendance with therapist and client.

He leaned back in his seat and wondered about who watched him through the observation window.

He stretched his legs out and put his hands at the top of his head. When he heard the doorknob, he sat upright and ready for the final phase of this unusual interview. Mr. Henderson entered and took Daniel's case notes.

"We'll be with you in a moment."

Mr. Henderson did not reenter the room. Instead, three aged men in sharp business suits came through the door. Daniel's heart raised a few rhythms, and his emotional nervousness rumbled as one of them spoke:

"Hello, my boy. I am Dr. Tom Miller… This is Dr. Roland Kushner... And this is Dr. Kevin Allison… We're here to ask you a few questions…"

Daniel felt confused but he was not worried because he had done nothing wrong. But what happened to Mr. Henderson and who were these three elderly men who looked more like senior executives than the usual laid back outpatient clinical psychologists he got to know over the years?

"Daniel we would like to continue the interview now," Miller said.

The three men sat next to each other across from their subject.

"First, can you touch on how you would handle a patient who had intrusive unwanted thoughts," Kushner asked.

Daniel graciously proceeded to continue the interview and said:

"Well, instinctively if it's something that's bad or something that is loathed, unwanted and intrusive people need to learn to control the intrusive thought, idea, memory or feeling. They need to minimize and to diminish the unwanted words and to put them into their place because those thoughts are unwanted and stem from the dark catacombs of our minds and they do not serve us because they're only there to teach us lessons and to test and challenge us, and until they're subdued it'll remain a thorn of psychological pain. But, once controlled and put into its proper place it'll teach us great lessons, which are lessons, which unite the soul with self and place us into our glory instead of dividing us into our despair."

Dr. Miller took a deep breath, and all three men studied Daniel for several seconds before the proceeded.

"Would you like some water, Daniel?" Miller asked.

"Yes, sir, I would."

Miller stood up and opened the door. He motioned for a man who must have stood nearby and gave him instructions. Allison made eye contact with Daniel and smiled. The fifty-two-year-old, hardly a boy, smiled back.

"Daniel what is your purpose in life?" Allison asked.

Daniel looked at Dr. Allison directly and readjusted his body orientation, so he faced him.

"I would say it is to serve the mentally ill."

"That's a noble purpose. Did you always have that purpose in your life?"

Daniel wanted to answer yes, but because of his gap in employment he said:

"Everybody has a purpose to serve and some people's purpose, unfortunately, is to serve no purpose. I found myself in that position for a while. As you're probably aware I resigned from my last mental health position. But it was voluntarily because of medical issues, but they've now been resolved, and I am ready to work again because for a while I wasn't sure that would happen."

Miller returned to the table and sat down. There was a knock at the door and Daniel began to move to answer it.

"That's all right," Miller said.

The door opened and another man in a well-styled suit entered with four small bottles of water.

"Thank you, Steven," Miller said.

Each party in the room opened their water. The three doctors took a small sip almost simultaneously while Daniel drank it fast.

"So, what is your philosophy about purpose, Daniel?" Kushner asked.

"Dr. Kushner I think some people serve a good purpose and they end up happy. Some people serve a bad purpose, and they end up mean, mad and miserable. We all want to serve a purpose in life and most people would make the first choice because I think most people want to serve a good purpose."

"What do you see as the major obstacle to that Mr. Sherman?" Allison asked.

"Taking gibberish to heart because gibberish sticks to a soul like burnt soup sticks to the bottom of a stove pot. Gibberish is stupid and irrational."

"What is gibberish to you?" Miller interjected.

"Unwanted, intrusive thoughts, feelings or memories…"

"You have a real flare for vocabulary Daniel. Do you like words?" Miller asked.

Daniel looked more relaxed as the conversation seemed to turn into a friendly one.

"Yes, I do."

"Did you know we've been watching and listening to your interview through the observation window?" Kushner asked.

"No, sir…"

"We heard you talk a lot about self. What would you say the biggest danger to self is and how would you suggest a person handle it?" Kushner wondered.

Daniel looked at all three men before he answered:

"Well, don't let self-become purposeless or of no use to anyone, especially to its live-in guest because we have the power to see that being without a purpose in life doesn't happen, and we need to learn to stay in control of each event. Self isn't the enemy because our vehicle for life is the only true friend we've got. And as to the second part of your question: How to handle it I would say it's important to learn skills that walk an individual through the steps of how to go from where they are now, to where they want to be, and to strive toward doing our best and having peace of mind."

"So, people need to heal," Dr. Miller said.

Daniel finished his water.

"Yes, sir, they do. When we heal, we begin to enjoy things that we formally would take for granted or could never appreciate before. For isolated people and a lot of mentally ill people who find themselves in that boat when they heal, they begin to enjoy things like self and others, nature and the world, and most importantly freedom, because they are no longer enslaved to whatever it is that is subduing them all these many years. They are free now."

Each doctor revealed his enthusiasm and smiled broadly.

"What is your prescription for someone who needs to find freedom?" Allison asked.

Daniel hijacked their revelry for a moment and told the threesome:

"Connect with self and others. Don't fall apart because when we fall apart reconnecting must occur and soul and self-must be put back together again! Soul and self must live and stand as one!" Daniel proclaimed.

Dr. Miller stood up and walked behind his seat as Daniel curiously looked at him.

"Daniel, we've been studying you since you were admitted into the hospital on two-south."

Daniel was taken aback.

"I don't know what you mean. What do you mean?"

"Daniel, do you believe in God…" Kushner asked?

Daniel's level of nervousness rose within him as his voice began to quiver.

"Excuse me, sir...?"

"Dr. Kushner, Dr. Allison and I have been on a long search over many decades. Over the past year it has all changed and led us to you. I give you my word that you're in no trouble," Miller said.

He leaned over his seat and the table so that his face was about two feet from Daniel's. Daniel recoiled a little in dismay and his composure felt like it slipped on a fresh sheet of ice in freezing weather.

"What happened to you on two-south?" Miller wanted to know.

"I don't understand," Daniel said as he held back tears.

Dr. Kushner pulled a pocket size MP4 from the breast pocket of the jacket he wore.

"I want you to take a look at some of this," Kushner said.

He turned on the MP4 and Daniel saw himself walking back and forth through the hallways of two-south with a spring in his step and a smile on his face and touching the word "Thank You" on each exit door sign. Daniel blushed and sat back in his seat.

"What's…? I don't know what… Can you tell me what…?" Daniel fumbled.

"Play the second part Roland," Miller insisted.

Kushner pressed a button on the MP4, and Daniel popped again with Ken by his side. The young man told Daniel that he was the Son of God and that he was: "…One of God's children."

Kushner froze the screen with the two patients on it.

"Do you know what is next, Daniel" Miller asked?

Daniel looked at Kushner then Allison and then back at Miller again and remained silent.

"But Daniel what did you say after Ken told you he was the Son of God," Miller asked?

"I don't remember, sir…"

"Show it Roland," Miller requested.

Dr. Kushner pressed the play button as Daniel declared with his arms outstretched to their limit:

"We are all God's children."

Daniel's body began to tremble.

"So, and so we are, I believe," Daniel defensively stated as a tear dripped down his cheek.

"What religion do you believe in Daniel," Allison asked.

"Well, I was raised Jewish if that's what you mean. But I stopped following religion when I was a teenager."

Daniel wiped his eyes and blew his nose on a tissue that Dr. Allison passed to him.

"Well, which of the religions do you believe is right, if I may?" Kushner kindly requested.

"Actually, I think they're all right. They're all working toward the same end…"

Daniel scooped up his composure and declared:

"I wish I could help you. But I don't know what you need help with. I take it that this whole interview, the role plays with the fake client, it was all a set-up just to get to a point and I don't know what that point is. I can't be of any further assistance to you, I'm afraid."

"Please, Daniel…" Allison softly requested.

"Daniel, we think that you know where we're going with all of this," Miller said.

"I don't, sir… I really don't…"

"Daniel we've talked with your brother and sister-in-law in Israel," Kushner told him.

"What…? What's this all about?"

"We've been on a search for many years for a particular person and we have come to the conclusion that you are that person."

Daniel looked at them queerly.

"What person?"

"It's a very special person," Allison said.

"Well, I'm not special, sir, let me assure you of that."

"Well, we've crafted a particularly complicated criterion…"

"I don't know what you mean."

"Daniel, we think you are the Messiah. You meet every one of the criteria," Miller insisted.

Daniel looked up and down at each doctor and he became a little emotional.

"What… who…. you can't mean it… no… that's the biggest bunch of gibberish… me… why… I…. it's just not true… It's all gibberish… it's just not true at all… what criteria… I'm Daniel Howard Sherman and I understand something about self… I'm not the Messiah and I'm not the Son of God… I was in the hospital because I've been depressed for more than a year."

"More like decades," Miller insisted.

"Of incorrect conditioning," Kushner added tactfully.

"And you claimed that the quality of your life hasn't been so good over the years," Allison stated compassionately.

"You've got the wrong person… I am not the person you're… if there are such people…"

"The criteria list of characteristics fit," Allison said.

"…Like a glove," Miller added.

"Look, I came here to get a job. I don't know what you are all talking about. I'm not a religious person and I have never been. I don't give a damn about religion."

Daniel blew his nose and wiped his eyes again.

"We understand that you know about mental health and the mind… can't you just talk to us about what you believe," Miller inquired.

"No wonder Hal was writing me so much about Israel and politics," Daniel thought.

"You're all out of your minds… you don't understand… I am no Messiah... I simply came out of long depression, and I am a different person now. It's the medication, my antidepressant… It works very well and I'm fine now. I need a job and I've been looking for a year now. I can't understand what I'm doing wrong. But I do understand there's no way what you say could be true. I just want to get back to my work... I like my work, and I do a good job at what I do, I think… today, all this… it wasn't a real interview was it?"

The three doctors did not respond.

"Well, I'm going to keep trying and I will get a job because I'm qualified, and I have experience. That's all I've got to say," Daniel concluded.

Allison, Kushner and Miller huddled and quietly exchanged their thoughts. Daniel eyed Dr. Allison's water bottle because he was parched.

When they were done with the impromptu meeting Dr. Allison spoke first:

"Hippocrates once said it is through error that man tries and rises. It is through tragedy he learns. All the roads of learning begin in darkness and go out into the light… Daniel I think you've gone through that process, and I wish you the best of luck in your future."

Dr. Kushner looked down as he searched his mind for the right words to use.

"I always believed there was reasonable doubt about this. We could talk about what happened during World War II and what we believe has happened to ensure that World War III is just around the corner. But Daniel, I don't know what to say. I'm a little lost, frankly."

Miller sat across from Daniel and looked him in the eyes.

"I think you're too young to be the Messiah, but I think you've got a good head on your shoulders, and I believe you do good work. I want to see you continue. All these months we've kept tabs on your every move because we wanted to learn for ourselves who you are. Today, we were all educated a little more. But I must tell you young man we'll be watching you. Go to work. Get a job. Get a life, you deserve one."

Daniel stood and walked through the doorway and turned to face the three wise men. "I believe I'm headed in the right direction," he told them. He turned and walked away.

The End